Kennedy Trengrove was born and raised in Perth, Western Australia. She attended university there and in Melbourne, but once lived in a small country town deep in the bush for several years. After a career as a school counsellor, she moved to the more-bohemian port city of Fremantle to write books.

This is her first published novel.

To my late father, Hugh Quentin Kennedy, who taught me the power of laughter.

Kennedy Trengrove

Almost Down to Earth

AUSTIN MACAULEY PUBLISHERS™

LONDON * CAMBRIDGE * NEW YORK * SHARJAH

Copyright © Kennedy Trengrove 2023

The right of Kennedy Trengrove to be identified as author of this work has been asserted by the author in accordance with sections 77 and 78 of the Copyright, Designs and Patents Act 1988.

All rights reserved. No part of this publication may be reproduced, stored in a retrieval system, or transmitted in any form or by any means, electronic, mechanical, photocopying, recording, or otherwise, without the prior permission of the publishers.

Any person who commits any unauthorised act in relation to this publication may be liable to criminal prosecution and civil claims for damages.

This is a work of fiction. Names, characters, businesses, places, events, locales, and incidents are either the products of the author's imagination or used in a fictitious manner. Any resemblance to actual persons, living or dead, or actual events is purely coincidental.

A CIP catalogue record for this title is available from the British Library.

ISBN 9781398487697 (Paperback)
ISBN 9781398487710 (ePub e-book)
ISBN 9781398487703 (Audiobook)

www.austinmacauley.com

First Published 2023
Austin Macauley Publishers Ltd®
1 Canada Square
Canary Wharf
London
E14 5AA

Many thanks to The Manuscript Appraisal Agency for their sometimes-stern guidance. I could not have got here without you.

Special thanks go to my fellow-writer Kamille Roach for years of supportive chats over many coffees.

To my other good friends who have probably wondered whether I was doing anything in my study all these years–finally, you can see that I was not just watching cat videos.

Lastly, my gratitude to the editors at Austin Macauley for believing in my work.

The fault, dear Brutus, is not in our stars but in ourselves…
                                        William Shakespeare.

Aquarius

A moderately-good month for orangutans.
On Friday, you will meet a dark, handsome stranger.
He will shoot you with a tranquilliser gun,
check your teeth, eyes and genitals,
then set you "free" in a wildlife sanctuary.

One

Reader, I have such a tale to tell. It is a tale of cosmic foolishness, power, and love. It may amuse; it may bemuse. Mine is only the telling of it. Like all true fables, it begins in the traditional manner.

Once upon a time, under the impenetrable darkness of a country sky, a rangy tawny-haired woman was standing on her rooftop pointing her comet-seeking telescope at the heavens. This was to be a night on the tiles that M'bali Hoyle would never forget. She had been scanning the skies since 3 am. A couple of asteroids had fallen like broken promises, quickly extinguished. The stars had spun, and their glory and mystery were fading in the dawning light, as she prepared to climb down to the reality of daily life.

No luck again. I should muster the sense to give up, she thought.

As usual, she scanned her garden, enjoying the tranquil scene before she descended. Native trees stood in feathery silhouette against an eastern sky shot with misty golds. Suddenly, a flying saucer streaked from the firmament, moved to a point above the soughing trees, hovered majestically, then dived out of view into her garden. She sat in rigid disbelief for many seconds. Slowly, her fingers began to tug at her spiky hair, as though tweaking it could drag the image from her brain. Finally, she reacted. 'I did not frigging see that. If I saw that, I have lost my tiny marbles,' she whispered to herself.

But despite the early hour, M'bali was not the only one who saw it. On the nearby coast, two surfers had slipped into the summer ocean and begun to paddle unaware that what they were about to witness, strafing the dawn sky, would one day threaten the lives of every being in their world.

Once beyond the shore break, Mick and Richo just sat on their boards, sharing the odd manly grunt of communion before launching themselves into the glassy swells. They watched mindlessly as M'bali Hoyle's she-oak grove emerged as a dark blur on the eastern horizon.

Without warning, a silver shape tore from the heavens, hovered briefly, then appeared to dive into her garden. The surfers exchanged glances, each silently wondering whether to admit what he thought he had seen.

Esteemed reader, I must advise you that these men were not stupid, they were just fashionably inarticulate.

'Did you see that, mate?' Richo finally managed.

'You mean over M'bali's joint?' Mick was giving nothing away. His heart was racing.

'Yeah, big shiny thing. Flattish, going like the clappers.'

'Space junk?'

It was clearly not space junk.

'Yeah, has to be.'

'Reckon we should paddle in and see if she's okay?'

Richo was a science teacher at the local high school. Part of him wanted to stampede over for a look, but his street cred as a rational being would be dented by that. Each guessed that the other was probably as startled as himself, but each also had the discretion not to notice. As they both sat emotionally hamstrung on their boards, an athletic figure, clutching a surfboard and waving, appeared in silhouette on the beach.

'Here's Gaz, let's see if he saw anything first.'

They waited. Their mate, local sports champion Gavin Cooper, commonly known as Gaz, came paddling out at speed. His mane of scruffy sun-bleached hair was being thrown over his face by the easterly breeze. He occasionally thrust it back.

'Hi guys. Slept in. Why are you two just hangin' about like a pair of dead barnacles in such gnarly swell?'

'We saw something fallin' into M'bali's place, mate. Big, flat silver shape—goin' like the clappers. Space junk maybe?' Mick added hopefully.

'Was there an earth-shattering explosion?' Gaz asked in his slow drawl.

'Nah. Quiet as.'

'Fire then?' They looked embarrassed. Gaz stared thoughtfully at the lightening blur of the shore before he spoke. 'That rules out an airliner, a dirigible, a flat, shiny, lost terrorist and every other crazy thing I can think of. Let's catch some waves, boys.'

Neither man was willing to tell Gaz he'd just seen a flying saucer landing, so Mick and Richo began to surf. In their tiny hometown, they would be mercilessly teased if they stepped beyond the very firm bounds of what was viewed as "normal". Seeing flying saucers rated 10+ on the informal, but universally recognised, total-dingbat scale. With that in mind, neither surfer would speak a word about the incident to anyone until many weeks later.

Dawn's light struggled over the treetops and oozed down on nearby Quimbleton as it rested in the arms of its sheltered forest valley. Far away from the evils of the wicked world, furry critters nibbled the lawns of several houses on the outskirts. Feathered creatures, the descendants of dinosaurs, began to fight territorial battles in the trees, using only song as their weapons. Little black flies hid in the ferny shade. The good citizens of Quimbleton would soon stir and begin their day.

Reader, those innocent rubes have no idea what is about to befall them.

Taurus

Some rare rains will lift the spirits of
kangaroos and wallabies on the 3rd.
But beware of dazzling lights in the evening.
Copyright. Alpha Dawn.

Two

My reader may at this point be muttering, or even shrieking, that this is sci fi. Perhaps you don't care to read sci fi. I certainly do not myself. This tale unfolded before my unwilling eyes, and I sincerely wish that two honeymooning space persons had not catapulted themselves into it while in the grip of one of those reckless whims known only to lovers.

To resume. Nearly an hour later, as Gaz was paddling himself away from the pleasures of the sea, he noticed two figures emerging from the nearby coastal scrub. They headed towards the water. The male of the pair lowered his exquisitely toned body to the sand. Gaz didn't appraise other males' bodies in quite that way, but I must warn you what eye-popping beauty we are dealing with here. The citizens of nearby Quimbleton would soon be bedazzled by the woman as well. She lingered briefly, bent to kiss her partner, then knifed into the turquoise waves where she began swimming at astonishing speed.

These gorgeous beings, who you will presently know as Jeffrique and Zera, had arrived in the so-called flying saucer. Or to be specific, in *The Suzerator-6*, a top-of-the-range space craft (the high-end model with the jacuzzi and gold taps). They belonged to the ruling class of an inter-galactic civilisation in which all life-forms were bred, patented, and owned by the *Genes-R-Us* corporation for its exclusive use. No naughty little life-form was its own person on any of their worlds because its genes had been shuffled and changed to suite the uses of the company bottom line. Some might say that they were engineered slaves. That is a point of view you may or may not care to ponder.

On this little planet, identified on *Genes-R-Us* cosmic charts as 3159XZ, illegal life was sprouting up everywhere. The dominant species dwelling there was a hominid group whose self-esteem far outweighed their competence in looking after the paradise they had been gifted. It was they who had dubbed the little blue spec in the cosmos Earth.

Even before he emerged from the *Suzerator-6*, it was immediately evident to Jeffrique that there was something very wrong here. He drew a startled breath. He clenched his fists in rage. There was leaping and twittering unsanctioned life on this rarking cosmic backwater. Illegal spawn everywhere.

Oops, I mean he realised that these living beings were lacking the wise oversight and control of the *Genes-R-Us* corporation. The Creator-Of-All-Things would blow his beautifully crafted lid when Jeffrique got back to the ship and messaged him.

Gemini

This week will not be lovely weather for ducks.
It is hunting season. I have only one word for you.
Duck!

Three

Still in a state of bewilderment, M'bali somehow packed up the 'scope, climbed down the ladder, and mounted the veranda step. She hesitated for a moment in the open doorway. Next second, she was striding across the garden towards the area where she thought the saucer thing had landed. It was not there. Was that a fresh disturbance in the mulch a few feet from the base of her sturdy *Crimson Glory* rose bush? Warily, she poked at a small, jagged displacement of the surface such as a small burrower might make during its nightly foraging. 'Anyway, the thing was enormous when I saw it,' she told herself aloud.

Perhaps she had dozed off and dreamt it. She checked her watch. Five twenty-one. That meant nothing, she hadn't checked the time for hours. One of the joys of her country life was time to be as well as time to do. She had named this seaside property, once her holiday retreat and now her home, *The Briar Patch*. It was M'bali's haven from the world, if not from herself.

She put her nose to the dark velvet of a flower, inhaling deeply. Its sweet, heavy perfume swept through her senses. *It must have been one of those optical illusions, that every clod in a remote wheatfield assumes must be a UFO*, she thought. M'bali had a university degree in physiotherapy. She was not about to act like a clod in a wheatfield all over Quimbleton. There wasn't even any wheat.

Bare feet began padding across her nearby veranda. She whipped around, just managing to stifle a "Hi, Gaz". The vision with shoulder-length black curls, disturbingly dressed only in one of her sarongs, was not her old mate Gaz seeking a coffee on the way back from a surf. He was Hayes—kitchen hand at the Quimby pub and lead singer of the local rock band. Frigging hell, she'd become a cougar overnight. How many ouzos had that taken?

'Gardening so early?'

'Er, no, no. Remember I told you last night that I often get up on the roof at 3 am to comet watch? I just climbed down. Coffee?' she queried, changing the subject adroitly.

'Mmm please.'

Surely this must be a one-night stand. How do you conduct a one-night stand? Do you offer them breakfast? Last night, in the afterglow of their passion, Hayes had seemed surprisingly interested in who she was. M'bali had been named after a tiny, but fierce leopard which her parents had been privileged to observe at close quarters during their safari honeymoon. Fortunately, she had not grown up make a painful mockery of her name by being timid or chubby. She stood five feet ten in her bare feet and had a brown belt in *taekwondo*. If he were to brag all over Quimbleton that he'd had her, she would haul him up a tree like a dead antelope and have him for lunch—metaphorically speaking. Underneath her blustering thoughts lay a well of fear about how he might misuse her, as another had done in her past.

Soon they were seated on the living room sofa with toast and steaming coffees straight from her machine. (Was toast breakfast? Surely not. It seemed like a reasonable compromise.) He had admired her rustic décor. My god he was trying hard.

'Comet-watching in the early hours. Unusual. How did you get into that?'

He was leaning towards her. The look in those lustrous brown eyes seemed genuine enough.

'I'm searching for previously unseen ones. *Star Atlas* rules allow any finder to name their discovery, provided you register it. I want to honour my late brother, Jon.

'Wow, I didn't know a non-expert could name a comet. What a great way to immortalise Jon. You must have been close.'

Was he was doing that fake empathic listening thing some males do automatically to get a girl in the sack? Some she'd encountered had all the empathy of a dead rat. But he'd already got her into the sack. Maybe he was up for seconds (thirds actually). Her guts fluttered happily at the thought. 'Jon and I were close, but it's more complicated than that. He died in a car I was driving. A stoned junkie crossed to the wrong side of the road. It was head on. He was sixteen.'

She wouldn't tell him how very loved Jon had been in town and that half of Quimbleton had blamed her for his loss. The accusing rumours and sour looks had driven her away to the city for years.

'I hope you don't think I'm being cheeky. But are you likely to find a comet?'

'It is difficult. Most of them are discovered by robotic telescopes these days, but occasionally we obsessed amateurs latch onto a new one.'

'Why a comet? Was Jon a space geek by any chance?'

She grinned. 'You have to be sporty in a country town, and he was. But he was the ultimate nerdy boy in private. Silver flying saucer hung from the ceiling, sci fi posters—and he watched every docu on TV about space exploration.'

M'bali's eyes filled with tears. 'Sorry, it never really stops being raw.' He was holding her hand by now. The urge to hurl herself into his embrace was almost overwhelming. She held herself back. How could he know how many times she had held her little brother and comforted him while her mother was off in an opiate fog.

She had to change the subject. Was she going to tell him about the space craft? Was she going to tell anyone? M'bali was too shaken up to think. Spaceships and cosmic lovemaking in one night. Reader, as I am sure you know, the hominid brain is brilliant at building things but can be easily rattled by emotional issues.

'Sorry, but I have to feed my animals now.'

He reached over and kissed her softly on the cheek. 'I'll leave you to it then.'

*

As she lugged feed across her farmyard, she considered her other secret. She was a sceptic by nature, but a hopeful one. 'When I climb onto the roof to comet-watch, I also hope to see alien craft,' she could imagine herself confessing after too many wines at the golf club. Wouldn't they have fun with that admission? Thoughts like that had kept her wine intake just under blabbing level in the so-called nineteenth green, the gossip hub of the town. Most of the members were likable enough—but a little clique of bastards would love to nail her for something else on top of Jon's death.

Reader, our heroine, M'bali, is a member of a species known across the galaxies for its reckless curiosity. Many cautious souls on planet Earth, mostly mothers, have often warned with hands on hips that curiosity killed the cat. Compared to hominids, the cat is a careful and cautious little homebody. Her species' passion for adrenaline-charged thrills didn't always end well. I'll just climb this volcano to find out how hot those red flowing rocks really are; I'll just ride this forty-foot wave like death on a stick. I'll just wish that some vastly more advanced pan-galactic civilisation would pay a visit to our own.

Alas, M'bali's naïve wish has come true.

Cancer

Mars enters the planetary world of black rhinos in mid-month. Crazed hunters will be taking pot-shots. Take care of your health by lurking in thickets.

Four

The flying saucer, reduced to miniature form to escape detection, was now cosily tucked up under the mulch near the fragrant *Crimson Glory*, M'bali's favourite rose bush. No burrowing animal had made that little disturbance. A startled earthworm was already writhing around it. Reader, how can this be? It defies belief.

Please bear with me a little. To answer your unspoken questions, I must whiz you back a few billion years, cover a startling amount of back-story in a few brief pages. Then we can let the good citizens of the Quimbleton district deal with the visitors in their own primitive earthling way.

The appearance of life on what was then merely the planet 3159XZ was more accidental than is popularly believed. You know how it is with small boys and chemistry sets. Jeffrique was not just any small boy. He was the son of a being known as the nameless and unknowable Creator-Of-All-Things. That arrogant hound, his father, had given the preposterous title to himself. Power had not only gone to his head it inhabited his nose, toes, kidneys, bladder, and sundry other organs as well. For practical purposes, he was merely the founder and chief executive officer of the intergalactic corporation, *Genes-R-Us*. His company owned the gene-patent on all life-forms in every galaxy. Every living thing, from the merest microbial cell to the largest most awesome beast, now had the *Genes-R-Us* brand upon it. All had been designed to be tractable and were bred only for profit. Hominid peoples were among those enslaved. They lived only to please their masters—modified, micro-chipped, and confined to their miserable barracks at night.

Jeffrique was a very bright lad, if a touch impetuous. Like small boys everywhere, he had an attraction to muck, combined with a strong dislike of cleanliness and order. He'd been happily fiddling about with his chemistry set in the privacy of his own bedroom for some time, and had even created a tiny planet, which he made orbit his light bulb for several space-time months. After it had passed through her celestial being twice, it was finally obliterated by his mother, Alpha Dawn, with a fly swat.

The life of the youngest son of two enormous forces with inter-galactic aspirations can be a lonely one. Jeffrique welcomed his mother's regular visits to his room, however occasionally tyrannical. Kylee, Her Celestial Motherness, is a shadowy figure, long out of favour with the more male-oriented creation theorists. But she loomed large in young Jeffrique's world, as mothers do. She had entered a mid-eternity hippie phase and had recently changed her name from Kylee to Alpha Dawn, because she believed that the numbers were more auspicious.

Alpha Dawn had taken to seeking out minor stars to re-arrange their planets so that they fitted a lovely book she had written about Librans, Scorpios, Geminis, and such-like. The title of her book was originally *Hororscope*, although the spelling has varied over the ages. When she met a group of planets that did not fit her cosmology, she would have them moved about until they did. The residents of those planets, if any, briefly found their previously settled lives suddenly made turbulent and unpredictable by the movements of the once-stable heavens. This of course spawned that mainstay of the women's magazines, the zodiac columnist, again restoring at least a sense of peace and predictability to those of the populace who looked for hope in such places, or a laugh with the girls over a coffee.

Waldorf, the not-really-nameless Creator-Of-All-Things, liked to breed 'em tough. Mostly a painful absence in Jeffrique's world, his fierce, critical eye hurt the growing boy just as much as his usual unavailability. Was it worse to have every birthday forgotten, or to face his icy disapproval when the space-cart, which you had built to impress him, failed to meet his crushing standards of perfection?

But Alpha Dawn did greatly care for, and watch over, her youngest boy. She was presently about to manifest that love in Jeffrique's room. She clanked her bangles across his threshold and looked about. He hadn't seen her in there for a space-time week or so and was happily involved in a particularly entrancing chemical experiment involving some carefully chosen molecules mixed with a whiff of ammonia, which he'd snaffled from his older brother's meth lab. Before he could see how it turned out, her up-market drawl penetrated his thoughts.

'Dahlingest boy, you really marst get control of this space. Managing spaces is Us. It is the family thing. It is whart we do. My stars, what's that varle stench?

It's like the stairwell of a multi-storey car park after all the pubs have shut.' (Kylee had gotten around a fair bit before her marriage).

At this point, Jeffrique became aware that the ammonia fumes wafting from under his door had given him away. He resolved to use a draft-excluder at the base of his door during future experiments.

'You know my rules, dahlingest boy,' she continued. 'No clean room, no dessert for the foreseeable.'

'Yes, Your Gracious Celestial Motherness,' replied young Jeffrique, with only a tad of sarcasm. No dessert for the foreseeable, on their time scale, meant no dessert for a few dozen weeks. That is, eternity in small-boy time.

Alpha Dawn swept out in a cloud of incense, leaving her boy to "get control of this space". Naturally, he looked for the fastest and easiest way to do so. Kicking aside a few favourite toys and other useful bits and pieces, he scooped up the 243 dirty socks lying about, along with a month's supply of half-eaten fruit, a quantity of congealed hamburger, and the beaker containing the gurgling remains of his latest experiment. He lugged them to the nearest evacuation-portal, tossed them in and pressed the red eject button, without a thought as to where they would end up.

As it happened, their starship, the *Cosmic Hub*, was cruising past the lifeless small blue planet 3159 XZ. The planet was not lifeless in the sense of being a couch-potato. It had only just acquired the necessary conditions to sustain life. At that point in time, the future Earth did not yet have a flammable oxygen-ridden atmosphere. So, when the awful mass of boy-floor trash was ejected and dragged into 3159XZ's field of gravity, it did not burn to cinders but hurtled intact towards the primal seas below, striking them with a splash that doused a nearby volcano and would have startled residents thousands of kilometres away. If there had been any. The unwanted contents of young Jeffrique's room sank, still festering, to the pristine ocean floor. After a thousand years or so, it was fulfilling its destiny. Jeffrique had accidentally gotten the mix of foul old sock, elderly hamburger, rotting fruit, and random chemicals just right. He had created life in the sulphurous depths of the ocean on planet 3159XZ.

Happily unaware of the sock-astrophe that would soon begin, young Jeffrique watched the bundle hit the primal seas with a deeply-satisfying splash. His mind quickly drifted onto the succulent desserts that he had just saved himself from missing. Then he turned, picked up his Boobie and Benn space dolls, and began to play. (Boobie was to have an unfortunate influence on his choice of companions in his teenage years.)

Had His Gracious Celestial Daddyness, the nameless and unknowable Creator-Of-All-Things, been aware of this event, he would have been cosmically and stupendously furious. The adult Jeffrique would much later have cause to imagine his reaction many times.

'At the end of the day, vis a vis projected corporate outcomes, taking into account loss of hominid and other valuable life-resource input,' he would begin... 'you, you brainless idiot-boy have stuffed up my bottom-line far beyond the capacity of your moronic little mind to imagine!' (This tirade would have been accompanied by sundry random comets being torn apart and sent hurtling into the cosmos by the power of his quantum-computer-assisted mental energy.)

'Which one are you anyway, boy?'

'Er, er, Jeffrique, Your Gracious Celestial Fatherness.'

'Egads, one of my own! I have bred a fool. Who is the mother of this miscreant?'

His second-in-charge would have done some nervous foot shuffling, before he ventured, 'He's Kylee's youngest, sire.'

Some of the nameless Creator's wives were not particularly memorable, but Kylee, alias Alpha Dawn, was not amongst those. Her willowy beauty, luminous pale skin, and her startlingly large grey eyes, were equalled only by her strength of purpose.

'Kyleeeee!' he'd have boomed, creating sonic waves that would mystify astronomers for millions of years to come.

'I have absolutely nothing to say to you unless you address me as Alpha Dawn,' would be the haughty reply, when she finally manifested herself at his side.

'Your moronic child has stuffed up my bottom-line.'

'Well, it's about time somebody did. Your obsession with endlessly expanding the business has gone too far. You're like a greedy weed that needs spraying.'

His father would explode at that. Jeffrique shuddered at the thought.

As *Genes-R-Us* had grown over the millennia, Waldorf had begun selling his concept to franchisees. At great cost to each new franchisee, genetically modified useful life-forms were then introduced onto likely planets which had been forcibly acquired by *Genes-R-Us* and "purified" of any existing rogue beings. He maintained an erratic, yet fierce, vigilance over all aspects of their operations.

Planets capable of supporting more life just than a few very unfussy bacteria were particularly rare and valuable. But hapless Jeffrique had blundered upon a planet which was just ready to become a throbbing womb of creation. A few billion years later, life would morph into dinosaurs which could either steal your apple turnover or seize you by the jugular and start snacking. Not long after that (in space-time, you understand) hominids would appear. These two-legged primates with an urge to build things and breed like flies would take the planet into their tender care.

So far, luck was with Jeffrique. His father was not aware of what his youngest lad had done. On the day of the boy's mistake, the surveillance-minion who should have been examining the current state of planet 3159XZ, had started an argument with his wife the night before, got pissed, then crawled into work nursing a hangover of galactic proportions. The glare of the screen made him nauseous, and he'd spent most of the day in the john, throwing up and moaning faintly. Thus, the only comment he recorded about his target that day was "cooling very nicely".

So it began, life on Earth, four billion years ago last Tuesday. Although it still raged and belched volcanically from its molten core, the planet was just cool enough, watery enough, to sustain primitive life, yet close enough to its sun-star for warmth. You may not have wanted to holiday there, dear reader, even on a discount package. But the lower life forms are adaptable, and not prone to whining about the weather. They thrived.

How could the child Jeffrique know the horrendous pickle that his lazy housekeeping would land him in a few billion years later?

Leo

An excellent week for the industrious ant.
Probable nest disturbances on the 8th
can be repelled by mass biting.

Five

M'bali could not settle to anything. She normally approached each task of her day in an orderly manner. But now she was wandering haphazardly through her housework. Several times she arrived in doorways only to find that she had no idea what she had come there for. She felt that her head might explode in a blast of unanswered questions and bewilderment if she didn't tell someone about her saucer sighting. But *The Briar Patch* was a B&B as well as her home. If she failed to get rooms prepared in a timely manner, bankruptcy loomed.

As she sipped a fresh beverage on the sofa, M'bali's eyes wandered over the beams of her arched living room ceiling while she mulled over her choices. Who to tell? It must not be anyone connected to the golf club. One too many champers and they would be blabbing and teasing at her foolishness. Tell no-one connected to the Country Women's Association, of which she was president. She loved most of those women, but they also loved a glass, or four. She longed to share her story with her farmhand, Roxy, who was normally a discrete ear. But Roxy might share the story with her footy-playing partner, Jarrid. It seemed to M'bali that there was probably a bit too much pillow-talk between those two for an outlandish secret to be kept.

'I know,' she muttered. 'I'll drive out and tell Jess and Rivers'. This enterprising young couple had moved from the distant city of Slique a few years ago. Quimbleton called them "the ferals". The young couple did not like being called ferals—but alternatives was a label they could live with. Dread-locked and dressed in the uniform of market-hippie clothing worn by their group, they were part of a small colony attracted to living in the unspoilt wilderness outside the town. Most of the locals gave them only a grudging tolerance, provided they worked. They did. But, apart from lending a hand at fund-raising busy bees, they kept to themselves. M'bali felt sure that they did not participate in the Quimbleton gossip circuit. Both were far too different, and far too busy working at part-time jobs while they built their home in the deep woods, hand-made by hand-made mud brick. At the same time, they were trying to establish the beginnings of an organic farm.

Dear reader, it is a funny thing about hominids, if you told most of them to wear a uniform they would jack up and refuse. Yet Quimbleton had an accepted uniform—track suit or jeans and boots in winter, flip flops and shorts in summer. All items in the sensible subdued colours that any rational being would and should choose. The alternatives did not conform. They dressed like wild birds.

As she piloted her sturdy four-wheel drive down dusty forest tracks, M'bali recalled how they had first met a couple of years before. It was after an event to prepare the site for a town swimming pool. On noting how hard they had pitched in, despite how exhausted they both looked at the start, she had offered to shout them a coffee at *Pat's Coffee Parlour*—Quimbleton's only attempt at urban chic. Once they settled on a black leather booth in the prison-grey interior, she asked about their lives.

'Rivers wants to start a certified-organic farm,' Jess told her. Rivers raised his sandy eyebrows at her with a faint grin.

She corrected herself. 'I mean we *both* want to. I guess I had it pretty cushy living with my folks when I was a student. I'm finding it a slog building our own house here. It's hard not to get a bit disillusioned by back-bending labour in this heat.'

Mostly, she tried to hide those feelings from Rivers, but he was too tired and fired up with his dream to notice anyway.

'We are passionately against genetically-modified food,' Rivers told M'bali. He added that they belonged to an activist collective who had the same vision.

M'bali liked them both at once. Rivers with ideals close to her own heart, and Jess so candid and honest.

'We're so exhausted,' the girl confided. 'We fight now, we never used to fight. Rivers came home from a farmer's meeting last week and I totally lost it. I was up to my eyebrows in wet mud bricks. He started babbling on at me. I told him, "Don't you dare go off on some political campaign and leave me here alone slugging my guts out".'

Rivers butted in. 'I blew it even worse. I told her she was just tired.'

'Yeah,' Jess agreed. 'Then I yelled, "Don't you dare patronise me! I'm doing all I can, and it's already too much".' Sobbing angrily, she had stalked off to their makeshift cubby-hole of a bedroom, where she threw herself down on the quilt which had been sewn with her mother's sad and reluctant best wishes.

This should have been an idyllic stage of their lives, but it had suddenly turned into a nightmare. M'bali had immediately offered to lend her labour to the cause. 'I run my place along organic lines—no pesticides, no artificial fertilisers and nothing genetically-modified. I'd love to come and give you a hand occasionally.' They had accepted, a little reluctantly at first. But as she bent her wiry back to the task of shovelling clay and always brought tasty home-made treats for their brief breaks, they had gradually warmed to her.

Now she stopped the old vehicle next to their block—sending up a cloud of dust and a handful of shrieking birds into the air. The young couple were outside lugging barrows of mulch. M'bali ran her eyes over the growing house. She thought their half-completed mudbrick structure was charming. (All I can say is that it was not a bit charming by cosmic standards.) Both gave her a cheery wave as she trudged across torn up mud towards them.

'Smoko!' Rivers called. 'I'll go in and put the kettle on.'

Inside their shed they had cobbled together a semblance of home. Paintings and objects gifted by friends decorated the space, drawing attention from the corrugated metal walls. An old moss-green sofa looked out into the pale sheer trunks of the forest wall to the rear.

After they had chatted about various topics of mutual interest, M'bali ventured a question. 'How do you feel about the universe and all that?'

'Are you seriously asking whether we're old-school hippies who talk to the universe and ask it to solve our problems? I've got a bloody environmental science degree, M'bali,' Rivers replied irritably.

Jess put a calming hand on his clay-caked arm. 'What do you mean exactly, M'bali?' she asked.

'Well, for one thing I mean do you think there's life out there?'

'Has to be,' Rivers replied. 'Astronomers are finding so many planets with the right conditions these days.'

Jess nodded in agreement.

'Intelligent life? I mean far more than a few hardy microbes?' M'bali asked them.

'Sure, less likely, but why not.'

M'bali took a calming breath. This was it. 'You know how I climb onto my roof to comet-watch. Well... I saw a flying saucer land in my garden this morning.'

'Seriously?'

'Very seriously.'

'Did little green men take you in and probe you in the traditional manner?' Rivers asked.

M'bali grinned. 'I get plenty of probing without little green men, thanks very much.'

Jess took a sip of tea. 'What did it look like?'

'Silver, and like a sleek, updated version of the traditional shape, as fantasised by nutjobs who've taken too much voodoo juice.'

'What did you do? Where is it now?'

'I climbed down from the roof and walked over to where it seemed to have landed. Nothing there.'

'If anyone but you were telling me this, M'bali, I would think they were teasing, lying, or out of their tiny tree,' Jess told her.

Rivers looked thoughtful. 'Are you scared?'

'Confused, disbelieving, curious, scared—you name it.'

'Are you going to tell that old cop?'

M'bali threw back her head and laughed. 'Doug Dewar! No way. I know him pretty well, but only because we've worked on some community projects together. I reckon he'd just crack up laughing—and I wouldn't blame him.'

*

When she returned home, M'bali was surprised to see an exceptionally glamorous couple sitting on her sofa and sipping drinks with her friend Gaz. Whoever they were they hadn't booked.

Virgo

Be prepared to fly at a moment's notice.
This is the week when the pelican builds her nest.
Avoid oil slicks and fishhooks.

Six

Celestial boy prince Jeffrique had been whizzed away through the farthest galaxies, oblivious to the burgeoning life he had begun. Many space-years later, he had outgrown the chemistry set, discovered girls, been away to college, experimented with illegal substances, cleaned up his act a bit, and had assumed a certain amount of responsibility in *Genes-R-Us*. Initially, his role was limited to cleaning up space junk, and tossing it to oblivion in the nearest black hole. Reckless hominids building escape rockets were the main source of his work. Only last week, an entire transport fleet had been taken out by one lump of orbiting space junk which had ricocheted from ship to ship like a pea in a whistle. At least, the silly beasts provided him with employment.

Across the endless galaxies, he served his time on the lowest rung of the corporate ladder whilst hoping that His Gracious Celestial Daddyness would eventually notice his dedication. At least, a modicum of attention would be nice. Approval, followed by promotions, would be a dream come true.

Eventually, thanks to his mother's frequent interventions to hide his foolishness from his father, he gained a more responsible middle-management position in the *Planetary-Life Enhancement Division* (an ironic title and one we will learn more of later.)

By this time, celestial prince Jeffrique was a most desirable marriage prospect. And he was about to be preyed upon. One night, by the light of the several blue moons of Kizox, (a planet fashionable enough to have a name amongst the swinging younger set), Jeffrique was lounging on the outdoor terrace of Bar-bariq. He felt faintly bored by the same old, same old crowd.

Zera had a successful career of her own as a zoologist. But she had reached the age where her ovaries were twitching. As she draped herself in a variety of flimsy, expensive garments (all just short enough to be classily seductive) she consulted her mother on the effect produced. 'Do you think the silver is better than the blue, Mumsy?'

Her mother surveyed it from the comfort of her armchair. 'Give me a spin, darling girl.'

Zera twirled, smiling demurely.

'Ooh, yes. That will do nicely.'

Thus armed, Zera set off for Bar-bariq. As a celestial being of vast pedigree, she did not walk into a room. Having the necessary nano-chip to master teleportation, she manifested herself wherever she chose. That night, she manifested herself onto the dance floor, just as Jeffrique's lazy attention drifted onto it. As soon as he saw her, he knew that she was The One; the Ultimate She. 'I must have that girl by my side for all eternity,' he murmured to a friend.

'Settle down Jeffers boy, all the hot babes in the galaxies are at your disposal.'

'And most of them are so very disposable,' Jeffrique told him, having disposed of quite a few, in the nicest possible way. Her flimsy dress and flowing hair lived up to his wildest imaginings (She was already quite up to date with his wildest imaginings, having followed his Tweets for some time.) Their eyes met. Almost in a trance, he now rose, drifting to her side. Soon, their perfect bodies fell into a rhythmic love-dance, which didn't end until the last of the blue moons of Kizox had fallen below the horizon.

'I really must get home. Mumsy and Pater will be worried,' she whispered in response to an invitation back to his starship. She would make him work for this conquest. However, within weeks, Zera was caught in her own net. She also was hopelessly besotted. Ah yes, love is blind, even amongst the galaxies' elite.

The parental blessings of both sides were given. Zera's parents gave theirs with great pleasure. 'A celestial prince,' her mother cried. 'What a catch.' The grandchildren would be gorgeous and so well provided for.

Jeffrique's side gave theirs with much relief. 'The girl seems bright and sensible. And, fortunately, I sense a strong will under all that glamour,' Alpha Dawn told his father. Waldorf grunted. All this marital organising was her domain. He had a new hominid model on his computer screen. A few gene snips and it now had some limited powers of flight combined with a strong homing instinct which would hopefully overcome the creatures' tendency to escape. Perfect for swifter deliveries if they could master the droppings issue.

After a wedding ceremony that lit up the cosmos, the lovers embarked on a nuptial flight—a honeyflit in the parlance of their kind. One day, their roving life took them past the little blue planet known to him as 3159XZ. Some eons of time had passed since the child Jeffrique had jettisoned his junk onto it.

'Rark, babe! There's that little blue planet I told you about. You know, the one where I jettisoned the contents of my bedroom floor to avoid one of the cosmic tanties of The Mother. Do you mind if we land and look around?'

Zera, who was thoroughly sick of flying around and wanted to land somewhere exciting and new, immediately agreed.

They exited the craft into a world vibrating with life. The minion back at headquarters who had failed in his surveillance of 3159XZ's life status would be disposed of when Jeffrique got back in the ship and told his father what was growing here, out of control and unobserved. It was mayhem. A dense cloud of little black flies hovered around him like erratic miniature vultures. Although they did not land on his body, their persistent whine added to his irritation. He swatted at them irritably but ineffectually. For a few minutes, they darted in with the desperation of life-forms which had survived for hundreds of millions of years by finding the slightest moisture in a continent that was dry and getting drier in many parts. Surprisingly, the flies soon gave up and drifted dispiritedly away. No proper smelly animal life there, they buzzed to themselves, in some confusion. To avoid the pestilence, Zera had dived into the shining sea and begun to swim at what was to her a lazy pace.

Several minutes later, a hominid voice broke into Jeffrique's reverie. 'Hi, mate. I've been watchin' you having a swat at the flies. Persistent little bastards. Looks like ya forgot the Aeroswat. Have a spray of mine,' it said cheerfully.

Jeffrique left his reverie to find a six-foot-three-inch ape-brain, with a mass of scruffy blond hair on top, gazing down at him and proffering a red metal container. Soon he would have to tell headquarters to arrange the destruction of these primitive creatures. He didn't want to have a chat with one, but like all clever psychopaths, he was capable of being charming and affable when the occasion warranted it. A peaceful honeyflit warranted that effort.

'I see they're leaving you alone. You clearly have the antidote to those little pests. I am most grateful.' He accepted the can.

'So, I just push this thing on top?' The hominid nodded. Jeffrique sprayed himself. The substance stank like a *Genes-R-Us* chemical facility. Being both a genetically and nano-chip enhanced cosmic entity, he could understand the basics of any language in existence. He had just never seen a can of insect repellent before.

'You're not from around here, are yer mate?' said the cheerful voice.

Jeffrique favoured him with a grin. 'Why, no. As a matter of fact, I am on my honeyfl…er honeymoon with my lovely wife swimming out there.'

'Congratulations, mate. Brilliant swimmer. Is she an Olympian?'

'Olympian? That isn't a term I'm familiar with.'

'Not to worry. Name's Gavin Cooper, mate, but you can call me Gaz,' the hominid went on. 'What's yours?'

Mentally shuffling through the planets' list of popular names to select one that was similar to his own, the alien came up with Jeffree. It sounded frightfully common. It pained him to say it.

The hominid extended a water-dimpled brown hand. 'Pleased ter meetcha, Jeffree,' it said. Fortunately, Jeffrique had encountered the custom of shaking hands before. It wasn't nearly as unpleasant as the exchanges of random bodily fluids which formed part of greeting rituals on Qwozmos34WK, his least favourite planet in all of creation.

'So how long are you planning to stay around here?' the beast inquired.

Oh, how the lower lifeforms did go on. The hairy uncombed creature was as persistent as the little black flies. 'We actually haven't decided. Playing it by ear as they say.'

'You guys got a place to stay? Not much available at this time of year. Peak season, and all that,' it said.

'Well, er, we actually hadn't planned on staying, more like a flying visit,' Jeffrique replied with sly humour. As he spoke, he realised that they should stay for a while so he could survey just how much unauthorised life had infested this unsavoury little outpost. His father, the Creator-of-All-Things, would be impressed by his diligence for once.

'This this place does get to you, doesn't it? You know, I wouldn't mind hanging about for a while.'

The six-foot-three-inch hominid smiled revealing a quantity of white but uneven teeth. Jeffrique found such imperfections most unsettling.

'Cool as,' it said. 'It's peak season and the hotel-motel in town will be full, but I think my friend M'bali has a free room at her place. She does a bit of B&B for extra cash. The place isn't real five-star flash. No jacuzzi or free in-house movies, and such like. But she's a great cook, and she'll spoil you to death.'

'Zee-star,' Jeffrique called at the distant figure executing a better-than-Olympic standard crawl stroke thirty metres from shore. 'Do you mind if we stay here for a few days? This place is so relaxing. I wouldn't mind lingering a while.'

'Super-starry idea. Genius in fact,' Zera yelled back. As we know, she was more than ready to linger and relax somewhere. This place was lovely, if not exciting.

'Done, er…mate. Thanks so much for your assistance,' Jeffrique said. 'How do we get to this, er…B&B place then?'

The hairy hominid turned around. 'See the little track that breaks into the beach over there? M'bali lives a short distance down it.'

Jeffrique knew her shack only too well. The *Suzerator-6* had landed there and was presently hidden deep under layers of protective mulch.

As Zera rose out of the water like a revelation of the possibilities of female beauty, the ape-brain let out a sudden breath. 'Wow, she's a looker, your wife.'

But, when introduced to her, he shook her hand exactly as he'd shaken Jeffrique's, without a sign of the sleazy ogling she'd had aimed at her in other worlds. 'G'day, Zera, pleased to meet you. I'm Gavin, better known as Gaz to my mates,' he said. 'Almost everything will be booked out at this time of year. I've offered to see if I can get you and your old man a room with my friend, M'bali. She lives a short walk down that track.'

Signalling them to follow he strode off. As soon as he was out of hearing, Zera allowed herself to let out a giggle as her eyes followed him. Gaz was clad in a baggy floral number that flapped down to knee level. 'What is that bizarre garment he's wearing on his lower parts? Do they really need to camouflage their genitals so thoroughly and ridiculously on this planet?'

'I think they call them board-shorts,' her partner replied. 'They wear them on Botoz too. I remember seeing some on the pod screen on *Galaxies' Gooniest Gear*. I think they serve the purpose of giving the wearer's future kids a big laugh when they see their father's old shots on screen. I wish I had a video of my old man in a pair. Something that silly flapping around his majestic family jewels could bring even *him* down to a laughable level,' he said with a trace of sadness. His self-obsessed father seemed less a family member than a distant god to him.

'The ocean here is divine, star-dream,' Zera told him. 'I did want to stop *somewhere* to relax, but I was hoping we could find somewhere that's a bit more…evolved, for a longer stay. For one thing, I'm sure the food and service will be quite dreadful here.' She may have chosen to do a doctorate in hominid studies, but that didn't mean she wanted to live in their sordid little houses in her spare time. (Of course, she didn't. You don't expect your local zoologist, who specialises in giraffes, to pull up a ladder and have a beer with them, do you?)

'I don't want to here for too long, Zee-star. But these local peasant-apes are too stupid to twig who we are, and we both need a bit of fresh air.'

They both laughed.

'Yes, lots of swimming in this divine ocean. Maybe I'll learn to ride one of those planks out there too. And I can study a few hominid habits for my research in the process.'

They kept tracking metres behind Gaz down the sandy trail. Unseen things scuttled in the bushes and white birds circled overhead, screeching. When they arrived at the hominid hovel, no-one appeared to be home. To their surprise, Gaz slid open a door and invited them in. 'Don't stand on ceremony, folks. We don't lock doors here and M'bali won't mind at all.'

The hominid led them into an open-plan room with floor-length windows opening to the garden. He threw a few beans in a kitchen gadget which produced a fragrant substance they had never tasted before. As they were sipping it enjoyably and dealing with his impertinent questions, they heard a vehicle pull up outside. A four-legged hairy creature with floppy ears and a powerful underslung jaw, which had been drowsing in a corner, rose awkwardly then raced out the door.

'Wozzer, darling boy!' a female voice exclaimed. A tall woman, clad in mud-stained work gear, soon entered. She was trailed closely by the panting beast. As she smiled broadly at him, Jeffrique critiqued her teeth. Sound by hominid standards. She spoke, 'Hello. Has Gaz been recruiting some more guests by any chance?'

'M'bali, meet Jeffree and…sorry I forgot to ask your name.' Her dazzling beauty had sent his brain into a turmoil.

'It's Zera. So lovely to meet you, M'bali. I do hope you have a vacancy. Your house is delightful.'

Yes, dearest reader, they are charming. Gorgeous and charming. What a recipe for success on celebrity bedazzled Azua.

'I do have a vacancy. Some people just cancelled.'

Oh, M'bali. How different life might have been if you had been fully booked.

Libra

Foxes are advised to stay home
on the 10th and 16th of the week.
All pattering and galloping noises
should be viewed with dark suspicion.

Seven

Gaz rose to his feet. 'I'll be off now. Places to go, people to see. Zera, if you really want to learn to surf, I'd be happy to teach you. Teach you both, of course,' he corrected.

'Why thank you so much. You know where we live,' Zera said. Jeffrique managed to hide his annoyance from her but not from the searching brown eyes of M'bali was already striding towards a small counter. 'We've just got a few little booking formalities to go through before I see you to your room.'

They rose to join her.

'Just names and address, phone number and email address on this form here, and then…how are you paying, by the way?' People didn't usually arrive at her remote property without a vehicle and dressed only in swimming costumes.

The couple exchanged glances. Jeffrique focused his nanochip-assisted mind on the local banking network and its procedures. He came up with the word "credit card", and some other relevant information, in half a second. Without a noticeable pause, he answered with apparent innocence. 'Credit card. Actually, it's American Express.'

'Sorry, I don't take that card. But there's no problem though. You can get cash in Quimbleton. It's not too far away. There's a machine there in the general store. So, we'll say paying by cash then?' M'bali went on.

'Yes, yes, cash,' Zera cut in.

M'bali's mind was racing. These visitors had arrived on foot with no luggage and she didn't usually allow any travellers the privilege of not paying ahead. But they were both expensively groomed and Zera's slinky swimsuit was clearly designer label. *They could still be just thieves with great taste*, she warned herself.

'No offence, but do you have any other form of identification? I hate asking people like yourselves, but it's had to become my standard procedure to ask that. Unfortunately, I've had the odd group doing a midnight flit.'

'Yes, of course,' Jeffrique responded smoothly. 'What would you like as identification?'

'Driver's licence or passport will do just fine.'

'Certainly, I must have dropped my licence outside. I'll be back in a moment.' Jeffrique stepped out onto the veranda, cursing the hominid's suspicions. 'Rarking liberty. She'd be branded and held in a breeding-stall in any decent society,' he muttered to himself.

He began a rapid mental search of the country's registered driver's licences with the first name of Jeffree. At astonishing speed, he found one and had the actual licence appear in his hand within seconds. With a glance, he changed the photo to an image of himself. Funnily enough, he looked rather like Jeffree Bradlee Smith anyway. A few hundred miles away, in an isolated city named Slique, one Jeffree Smith would wonder for weeks how his licence had left his wallet and disappeared, leaving everything else intact.

'Identity theft, Jeff,' his girlfriend had concluded.

'Who by, the fuckin' fairies?'

Unaware of the chain of events he had just begun, Jeffrique strolled back into the entry hall. 'Here's my driver's licence.'

M'bali did not reach out a hand to take it. *Did he find his licence in his butt cheeks?* she wondered, snatching a quick glance at his purple bathing costume. He was forced to place the object on the counter in front of her. She ran eyes over its surface for an insulting length of time.

'Thanks. Can't be too careful,' she said, as she transcribed the number and address into the guest register.

The irony of that statement was lost on her until much later.

As soon the formalities were concluded, Jeffrique spoke, 'M'bali, you seem like a practical woman, and I'm wondering if you can help us. Our four-wheel drive motorhome is bogged on the beach, a few kilometres away. Could I trouble you to give us some help to get it out? The rest of our gear is in the vehicle, of course. I'm afraid we're the most helpless city types.'

'Well, sure. Your possessions will be fine. No-one around here would take them. But I hope that you're bogged well away from the rise of the tide. We've had a few accidental salt-water car-washes around here over the years.'

'Oh yes, well above the high-water mark, more by good luck than good judgment,' Zera chimed in. Jeffrique had better use his powers to move a vehicle from somewhere, and fast.

'In that case, how about I serve you a quick breakfast first?'

They agreed. As she worked and chatted M'bali took in their appearance. She could not believe that any woman could scrub up so well first thing in the morning. Her perfect cafe-au-lait skin, those huge black-lashed, and impossibly violet eyes; that abundant hair with not a tangle in it. She flicked toast onto a fine china plate. *And he's creepily perfect too*, she mused. *That six-pack looks like a rock carving.*

'What can we visitors do for fun around here?' Mr Perfection asked her.

'We're not exactly a major centre for the arts, but that isn't why most people come here. Beaches, swimming, some great surf breaks; fishing, bushwalking, riding, or just lying about reading, that sort of thing. If you like fauna, you won't see much native wildlife unless you go out at night because they're mostly nocturnal, on account of the heat.'

Jeffrique laughed internally. As far as he was concerned, one of the native animals had just been cooking and serving them breakfast.

Once her guests had eaten, M'bali was ready to retrieve their vehicle. Her mind switched to that topic. A few kilometres away? How had they got here? The day was extremely hot, they had brought no water with them, and she could neither see nor smell slightest hint of sweat. Mind you, Zera had been in the ocean, her waist-length locks were still drying. But he had not, his hair was bone dry and yet he smelled totally fresh and fragrant. M'bali detached herself from the mantelpiece and strolled over to the kitchen with her cup. 'Well, if you're sure you're rehydrated, I'll get the ute, and take you down to your vehicle,' she said. 'Wait here a bit.'

Zera and Jeffrique wandered out into the yard at the sound of an engine starting up. A quaint farm vehicle soon appeared, followed at a distance by the tan four-legged creature with the slobbery mouth. Wozzer-the-dog let out a series of wheezy, indignant barks. Keeping up with the ute was getting harder for him these days.

M'bali climbed from the cabin to stride towards the old beast. 'Up until a year ago, he could leap into the tray of my ute unaided. He still likes a frolic, but the arthritis in his back legs affects his jumping, so he gives me a yell to tell me lift him up there.' In a softer aside to the animal, she added, 'You just can't bear to be left behind, can you, old mate?' She turned towards the visitors. 'Hop in, guys. Don't stand on ceremony round here.'

Jeffrique wondered why these silly creatures kept saying not to stand on ceremony. They wouldn't know what a real ceremony looked like.

Her animal pal safely stowed and secured, M'bali joined them in the cabin, then started the engine. Dust rose, and her domestic birds scattered, as they eased out of the yard towards the narrow, sandy track leading to the beach. Once there, M'bali got out and lowered the tire pressure. 'Now where is that famous bogged Toorak Tractor of yours hiding then?'

'Did I give the impression that we drive a farm vehicle? How silly of me. No, it's a four wheel drive motorhome,' Jeffrique replied. 'Anyway, turn left and, as I said, it's a few kilometres down the beach.'

He doesn't know much local slang, M'bali thought idly. *Where are these guys from?*

As they sped down the sand with windows down, the iodine tang of the sea took over from the warm earth and peppermint scents of the scrub. They drove in silence until the bogged vehicle came into view. When he'd put his mind to seizing a means of transport for themselves, and mentally moving it, Jeffrique had done his research first. A brand-new blue *Mercedes Sidebottom* motor-home floundered up to its axles in the powdery sand (The vehicle having been named after the daughter of its inventor, a Mr Sidebottom.) Two surfboards, once the property of a world champion who was holidaying in a nearby town, were strapped to the roof. The vehicle had been his too. *Surfboards, a nice touch*, Jeffrique told himself.

'Wowee, cool wheels, and you sure made a good job of digging it in, my friends. I won't ask who was driving. I hate to see smart people blush. But not to worry, I've seen worse predicaments, and some of them I got into myself. I'll need your help, both of you. This is how we do it…'

After half-an-hour of demeaning physical labour, Jeffrique was unbelievably relieved that their machine was free. But to his irritation the M'bali-hominid then delivered a lecture on how to drive on sand, as well as how to get out if they got bogged again. She had also lent them her shovel and a tire pump, in case of future dramas.

'Well-earned refreshments,' M'bali told them, pulling a berry cake, plates, a chilled bottle of fresh fruit juice, and three elegant glasses out of a rectangular box. Deftly she divided up the spoils, and then lay back on one elbow looking about her, taking in the sea haze, and the swirling flight of the seabirds. The old dog lay beside her in the meagre shade of a bush as she absentmindedly stroked his head. Jeffrique stifled a yawn. He was feeding with the natives again.

'Have you two done much travelling?' M'bali asked. It was a standard question of hers. It usually brought out fantastic stories of adventures, blunders, and exotic scenes far away from her own fierce wilderness.

The two exchanged glances. A brief frown disturbed the perfection of Jeffrique's chiselled dial. 'Yes, rather lot. We have been incredibly fortunate. But we really hate to show off about it, you know,' he said, in tones that were clearly intended to close the subject.

M'bali grinned. 'Not travel wankers—that's a likeable trait.' They had no idea what that term meant but both smiled agreeably exposing the most impossibly perfect white teeth she had ever seen. *Some cosmetic dentist made a fortune and retired to the coast after they turned up*, she thought.

'We thought we'd spend our honeymoon exploring our own country now, but as you see, we're not very expert at it yet,' Zera put in.

As a child, M'bali had been a wiry-limbed thrill-seeker, the one who always responded to a dare or jumped off the high-dive board first. Her careful parents, whose genetic gifts were otherwise, had been at pains to rein her in. Sometimes, her impetuous side still broke out, surprising even herself. There was something not quite right about these two.

'You're not from around these parts, are you?'

'Er, no, we're city folk from Slique,' Jeffrique responded dredging up the name of the nearest city which was on his purloined driver's licence.

'No, I mean you aren't from this planet. I watched your space-ship land last night.'

Zera could not suppress a start. Her glance flew to her husband.

'Spaceship? You can't be serious. Just what were you drinking or inhaling last night, M'bali?' he asked with a cool grin.

'I'm a comet-hunter. I have a telescope on the roof. I also believe there is life out there somewhere in space and I'm just curious and stupid enough to want to meet it. Last night I saw a spaceship come in over my garden. But by the time I climbed down, it had disappeared. Then you two turned up.'

'What a fascinating hobby you have. But I'm afraid you're mistaken about us. We're just boring honeymooners from Slique,' Jeffrique went on.

Zera had now recovered enough to back him up. 'Yes, it is our honeyfl...moon.' She cast Jeffrique an adoring glance. 'We have many months to go...such heaven,' she added.

'It's a lovely change to be able to wander our own country without a plan. I'm usually such a perfectionist, some might say a control freak,' Jeffrique purred. *Rarking nosy hominid*, he thought. *She needs her nose put in a vice.*

'Sorry, it's been a confusing twenty-four hours, and I haven't slept much.' M'bali was inwardly kicking herself for opening her big mouth. She stowed the plates, glasses, and the bottle in her picnic basket, then stood up.

'I notice that you have GPS, so you'll have no trouble getting into Quimbleton. I'll leave you to it,' she said. Unaided, she loaded the morning-tea gear into the left-hand passenger's side of the ute, then lifted Wozzer into the tray and secured him.

'Have fun. If you want a meal tonight, I do cater sometimes, but it will cost extra. No need to tell me now if you don't want. You do your own thing, and I'll see you when I see you.'

'Thanks, M'bali, you really have been most helpful,' said Zera, favouring her with a smile of cosmic warmth.

'No worries, it was my pleasure.' *Why in heck did I open my stupid mouth*, she berated herself yet again.

Yes, M'bali, there are times when you do need to be a lot more careful how you use that mouth in the speech department.

Scorpio

Sloths are advised to live up to their name
on the 4th and 5th of the week.
Stay treed to avoid the fast, fanged or feisty.

Eight

As their hostess drove off into the distance, Jeffrique's carefully maintained air of casual sophistication dropped at once. 'You drive, Zee. How dare that hominid bovine lecture me. Don't say a word. And don't for rark's sake make any more plans for me to do rustic sports with these savages.'

'I'll thank you not to speak to me in that tone. I won't put up with it,' she warned him. When he didn't reply, she went on. 'If she saw us land, it was perfectly reasonable question. You know hominids—they have their noses into everything. It's just their nature. I find it a rather attractive quality myself, that's why I study them.'

'So sorry, my star. I'm just not used to socialising with the help.' He threw her a mischievous smile.

Zera drove on. The lone voice in the cabin was the impersonal one of the GPS telling her where to go. Her lovely eyes floated over the ancient landscape. Most life-forms didn't notice the brilliant curiosity hiding behind those eyes. They were too distracted by her beauty. She didn't entirely mind, at least it gave her privacy to think her own thoughts.

Her gaze flitted over the vigorous coastal scrub as it began to give way to the soaring forest of the hinterland. There was not a dwelling or person in sight. Tiny insects with transparent wings floated up and splattered on the windscreen. A larger winged creature hung like a distant threat, suspended from the blue ceiling of the sky. Shrieks and twittering hinted of life hidden amongst the dense bushes, and something long and scaly writhed off the road just in time.

'Wow! It's all so random and crazy, and yet it seems to work. Beautiful, too,' she mused aloud. Jeffrique appeared not to hear.

Zera had grown up on a large estate, the only child of mega-wealthy, but not too indulgent parents, who had home base on planet 210YQ, commonly known as Kizox. Their fields of goats produced silk-milk for the weaving industry. They could not nurture their own offspring, but the *Genes-R-Us* company cloned and hand-fed its own goats so that was of no consequence, except to the animals. Trees along the roadsides were engineered to glow in the dark, to guide the sleepy traveller. Zera missed that orderly, designer-world of her childhood. It was the nearest thing she had known to nature, until now.

As she piloted the van, Zera occasionally glanced tenderly at Jeffrique's perfect profile. But he remained lost in thought. After she had had driven steadily for half an hour, they entered a valley of farms leading to a small settlement. The amount of litter scattered on the roadsides was increasing, and now there was a sign. Quimbleton, Tidy Town of the Year, she read. The scattering of bottles, cans, wrappers, and plastic bags ended quite abruptly at the sign. Troop One of the local scouts has been on a re-cycling and fund-raising drive the day before, and Quimby, as the locals called it, once more resembled the tidy town of legend. There was only one troop of boy scouts in town, but Troop One had a nice ring to it. It signalled the possibility of two.

The original inhabitants of the area, a tribe of displaced indigenous people, had bestowed the name Quimbleton. I believe it means, roughly translated, "place of very many annoying small black flies". The name is apt. They are an abomination.

It wasn't much of a town as far as Zera could see, more like a village really, and not a very big or picturesque one. On the outskirts, several signs announced the approach of civilisation of some primitive kind. "Best burger in town at *Pat's Coffee Parlour*", a billboard screamed in discordant orange and reds. They passed a few weather-board cottages with strange flower gardens, then the small business district straggled by. A post office, petrol station, pharmacy, pub, cafe, clothing store, a humble little hall, a small school, and finally a large general store, lined this main street. Most of the buildings had wooden veranda posts.

'We're here, Jeffrique,' she told her silent partner.

He stirred. 'Have you seen the Bank of Festering-Ape-Shelter yet?' he asked, lifting his head and gazing about.

She laughed and ruffled his shining dark hair. 'There doesn't appear to be one.'

'But the M'bali creature said we could get cash here,' he replied irritably. 'Anyway, it doesn't matter. Give me a few minutes, and I can easily focus my mind and think some here. We don't have to go through their silly rigmarole.'

'Jeffy-star, I think we should. I grew up in the countryside. People in these small towns notice everything. Let's just fit in. I want to play hominid for a day or two.'

'Okay, okay, I bow to your wisdom. But where the rark do they get their currency? I wasn't really listening to her hominid drivel.'

'I'm going to pull in near that big shed that says *Quimby General Store*, so I can ask someone,' said Zera, with the humble practicality of wives everywhere.

Without waiting for Jeffrique's reply, she turned into the only free space in the carpark. They both clambered out. A shrivelled, yet alert, old couple was seated on the only bench outside the building. The bench was painted green and flanked by two pots of flowers. 'This bench was donated by Councillor Augustus Tinelli, for the comfort of our valued senior citizens,' a plaque on the back said.

Norbert and Francis watched Zera and Jeffrique approach with intent interest. Such a beautiful couple, so stylish—and they were new to the area. The girl looked like a princess—her glossy, flowing hair, the tailored linen shorts, the silk shirt, the fancy canvas espadrilles, the dazzling rock on her left hand and her general air of expensive well-being. Francis noted all that for purposes of gossip. Norbert had other interests, as will be seen.

'Hello there,' said the vision, taking off her designer-shades and bestowing the radiance of her smile upon them. 'I wonder if you would mind helping us. My husband and I are looking for somewhere to withdraw cash.'

'Of course, lovey,' replied Francis. 'There's one of those fancy cash-dispensing machines inside the general store over there. Not that I ever use it myself, I like a chat with Bert at the bank,' she said. 'Anyway, where are you people from, dear?'

'Slique,' said Zera carefully. 'We're down here on our honeymoon.'

The old woman's face lit up. 'Isn't that lovely? And where are you staying, dear?'

'Out at *The Briar Patch* with M'bali. Her friend Gaz is going to teach us to surf one day. I can't wait.' There, how ordinary and normal was that?

'We know M'bali, dear.'

'Soo lovely to meet you,' Zera cooed as she began to walk away. 'I'm afraid we are in rather a hurry,' she called over her shoulder.

Norbert's eyes had never left their vehicle. He could describe the grill-pattern of every *Mercedes Sidebottom* vehicle going back sixty years, and often did. Not that he'd ever owned one. He just had that kind of mind. Francis loved him anyway; she was a patient woman. Only Doug Dewar, the town copper, appreciated his obsession. Zera and Jeffrique's van had just been catalogued and they would later have cause to regret it.

As they entered the general store, Jeffrique's laser-gaze took in a bizarre collection of items from groceries to crude hominid garments. Where was the rarking money-machine? Turning, he saw that it was near the front wall behind them. Reaching for his card he walked over to it, followed by Zera. 'These primitive machines are always pretty self-explanatory,' he said as he swept his eyes over the face of it. 'Yeesss, card in there, key in your pin, and away we go. Just as well I thought to extract the pin from Jeffree Bradlee Smith's rather addled brain when I lifted his card,' he whispered to Zera as he keyed in the numbers. Money spewed out. He pocketed half and handed half to her. 'Come on Zee-star, I owe you a drink and the best meal these creatures can supply, from their no doubt revolting regional larders.' He threw a beautifully muscled arm around her waist to lead her out.

'Phwoah, did you get a good eyeful of him?' hissed Krystal, one of the teenage girls at the front cash registers, after the couple had paid and were traipsing back to the Merc. 'Talk about hot, hot, hot!'

'Who are they, do you reckon? They look like they've been on telly or something.'

'Maybe. We'll ask Parys at the pub tonight. She knows who's cool. Her mum buys all the best celebrity magazines like "Bad Idea" and "Hoo Who". And they've got Wolftel.' They both sighed for the lack of such a coo-ool parent.

Patient reader, it was ever thus with teenagers all over the many universes.

Jeffrique's search for the best meal in town didn't take long. The choice was either the hotel or *Pat's Coffee Parlour*. Not really fancying either, they reluctantly chose the former.

'*Quimby Quality Beefery*,' he read aloud at the entrance to the hotel dining room. 'I can hear my taste buds positively screaming with joy at the prospect of what I am about to receive.'

Relieved that his cosmic wit had returned at last, Zera laughed. 'Well, I'm game if you are. Do you remember that awful Globber Burga we were served on planet 376QK?' she asked.

'Unforgettable in every way. I couldn't get past the smell of rotting reptile on a bed of compost. Now, will this next experience set a new low in disgusting hog-swill? If it does, we're leaving. I don't care whether that makes us conspicuous or not.'

The Quimby pub, as in most small country towns, had a great deal of difficulty in attracting and holding chefs from the city. The visiting chefs were usually men, and unfortunately not the hunt'n, shoot'n and fish'n type. After a few weeks of after-hours boredom, they'd either hot-foot it back to the delights of the city or attack the kitchen hand with a meat-cleaver and then hot-foot it back to the city. That week, Zera and Jeffrique were amazingly lucky. The chef's job had just attracted a talented young female named Klaire who had two kids in need of a country up-bringing. She was going to stick it out no matter what.

A busty middle-aged woman, hiding her charms under a cakey layer of badly applied make-up, ushered them to a table. The *Quimby Quality Beefery* was almost full. Marj, the publican's wife, was stomping about on skinny, veined legs. Word about the new chef had spread rapidly down the bush telegraph, and she was stretched to the limit. She tossed a couple of menus on their table and charged off.

'I *would* like to order a drink. Thank you so much for asking,' Jeffrique commented sarcastically to her retreating back. She kept going, muttering under her breath about wankers in fancy footwear. He raised his eyebrows. Before he could react further, Zera handed him a menu, and they both began to read.

'Star-dream, I don't recognise a single ingredient, yet again.' Zera was used to this. When you travelled cosmic distances to strange worlds, it was a common experience. 'I'm just going to ask her what she'd recommend, as I usually do.'

'I'm in the same situation on this one. We'll ask the old painted savage when she finally comes back. By the way, I'm sorry I've been so distant. I'll make it up to you, in very many ways,' he added, reaching for her hand and bestowing a tender kiss on it.

'I did wonder where my Jeffrique had gone for a while there.'

After a few minutes, Marj came bustling back, taking their food order, slamming a drinks menu on the table, and fleeing before this demanding-looking pair of urban princesses could waste her precious time. Again they waited, now happily lost in the inane small-talk of lovers. Both the meal and their drinks eventually arrived. Surprisingly, both were not too bad by cosmic standards. The lovers communicated their pleasure to each other with lingering gazes.

'Honeymooners, are you?' the voice broke into their romantic moment. Jeffrique turned to see an ape-brain whose horribly sun-damaged skin was splotched like rotting fruit. It was leaning towards them, giving a truly awful display of teeth. Fortunately, Zera had warned him that giving the teeth was considered part of friendly hominid greeting.

'Honeymooners, yes we are. Does it show that much? I am Zera Smith, and this is my husband Jeffree.'

The creature extended a horny, calloused hand. 'Matt Vigano, farmer,' it said, 'and this is my wife, Joelene.' The stringy grey-headed woman, in jeans and faded tee shirt, was also delivering a gruesome display of middle-aged choppers. Jeffrique was smiling agreeably, but Zera realised that he seemed to find these encounters with the natives quite revolting, so she took over again. 'Very nice to meet you both. What is it that you farm then?'

'That, my dear, is the sixty-four-thousand-dollar question. What I *want* to farm is the new genetically modified bean called aneera. But do you think anyone else in this town can see my wisdom?' Without waiting for a reply, he continued, 'Move with the times, I tell them. More money for me, more money spent in town.'

Jeffrique had suddenly snapped to attention. 'Genetically modified. I'm not sure what you mean…' he began.

'Well, Son, I'm surprised you haven't heard. This country is finally catching up with the rest of the world. Some corporate geniuses overseas own the patent for a genetically engineered new form of aneera. It's bigger, better, and blooming be-yoootiful. But I'm afraid some of my neighbours are too hide-bound to see it. They're trying to lean on me not to go ahead with my project.'

Jeffrique bent his head, attempting to hide his reaction. His thoughts raced. *Rark! The ape-brains are designing organisms. You can't leave them unsupervised for a minute.* He suddenly recalled the space-junk he had barely noticed on their way to land. *And they must have rockets. What if they're already exporting new life-forms? The old man will explode. He'll shoot the messenger, and that would be me.*

The alien prince managed to keep his veneer of easy charm, despite his seething thoughts. 'So, what is to stop you planting this genetically modified aneera crop?' he asked.

'Nothing much, it's perfectly legal. But we'd sorta like to keep friendly relations with the neighbours,' Joelene told her. 'We've talked to a few movers and shakers in the district, and soon we'll have a lobby-group and big, big funding from the manufacturer too. That will get our message across, guaranteed. You can't stop progress.'

Ah yes, esteemed reader, "progress". A label applied to change by those who stand to profit from it.

Vigano fumbled in his shirt pocket, pulling out a business card. 'Here's our address. Drop by any time.'

'Thanks so much. And I wish you every success with your enterprise,' Zera told them. She and her partner rose to go, leaving the room in a flurry at their gorgeousness as they retreated.

Once in the vehicle, Jeffrique's charm offensive ended. She had expected to drive again but he pushed her aside and jumped in. 'I'll drive. I want out of here.'

'Don't ever shove me like that! In case you hadn't noticed, I'm not one of your minions. I'm your wife and you can quit ordering me about too.' This was a side of him she hadn't seen. He was a wildly exciting lover, but Zera would increasingly suspect that his vast intellect was flawed by psychic wounds she hadn't noticed during their whirlwind courtship. Reluctantly, she took the passenger's seat.

Without a word in reply, he started the engine, gunned it with a stab of his foot, and took off down the main street in a squeal of rubber. The van jack-knifed, spewing the contents of a loaded rubbish bin down the street. It ricocheted on.

'Rarking primitive tin can. Rarking useless piece of monkey-junk,' Jeffrique snarled as he took out his venom on the controls.

Sundry pieces of garbage, including an exploded *Doggy Doo* bag and three used condoms, were now pressed flat to the windscreen glass like peeping toms ogling a window. Zera collapsed in helpless laughter as their obscene cargo slid crazily up the glass. Further infuriated, Jeffrique accelerated, charging the heavy vehicle back towards the coast. They flew down a narrow, forested road which was not engineered for such insane speed. At times, he hugged the curves, at others he veered crazily towards the crumbling gravel edges on the other side. Zera thought of the soft watery bodies of Earth creatures who might blunder into their path. She guessed that they probably weren't very repairable with only the primitive technologies available to them. Superior technology had rendered the cosmic elite more-or-less immortal. Every organ was replaceable.

If Jeffrique had glanced in the rear vision mirror, he'd have seen a white shape battling down the road behind them. As it grew closer, blue and red lights began to flash on its roof. A siren began to wail. Norbert had put the town cop on their trail.

'Oh, rark! Hominid plod, that's all we need!' Jeffrique shouted. He braked sharply before reluctantly guiding the vehicle onto the narrow road verge. A cloud of dust briefly enveloped the car behind them. When it had cleared, a beer-gutted, but heavily muscled, middle-aged man, wearing unfashionable but sturdy plastic shades on his bulbous nose, was trudging towards them. Senior Sergeant Doug Dewar had been in the force for thirty-nine years. He was hoping to accept the government-issue retirement biro before too long, then throw it in a drawer somewhere. His dream was to settle down to golfing, fishing, and enjoying the company of his wife and his many mates in the district.

'Was there some good reason for you to be travelling at one-hundred-and-fifty while passing through the eighty-kilometre-an-hour zone back there, sir?' he asked.

'Officer I am so embarrassed and sorry,' Jeffrique replied. 'I'm on my honeymoon with this gorgeous lady, and I must have had a moment of carelessness. It won't happen again, I assure you,' he went on smoothly.

"Smoothly" was a manner which irritated Doug Dewar beyond anything else. 'A speeding Merc with this registration plate was just witnessed destroying a bin and road sign in Quimbleton, sir. (First strike to Norbert.) Any reason for the festive windscreen decorations, and your hasty departure from town?'

'My foot must have got jammed under the accelerator. I'm so sorry and embarrassed, officer.'

'Permanently, it seems. Do you realise that little kiddies live near this road, sir? What would happen if one of them ran out after a ball and you were going through at that speed?' Dewar's voice was calm, but his eyes were steely. He'd seen too many mangled little bodies pulled out of wrecks to be taken in by easy charm. *Smug city bastard with designer shoes. Probably had a designer dick as well*, he thought. But he kept his actions professional. 'Please blow into this instrument now, sir.' He appeared surprised that he had to teach the driver how to do it. 'Now, I need to see your driver's licence.'

Jeffrique reached for his wallet and produced the document. Dewar passed it to his female colleague without comment. She took a few steps away and began to check it on her hand-held computer. The policeman went on more conversationally.

'Surfing honeymoon, is it?' They nodded. 'Nice boards, verrry nice. Must have set you back a bit. Where are you folks heading next?' Dewar had learned to work at keeping the situation as calm and normal as possible in case the computer threw up something his suspects were likely to get over-excited about. No sense in revving them up first by being unfriendly and officious.

'We're staying locally, with M'bali Hoyle. She's been so good to us, and the beaches are so lovely that we've decided not to move on for a while,' Zera answered, hoping to win him over with her radiant attention and the fact that they were contributing to the local economy.

'With M'bali, eh. Great choice.'

'Doug, can I have a word?' his burly female colleague asked, in matter-of-fact tones. They stepped away a few paces away while she spoke to him briefly. He nodded, returned to the Mercedes, and spoke to Jeffrique again. 'Hand me the keys please, sir, then step out of the vehicle,' he said.

'Look, I know I was in the wrong, and I'm sorry. Just tell me what the fine is so we can get going, thanks,' Jeffrique said firmly. He'd dealt with local plod across the galaxies. You had to be polite but assertive. Don't let them intimidate you.

'Keys to me, and out of the car *now*,' Dewar told him, in a tone which said it would be a mistake to continue arguing. Jeffrique handed over the keys, undid his seat belt, and grudgingly stepped out.

'Jeffree Bradlee Smith, I am arresting you for the murder of Jo-Ellen Lambert. Anything you say will be taken down in evidence, and may be used against you as evidence,' the plodder informed him.

Jeffree Bradlee Smith was the original owner of the driver's licence. His single mother had succumbed to the current fashion for dyslexic spelling when she'd named him. As a child, Jeffree Bradlee had watched helplessly as a succession of violent partners belted her around her various sparsely furnished government houses leaving his mother battered, bruised yet still pathetically forgiving; and him full of a helpless rage which had never left him. After a childhood of petty theft, and cruelty to small animals, he had self-medicated with any sort of street drug he could get his hands on. Finally, he'd begun to deal in crystal meth, to fund a heroin habit of long-standing. Jeffrique, son of the nameless and unknowable Creator-Of-All-Things, had chosen the wrong driver's licence to steal.

After a long night of boozing and drugging in her seedy flat, Jeffree Bradlee had injected a little hooker with a little something to wake her up. But she'd remained unconscious. Even a few sharp slaps hadn't stirred her. He'd felt for a pulse, but there was none. He had grabbed most of his clothes and fled both her lifeless corpse, and the state of West Coast, and was presently on the other side of the continent, three thousand kilometres away. Lurking in Reef City with a beard and a new hairstyle, he was hoping that the fuss in Slique would die down. His long-term girlfriend was enjoying the break, unaware of the reason for their sudden departure.

Cosmic Jeffree could have chosen to un-manifest himself from his present position, and instantly escape Dewar. He briefly contemplated the idea but decided against it. His anger was fading. If he used his power to teleport himself away, he would draw attention to their presence and annoy his lovely Zera immensely.

He held out his wrists to be cuffed. 'I have no intention of resisting. I am innocent, as you will quickly find.'

'I'll have to ask you to drive the vehicle and follow us, ma'am,' Dewar told Zera. 'You'll be helping us with our inquiries.'

Sagittarius

This week, elephants will find it necessary to tramp through hominid crops in a desperate quest for food. Beware of poison arrows on the 4th.

Nine

On her return to the house, M'bali unpacked the picnic gear and immediately set out for her vegetable and herb paddocks followed by a shambling and sniffing Wozzer. She was in her third year of building the little property towards being an accredited organic farm. At night, she muttered and swore as her tired eyes wandered over a sea of compulsory paperwork. She was required to have a conversion plan documenting every step she made towards a biologically based farming system. And she had to sign a legal pledge that she was adhering to the rules—no artificial fertilisers or pesticides, and no genetically-modified plants. She worried about the water quality of the stream which flowed across her land because, as it wound down Quimbleton's lovely valley, it was shared by farmers with different agendas. Her water source would be tested, and it must be pure. Muscle soreness and backache had plagued her first year as she shovelled animal manure and compost and dragged heavy rolls of fabric to deprive weeds of light. Now her lithe body easily managed the physical load. It was the paperwork and planning for her integrated-pest-management system which tired her most.

At the far boundary, she could see Roxy, her young farm assistant, wielding a hoe amongst the vegetables. 'Hi, boss-lady,' she called. 'You're out late this morning, I mean this afternoon. Just as well I'm the stoic reliable type. I've fed the horses.'

'Oh, mega apologies. I can't believe I didn't let you know I'd be delayed. I shot out to Jess and Rivers' place. They're finding it very tough trying to work paid jobs, build the house, start farming—you know how it is. They needed a bit of an ear.'

Roxy understood. At the start of these enterprises, there was very little income, and a lot of outgoings. 'I thought it might be something like that. I know you, mothering the tired, wounded and worried.'

They worked on in silence for several hours before M'bali signalled afternoon smoko.

Wozzer, in the manner of dogs, had found the shadiest tree to lounge beneath so they joined him there. Roxy promptly lay on her back stretching her tired body. M'bali doled out cold water and slices of a chocolate cake she'd hurriedly pulled from the freezer when she hit the house. The herbal scents were soporific, insects hummed a lullaby, and the girl was almost asleep by the time M'bali tapped her leg before handing her a mug.

'Jarrid been keeping you up nights, has he?'

'No, I've just been slaving alone all morning while my employer swanned around the neighbourhood.'

'Ouch, I deserved that.'

'How's your love life anyway? Rumour has it you were seen leaving the pub with a certain Hayes Slavich.' Roxy smirked happily, then took a bite of cake.

'Who the heck told you that?'

'Don't worry, everyone knows. I've had three texts, two phone calls and been stopped in the Quimby store and pumped for details.'

M'bali groaned. 'I've made a total prat of myself. A one-night stand with the kitchen hand at the local pub. Oh, and part-time singer—delectable as he may be.'

Roxy sat up to stare at her. 'You think you're slumming?'

Now M'bali was embarrassed. She teased the girl to cover it. 'Slumming? Where did you pick up a quaint old expression like that?'

'My nan. She's a treasure trove of ancient sayings.'

'Look we did the deed, it was wonderful, very wonderful, but how likely is it to go on? It's not…'

'You mean what with you being C.W.A. president and teaching *taekwondo* to the high school kids on Tuesdays he's not respectable enough for you?'

'Look, I deny that. I mean he's six years my junior and very hunky and probably widely available.'

'And just the kitchen hand at the pub and only a bit of a part-time singer.'

'Okay, there's a bit of both if you must insist.'

'Seriously, you really don't know who he is?' Roxy was laughing now. She choked on a cake crumb. Wozzer looked up and gave her one of his I-feel-for-you-but-I-can't-be-bothered-rising looks. When she had cleared her throat, he sank into slumber again.

'So, what's so funny and who is he?' M'bali was irritated now.

'He was only the lead singer of the *Superchargers*. They toured overseas as backup to some of the best rock groups in the world. What planet have you been on, girl?'

'Planet he's-too-young-for-me and I'm only an aging farmer in Quimbleton who apparently doesn't know what's going on in the cool people's world.'

'Jarrid says Hayes has built an amazing house outside town on the old Jones property. He and the boys did some of the tiling.'

'What is he doing down here? Slumming, as you so charmingly put it?'

'He told the boys he was sick of the road life. And he wanted to get out of the band before their career planked—as they mostly do. And he said he wants to invest his earnings into setting up an organic farm and to just dabble in other things for a bit of cash to pay for materials, plants. You know how much it costs to set these things up.'

'An international rock god. Definitely a one-night stand. I feel such an idiot.'

Roxy's voice softened. 'Look M'bali, you are a gorgeous, smart woman and you have lots in common with him now. The high school kids will think you're the coolest teacher ever, and the jealous old bags at the golf club will lie awake twitching for weeks.'

M'bali jumped up. 'This isn't getting any work done. Pack up this gear for me, please. I need to dash inside for a pee.'

She jogged off towards the house. Wozzer considered following her but decided to stay with his friend Roxy who was always good for a sneaky snack. When M'bali reached the privacy of the house, she threw herself onto her bed and began to cry. Why had she ever thought she'd find a suitable partner in this godforsaken hick town she'd been born in? Why had she ever been silly enough leave city opportunities in Slique?

Before she could return to her labours in the vegetable field, the house phone rang. It was Zera. She could hear erratic breathing, as though the girl was struggling to control herself.

'Is something wrong, you sound upset?'

'It's…it's Jeffree. He's been arrested and charged with the murder of some girl in Slique.'

Now M'bali was the one struggling to control her emotions. Murder! She had harboured a murderer. And she'd allowed him to book in with no deposit because he looked affluent. Her judgement was really off these days.

'You poor girl. Where is he now? And where are you?'

'I'm at the police station in Moobalup. They say that I'm helping with inquiries. How can I help them? He didn't do it; he wouldn't do it…' Zera trailed off, sobbing.

'It's okay. Take your time. Is your husband still there or have they taken him to Slique?'

'I think he's still here—but they won't tell me anything.'

M'bali's mothering instincts got the better of her. 'Do you want me to come up to get you.'

Zera was managing to hold herself together now. 'No, no. I have no idea when they'll let me go. And I have the van.'

As she spoke, esteemed reader, the town's one detective was all over the van like a particularly bad rash. Its contents were systematically spread over the tarmac of the police station forecourt. The local hominid plod had not come down in the last shower of rain. They should have discovered that the vehicle was stolen but Jeffrique had ways of covering his tracks on that score.

'If you need any help, don't hesitate to call me. It doesn't matter what the time is. Okay?'

'Yes, thanks so much. You are kind.' With those words, Zera hung up.

Capricorn

Venus rules lion life this week.
Spend several days bonking yourself witless.
Beware of poachers on the 11th and 15th.

Ten

It was after midnight when the exhausted intergalactic princess known as Zera drove the van back to M'bali's door, groping blindly for the bell. In her distress, she had forgotten that it was always unlocked. M'bali started from sleep, wide-eyed and breathing sharply. The events of the previous night were still driving an anxiety she normally didn't experience. Wozzer exploded off his bedside rug and disappeared, sending several booming barks into the night. Then he was abruptly silent. It must be someone she knew. Or maybe someone had hurt him to shut him up. A sob escaped her throat. She jumped up, grabbed her old silk kimono, and ran for the front door, thrusting her arms into its flapping sleeves as she moved. With his white face and heavy body, the dog had the air of a dignified aging cowboy, but he was slowly becoming her baby now that his youthful power was diminishing. She would throw any bastard who hurt him through a plate glass window if she had to. Her martial arts master wouldn't approve but that was too frigging bad. Adrenaline pumped into her muscles tightening them for action.

At the front door, Wozzer was standing quietly looking out. In the dim light of the waxing moon, she could just make out Zera's vague outline through the glass. M'bali thrust open the door. As the girl staggered in, sobbing, she threw a wiry arm around her sagging shoulders, helping her to the couch. Wozzer wagged his tail apologetically as he followed them. Once Zera was settled, M'bali strode into the kitchen to turn on the jug. *A cuppa always added a touch of normalcy to any desperate situation*, she thought. 'Hot chocolate okay?' she called (chocolate—a substance which evolves wherever hominid females exist).

'Anything hot, please.' Zera resumed crying uncontrollably. She'd been stoic during the police interrogations, but now the pressure to perform was now off. M'bali let her cry it out while she prepared the drinks. Mugs of steaming comfort in hand, she walked over to sit next to her, taking her hand as she did so. 'Now, sweetie, what's happened?'

'As I told you, Jeffree's been arrested for a murder in Slique that he didn't do. My darling boy wouldn't hurt anyone. (How very wrong she is, dear reader.) And he couldn't have done it, we haven't even been there,' she let slip.

'It doesn't surprise me you haven't been there, Zera. I noticed your reaction when I said I'd seen your spaceship land. You were stunned at being sprung, weren't you?'

This nosy hominid just can't help herself. Prod, prod, prod.

There was a tense pause, during which M'bali's dark eyes never strayed from Zera's face. The girl raised her own eyes to the ceiling, biting her lower lip. Finally, she gave a great sigh, and replied, 'You're mistaken, as Jeffree already told you. Please, please don't interrogate me. It's bad enough already that my new husband has been falsely accused of murder on our honeymoon. I can't take any more.' She resumed sobbing, aware of the hominid M'bali watching her, not without sympathy.

'Sorry, I'll help you in any way I can, Zera. But, if Jeffree wasn't ever in Slique, then the police will have no concrete evidence. They'll have to let him go. You can trust our legal system that far, I assure you.' (She wasn't totally sure about that, as several recent miscarriages of justice crossed her mind.)

'My lovely honeyflit…er, moon,' moaned Zera. She sat up to take a sip of the warm liquid. 'I don't know what's wrong with me. I'm usually so good in a crisis. You must think I'm such a spoiled baby.'

'I certainly don't. Everyone dreams of a perfectly idyllic honeymoon. I had one myself. (It all went pear-shaped a few years later, esteemed reader, but that is irrelevant to my story.) Do you have any idea when you can see your Jeffree?'

'No, they wouldn't tell me.'

'Who was it that made the arrest?'

'He was an oldish fellow, quite fat. Dewaz, or something like that.'

'That would be Doug Dewar. I know old Dougy quite well. We both play golf, and we're on a little committee together too. He's not a bad cop, one of the good ones. I'll give him a call for you and see what's going on.'

Relieved at finding something practical to do, she escaped to the wall-phone, pulled it off its cradle, and went into her own bedroom to make the call. *Not much prospect of looking for comets tonight,* she mourned to herself, as she punched in the numbers. She heard only a recorded message. 'This station is not manned after 5.00 pm,' it said. 'In case of emergency, dial 000. In all other events, call 1231234 and leave a message.'

Be prepared to fight off a gang of armed bandits by yourself with your teeth and half a large German sausage, she thought to herself. *Ah, the glorious state of rural policing.* Never mind, she had Doug's personal mobile number. She felt they had a friendship which was good enough to chance a call on his private number.

Fast dial brought her the distinctive deep ring of his personal phone, followed by his usual recorded message. 'I'm either fishing or fucking. In either case, I don't wish to be disturbed. Please leave a message.'

Fat chance of the latter, she thought. Doug's wife Ros had gone a bit strange after they lost that last-chance baby. She had joined a fundamentalist sect. Rumour had it that they were waiting for the imminent arrival of their messiah. M'bali doubted whether the poor guy had been getting any for ten years or so. Not that he ever said it as such, but you could tell. It was amazing the unstated courage with which some people carried on. Doug was the life of the party around a campfire, or at the nineteenth hole.

'No, I was not going down on my boyfriend at the time of the accident,' he once mimicked in the nasal and insolent tones of a well-known local teenage girl, who was under police interview. 'Anyway, you can't take his licence 'cos he hasn't got one yet.' That night, Dewar had dragged out two people from the other car as it burned. Both were badly injured, but she didn't seem to get it. He carried a lot around, old Doug, but he managed somehow to be fun.

'Doug, it's M'bali here. Sorry to ring so late, but I seem to have lost one of my clients to your tender care. Jeffree Smith's wife is staying with me, and she's pretty upset. Give us a call when you can,' she recorded.

By the time she made her way back to the lounge-room, the exhausted Zera told her she was going to bed. 'I don't suppose I'll sleep much. But I need to try.'

M'bali walked over to envelop her in a hug before she left. Having stowed their cups in the dishwasher, she threw off her kimono and slid into her own silky sheets. She tossed restlessly for an hour or so before giving up on slumber. Her right hand groped for the mobile phone on the bedside table and found it. Night-owl Hayes would still be awake. She knew he had a gig that night and he had told her that it always took him a couple of hours to wind down after that. She hesitated. Roxy's revelations had left her even more confused about him than she had been before. A couple of toxic past relationships had left her wary. Too bad no-one else would be awake. And anyway, she had a bone to pick with him.

'Hi, Hayes, hope I didn't disturb you.' *Hope I didn't disturb you bonking some small-town groupie.*

'No, babe. It's cool. What's up?'

'Zera, my house guest, just arrived at my door minus husband-arrested-for-murder. She's very shaken up, as you'd expect. I had a gut feeling that there was something not quite right about those two, but I certainly didn't consider homicide. Fraud perhaps, he could charm the stars out of the sky.'

'I see. You fancy him like mad.'

'I certainly do not. He's not my type—way too sleek and oily.'

'Do you reckon he did it then?'

'I haven't a clue. The sooner the two of them piss off out of my life the better.' She considered voicing her growing list of suspicions to him but quickly decided that it was far too early in their relationship to talk about seeing aliens.

'So, you don't know if he did it, but you don't trust him anyway—in line with your general paranoia about us poor blokes' intentions.'

Paranoia? How dare he. He hadn't told her who he really was, which was lying by omission, and *she* was too bloody suspicious? 'I hear you've had an international music career you plum forgot to mention to me, Hayes.'

He groaned. 'I can't win. If they know who I am... I mean was, too many women see me as a notch on their belt. I'm just an ordinary man with faults and foibles who wants to start a new life and be accepted for who he is now. And I decline to be just a financial investment in some chick's future. You have no idea.'

'No. I don't suppose I do. Perhaps I'm the local gold-digger then?'

'Look, you rang me in the middle of the night. I've just sung and played for hours, and I'm totally bushed. If you want to pick a fight, phone someone else. I don't need it. Goodnight.' He hung up.

Hmm, that went well.

Aquarius

Funny-looking luminous creatures
in the ocean depths will have an excellent week.
Hominid nets can't reach you—not yet.

Eleven

By 7.00 am, M'bali was back in the kitchen, fully dressed and with her horses already fed and watered. She knew Dewar to be an early riser, but he hadn't called yet. Zera hadn't appeared either. M'bali hoped that meant she had achieved sleep.

The harsh warning cries of birds in the native shrubbery outside the kitchen told her of the approach of Gaz, well before she heard his bare feet slapping across the veranda. As he entered, dressed in his usual boardies and fresh from the ocean, he looked about to see if they were alone before he spoke. 'What's this I hear about you harbouring a murderer, then?'

'Keep it down, Zera is back here. He's only a suspected murderer. Anyway, how do you know? The rumour-mill is starting exceptionally early.'

Gaz moved to the kitchen to help himself to a brew. 'Jamie Gamble was driving back home when he saw they'd been pulled over by Dewar, and he saw Jeffree was standing out of the van with the cuffs on. James' mum cleans the Police Station, so he waited a while and rang her. As she cleaned the place this morning, she heard them talking about city cops being on the way down because of murder charges. Naturally, she passed that on to Jamie and the grapevine. That's all I know. She couldn't exactly hang around outside the interview room door. It's sound-proofed, anyway.'

'That's more than I knew. Cops from Slique, he's not getting out of it easily then. Zera arrived back just after midnight. She was very distressed, as you'd expect. She's still asleep, or at least in bed. I don't know how anyone could sleep after that shock. I rang old Dougy, and we're hoping for a call back.'

'It'll get taken out of his hands pretty quickly if the city homicide boys are onto it,' Gaz said, as he settled onto the sofa next to her with his coffee.

'Yes, I know, but Doug will surely know if Jeffree's to be held here, or in Slique and whether he can be bailed. We have to think of that poor girl in there. She's totally alone.'

'Once I've swallowed this cuppa, I have to get to work and it's a fair drive today.' Gaz was a builder and sometimes worked some distance from town. 'Zera's an amazing swimmer. When she wakes up, if she wants to have a little surfing lesson to take her mind off things, give me a call on my mobile. I can pick her up at about 4.30.'

When the young woman finally surfaced at ten o'clock, a note in M'bali's spiky handwriting lay on the kitchen benchtop. 'Your breakfast is on a plate in the fridge. Just pop it in the microwave. Brewed coffee is still on the warmer, and some fresh bread is next to the toaster. If you need some company or any help, just give me a yell. I'm out in the paddock feeding plants. I haven't heard from Doug Dewar yet, or I would have woken you, Cheers, M'bali.'

Zera put her considerable intellect to working out the unfamiliar appliances, and quickly had the waiting food heated. She didn't want company, however well-intended. As the aromas of warmed eggs and a strange meaty substance hit her nose, a surge of nausea hit. She emptied her plate into the bin before pouring a coffee without adding milk. At the dark wooden dining table, she gazed blankly as she sipped. Her mind was truly in out in space, dwelling on the night she had manifested herself by Jeffrique's side in Bar-bariq. It now seemed an impulsive decision to marry in lust and so soon. But, of course, he would get out of this dilemma, and they would soon fly away to the honeyflit of her dreams.

The telephone rang. Without waiting to see if M'bali would appear, she leaped to grab it.

'Hello M'bali, Doug here,' said a rough, throaty voice.

'This is not M'bali, this is Zera Smith. You have my husband in custody. What is going on please?' she asked.

'All I know is that the city homicide squad drove down and took him up to Slique for questioning, ma'am,' he replied. 'I've only just finished my paperwork, and I'm about to turn in. It's been a long, long night. I expect you'll hear something from Slique soon. It's totally out of my hands now. Sorry to not be able to help you more.'

Zera flinched as the cop hung up in her ear. She was about to put the handpiece back into its cradle when M'bali breezed in through the back door. 'Any news?'

'That was Dewar, but he didn't tell me much. Jeffree was taken to Slique for questioning, as you thought. Coffee?' (Coffee, an addictive bean attracted to hominids in many galaxies.)

M'bali dropped her supple body into a dining chair. 'Mmm, please.'

Zera returned with the cups. 'I feel much better this morning. It's all too silly. My darling boy is innocent. They will soon find that out.'

'You do look awfully stiff though. I'll bet your neck is aching. I have a degree in physiotherapy. I still practice two days a week, so I have a pretty useful pair of hands. How does a relaxing massage sound to you?'

'It sounds just what I need,' Zera said. Her life to this point had been an exceptionally charmed one but she was now discovering that even the enhanced bodies of the cosmic elite harboured painful tensions when their owners were extremely upset.

As they sipped their drinks, M'bali briefly explained what the massage would entail.

Soon, Zera was in the ensuite bathroom, sliding out of her clothing and into the folds of a white bath-sheet. She emerged into the bedroom, calling as she did so, 'Okay, I'm ready.'

M'bali came softly in, rummaging in her leather tote bag. Seizing the bottle of fragrant massage oil which she'd been seeking, she poured a pool of it onto one hand before commencing to warm it between her capable palms. Standing beside Zera, she began the first sweeping passes over her back. Soothing aromas filled the air. For more than forty minutes, only the minute sounds of Zera's breathing, and the soft slap and slide of M'bali's healing hands could be heard.

As her slender fingers automatically plied the knotted flesh, M'bali's spiky-haired head buzzed with a torment of unasked questions. She seriously doubted her visitors' denials.

But if they were aliens, why were they here? Was an invasion likely? Was Earth a frequent holiday destination for their race? What was their own world like? With difficulty, she spared the suffering girl an interrogation. Finally, she ceased work and began drying her hands on a towel. 'You're done. How does that feel?'

'Mmmmm, just wonderful. Thank you so much.'

'I'll leave you to relax then. Don't hurry to get up. Enjoy the calm.' She stowed the fragrant oils back into her tote, picked it up, and left the room.

*

With her heavy bedroom door firmly closed, she rang Jess and Rivers. After a long pause, the girl answered.

'Sorry to interrupt your work, but glad I got through.' (Telephone reception out on their forest block was variable.) 'How are you doing?'

'Bushed as usual, but we just got the windows into the house.'

'Wow! That's a big step. Congratulations.'

'Why aren't you out in a paddock shovelling muck, M'bali?'

'Big dramas at this end. The male of my maybe-aliens has been arrested for the murder of a girl in Slique.'

Jess gasped. 'My god, that is scary. Where's the other one?'

'Resting in one of my B&B rooms. She got in some time after midnight last night. Very distraught. I just gave her a massage…'

'M'bali, you can't be alone with them. Who knows what they can do?'

'I want them out of here pronto, but I can't throw her into the street. She's on her honeymoon…'

Jess interrupted again. 'So she claims! Who knows what they're really up to?'

'Thanks for your concern. I must admit I am feeling very unsettled. As I said, I just gave Zera a massage. I feel very foolish saying this, but I need to say it to someone I can trust. As you know, I have been a physio for…quite a few years. These hands have felt every size, shape and condition of the human frame and that body doesn't feel like any human body I ever touched in my entire career.'

'Omigod!'

'They look like human muscles, but they don't *feel* like human muscles. It's a textural thing.'

'M'bali I don't know what to say. If I didn't know you so well, I'd say that was crazy.'

'Me too. But these hands don't lie. Anyway, I must go. Promise me you'll keep this to yourself?'

'Can I tell Rivers?'

'Of course. Great about the windows. Don't worry, I'll be careful. Must go now—bye.'

*

At the Quimbleton General Store, the doors opened at 7.30 am. Krystal had already heard the news about the murder allegations via her mum, a close friend of James' mother. She had passed it on excitedly to Skye, adding a few speculative touches of her own which were soon to circulate around the district as fact. 'And he strangled her with her own dressing gown cord,' she'd said, voicing the plot of a paperback which she'd recently devoured. She had already imagined herself visiting the gorgeous Jeffree in his lonely prison cell and his powerful gratitude turning slowly to love.

Why are these bad boys always so attractive to the fair sex, dearest reader? Princely Jeffrique, son of the self-titled Creator-of-All-Things, has the temperament and powers to be a very bad boy indeed.

Pisces

This will be a patchy week for dolphins.
Avoid trawler nets on the 7th and 10th.
Frolic near tourist boats and smile a lot. Good PR helps.

Twelve

It was at least true that the city homicide boys were onto it. As the alleged murder had happened in the city, Jeffrique was briefly interviewed by the visiting detectives, then ushered into a paddy-wagon to be transported closer to the scene of the crime. Meeting the two men who were to handle his case had given him an opportunity to size them up. Detective Sergeant Papadopo was a swarthy, thickset hominid of middle height, with a shaved head and coolly appraising eyes. Jeffrique noted that those cool eyes didn't quite go with the worry-lines etched deeply into his forehead. Constable Browning, his skinny offsider with the under-slung jaw and acne-drizzled skin, had the anxious look of a perpetual underling. He'd do as he was told. The older man was probably a slightly above-average ape-brain, he guessed. *They can both be pushed where I want if their careers or families are threatened*, he concluded.

The long journey by road gave Jeffrique plenty of time to consider his options. When they let him out at the other end, he appeared surprisingly unperturbed.

'Either he didn't do it, and he can prove it, or he must be one of them sociopaths,' commented one of the front office staff, after he'd passed through with his escort. As a result of hours of dedicated crime-show viewing, she could now bandy around psychological terms as though she knew what they meant.

The prisoner was ushered into a boxy room furnished with a table, three chairs and recording equipment. So far, Jeffrique had been very polite and co-operative. The moment the door had closed on himself and the two plod he used his nanochip-assisted mind to disable the electrical equipment. Then he struck.

'Right, let's get one thing clear. I am the son of the Creator-Of-All-Things, and I'm in charge here,' he snarled.

Sergeant Papadopo stifled a guffaw.

'Oh, yes, I rarking am,' Jeffrique continued. 'And you two ape-brains are going to come up with a sudden reason why I am innocent of all charges, including bashing bins and exceeding the speed limit, right now or I am going to turn you both into the stardust from whence you came.'

'Whence you came—very fancy,' said Browning.

But Papadopo broke in. 'I am not in any way impressed by threats, young man. The one under pressure here is *you*. Sit down and tell me where you were on the night of December 28.'

Jeffrique now realised that these two hominids needed instant persuasion towards his point of view. He promptly spent twenty seconds teleporting a nine-foot megazoid from 2187KF into the room. The animal looked terrifying but had a passive nature. Its species was engineered to kill mould on tall crops with its fierce breath. Papadopo's eyebrows were singed, and the blast wiped out every invisible organism on his face. Jeffrique replaced it with a multi-tentacled purple and black medusazoid from 4237QM (useful for packing goods quickly and efficiently on two assembly lines at once). Browning screamed. Sergeant Papadopo merely shook his shaved cranium, leaned on one hand, and tried to focus more clearly. He had more than a few domestic worries at present, and unusually for him, had resorted to a little chemical help beyond a few lagers with the boys. It suddenly occurred to him that the last *eccie* he'd taken must've had some more serious stuff cut into it. But he'd had too many years of experience to be bluffed by this bozo. He leaned forward, glaring fiercely. The creatures were gone. If they had ever been there.

'Now you listen here, sunshine…' he began.

'No, you listen, ape-brain,' hissed Jeffrique. As he spoke, he caused all the clothing of both officers to teleport elsewhere. 'I am going to start screaming and yelling and flying to the door crying "attempted rape" in five seconds time if you two don't shut up and pay attention.'

This was a new one. Papadopo and Browning looked at each other in bewilderment.

'Don't threaten me young man…' the sergeant began.

Browning was clutching his groin with both hands.

'We can't release you. We have a chain of command. They know you're here,' Papadopo added. His attempt at a dignified reply was spoiled by the uncontrollable shaking of his hands.

'I want you to find out that I am *not* the Jeffree Bradlee Smith who murdered that woman. He has fled this state and is currently hiding out at the Sunnyside Motel in Reef City. Room thirty-four to be exact. You will have him arrested, then you will discover that his DNA matches the samples which you have taken from the crime scene. You will then make sure I am cleared of this very inconvenient murder charge, and the speeding charge the fat rural plodder threw at me. Then you will release me.'

Sergeant Papadopo was not a cowardly man. He had a citation for bravery, gained by saving a four-year-old girl from the clutches of her gun-toting aggrieved father. The man had been on a vicious pathway towards teaching his estranged wife a lesson she'd live with forever. Now the sergeant made a last-ditch attempt to pick up his gun from the floor. Jeffrique instantly deposited both men elsewhere. A still-naked Browning appeared in the middle of a Country Women's Association meeting in Coffitup. The gathering of earthy farmer's wives eyed him appraisingly. He shrank visibly in the chill of their humorous gazes.

'If you're a stripper-gram, I want a refund.'

'He's not a stripper-gram. He's a nasty little pervert. Let's rope and throw and brand him, girls.' Several burly women lunged towards him with giggling intent. Constable Browning was still screaming as Jeffrique transported him back into the interview room.

Papadopo fared no better. The alien prince had deposited him in the middle of the nation's greatest sporting arena during a particularly tense moment of a grand-final. Only one meagre point separated the struggling gladiators, with a minute to go. At his streaking interruption, the two teams turned on him as one, bringing him down in one great heaving scrum of hairy indignation. Under the struggling heap, multiple rules were being broken and so was his body. He too arrived back in the interview room screaming for mercy.

'You are powerless to oppose me. Do I make my point?' Jeffrique asked, with a wry smile. 'And, just in case you think that you are safe to blab when you go out that door, here is an image of your wife at her domestic duties, Sergeant.' Using yet another brain-located nano chip, he projected the scene of Anna Papadopo shampooing the living-room carpet onto the wall in front of them. A pistol floated nearby. It was aimed at her head.

'I know where you both live. I can go there anytime I want, do anything I want, and disappear without a trace,' he warned. 'Now, do we have a clear agreement on what you are to do?'

Papadopo swallowed heavily and frowned. 'Yeah, you win.' However badly things were going at home, he loved his wife. And the kids adored her. 'But you'll have to remain in custody for questioning until I can get Smith arrested on the Tinny Coast. Getting the other charges dropped will be more complicated.'

'Perhaps you will explain to your superiors that I am a fabulously wealthy businessman with an excellent reputation to maintain, and I will sue the pants off this department for wrongful arrest if they don't quash all charges? And I don't want any leaks to the tabloid press, or to anyone else.'

The two nodded glumly.

'And remember, you are under my particular surveillance at all times, even when I am ravishing my lovely new bride.'

'Oh, honeymoon. Congratulations,' said Constable Browning weakly. Jeffrique glared at him. 'And you can shut up about her too. Got it?'

'Yes.'

Satisfied that he had them right where he wanted them, Jeffrique restored their uniforms to two bodies in which hearts raced in terror, then held out his hands to be hand-cuffed again. 'I can hurt you with my mind alone,' he warned. He needn't have bothered. They were in his power.

The police chaplain was to wonder for weeks why two previously stable officers had simultaneously gone off on stress leave after an interview with a well-dressed businessman who had entered headquarters meekly enough. And the man that forensics showed to be the real murderer had been arrested on the other side of the continent. Despite that, the shrink's report indicated that neither could work, sleep, concentrate, nor hold a cup of coffee without shaking. Both men had talked very evasively about their interview with the suspect and, strangely, the electronic recording device had failed. Naturally, suspicions were aroused, but Papadopo was an experienced and trusted officer. At this stage, the truth was hidden in the recesses of two terrified minds.

As he waited for his release, Jeffrique was gloating. On the hard bunk of the holding-cell, he laughed to himself as he pictured what he'd done to the older plod. Stark naked in a pile of enraged hominids on national prime-time television. *One of my better jokes*, he thought.

Esteemed reader, this is not a personage we want our heroine M'bali to annoy. And I'm not just worried about the no clothes bit.

Aries

Antibiotic-resistant bacteria will find the planets moving in their favour this week. Party, party, party while you still can. New drugs are on their way.

Thirteen

Life was stirring in the musty gloom of *Crimson Glory's* mulch, and it wasn't an earthworm, or even a dung beetle. A tiny two-legged figure was gasping and snorting its way to the surface. Soon, a pair of bloodshot hazel eyes surveyed the garden. All clear. Cursing and grunting in piping tones, the creature hauled itself out. Once beyond the *Soozerator-6's* force field, it began growing rapidly. By the time it had launched into a shambling run, with all the grace of a hobbled hyaena, it had enlarged to a burly eight foot or so and was having difficulty finding a place to hide. Galumphing past a clothesline it seized a sheet in case the local inhabitants were into more clothing than just a *nid* loin cloth. On reaching the apparent shelter of a large shed, it paused, gasping for breath. Its clumsy hands were struggling to wrap the flapping fabric around its mighty bulk.

Suddenly, racing footsteps pounded towards its hiding place.

'Zwyf ca rarking oort?' the space-escapee whimpered. A hairy four-legged beast with great slobbering jowls had bounded around the building, confronting the newcomer with a series of deep, indignant barks.

'Gooq moofer xem,' the intruder said hopefully, holding out a friendly hand. Wozzer stood his ground, continuing his outraged barking, until M'bali called from the house, 'Wozzy, leave those roos alone!'

Taking her familiar words as some sort of assurance that the intruder offered no threat, Wozzer moved confidently forward and thrust his nose into the space-hominid's crotch. Believing the hairy beast now wanted to mate with him, Slugg took off running again, with Wozzer romping cheerily at his heels. Panting desperately and fending off slobbering passes at his rear end every time the sheet lifted in the breeze, Slugg scrambled over the wooden fence marking M'bali's boundary. He landed gracelessly on his face. For several minutes, he lay unconscious under a bush.

Slugg was one of Zera and Jeffrique's five domestic hominids on the *Soozerator-6.* Commonly known as *nids,* they were genetically modified to be exceptionally strong, and capable of only slow, careful movements. *Nids* were also bred to have a low sex drive, be hopelessly plain, and do as they were told. All these factors added greatly to domestic harmony. No-one was tempted to bonk the help, and vice versa.

But left to their own devices in the *Soozerator-6*, the four other *nids* had ganged up on Slugg, leaving him lonely, and with little work to do in the absence of The Masters. It had proved a recipe for boredom and loneliness, followed by an urge to rebel. Slugg had opened a hatch and scrambled out, looking for company and diversion.

Esteemed reader, these hominid servants were bred for compliance, but every now and then one would turn rogue and escape. Reader, I expect you are no more surprised at that than I am.

After a few minutes on the ground beneath the fence, Slugg regained consciousness, and mentally checked his body for signs of injury. Apart from a bump on his forehead, and a few scratches, everything seemed in working order, if a little bruised in places.

He began to wonder how to meet the locals. A distant hum built to a roar as a silver car, full of tourists from Slique, sped by. Now he knew what to do. He rose and stood hopefully by the roadside. Passers-by saw a massive, bearded figure clad in a striped king-sized sheet, an assortment of exotic bracelets, and an identity tag around his neck proclaiming his owners' names and ship number in cosmic script. Slugg had been micro-chipped at birth as well, so it wasn't possible to him to escape for long in most places they visited. He hoped this planet, which he had heard The Master say might be feral, could be different. More than a dozen vehicles full of Quimby locals whizzed by, each one leaving him coughing in a cloud of red gravel-dust. He waved hopefully but was ignored. The evening was still hot, he was thirsty and hungry, and he was contemplating braving the slobbering creature again to at least slake his thirst in the stream. Just as he turned to go back, yet another hum formed itself in the distance. Out of the shimmering heat haze came a battered four-wheel drive, cheerily painted in rainbow colours. It puttered to a halt, and a male hominid as bearded, long-haired, and bangled as himself leaned out.

'Need a ride, friend?' it asked.

'Tharg,' Slugg muttered, opening the back door and scrambling in before they could object.

(Yes, astute reader, the hairy male in the rainbow van is indeed our friend Rivers.) Its two occupants turned to look at Slugg. The lady was very pretty. This could be a good planet for meeting girls. Although sex was of little interest, he yearned for a cuddle, and he hadn't been allowed to see his mother for many years. Jess surveyed their passenger's scratched dusty face, the egg on his forehead, and the makeshift garment.

'Man, you look all done in, and beaten up. Who did this to you?'

'Rarking narfuz moofer,' Slugg commented, having not without understood a word she said.

'My god, some bastard has robbed this poor defenceless foreign visitor, and left him with nothing. He'll have to come home with us, after we've been to Hayes's gig at the pub.'

'Sure, we can get Dewar to help sort out who he is tomorrow.'

Both smiled reassuringly at Slugg. Jess reached back to pat him on one hairy arm. Rivers gunned the old van into life, and they continued their jaunt into Moobalup.

Hair-endowed and robed Slugg didn't look entirely out of place at the ferals' table in the pub. He was overwhelmed with sympathy, a meal, the occasional drink, and a few puffs of weed in the carpark. Two amply breasted hominid women eyed his giant form with some interest and approval. Even his road-accident nose didn't seem to deter this lot. By then, Slugg was a very mellow genetically modified hominid, and profoundly grateful to his rescuers. By midnight, before they loaded him into the van for the forested drive home, he was joyfully entertaining the table with popular inter-cosmic love songs, sung in a strange minor key.

'Sounds a bit oriental,' a member of the group remarked.

The dark, winding journey to their furnished shed was interrupted only by the change of engine note as Rivers slowed for the glowing eyes of creatures frozen in the dazzle of headlights. Jess softly hummed some of Hayes's better-known songs. The music was odd, and the darkness scared him, but before long Slugg drifted into a substance-assisted sleep.

*

Despite their weariness, on the morning after his arrival, the young couple rose at 6 am, ate a hasty breakfast, and were soon working inside the slowly growing house. Now that the windows were in, at least they could work indoors without being drenched in sweat or being drenched by the elements.

At lunchtime, they walked, hand in hand, over to the house-shed for a break. As she opened the door, Jess yelped in astonishment. Slugg had worked all his life as a house *nid,* as had his parents and forebears, for countless generations. He saw mess, he cleaned it. He saw food, he cooked it. Waking in a state of profound gratitude, he had studied their dwelling, found it sadly in need of his tender care, and had laboured to put it to rights. It was clean. It was orderly. A glorious fragrance was steaming from a pot on the stove. He stood beaming by a kitchen sink where all the dishes were washed and sparkling.

'Dzibrig ga hoogar,' he announced. Jess rushed over and threw her small arms as far around his bulk as they could go. No female employer had ever touched him in any way before. He blushed. Even his vast nose blushed.

'You bloody great treasure, you angel from heaven,' she shouted from somewhere around the level of his stomach. Rivers came over and shook his hand. Smiling broadly, they sat down to their first cooked lunch in months.

The stranger seemed happy too. They had intended to inform Doug Dewar that they'd picked up a lost foreign visitor the next time they were in town. His wonderful ability to transform their lives suddenly made them postpone this intention. Anyway, their visiting benefactor seemed to be very happy. He sang and smiled as he worked. Their spirits rose, their exhausted bickering stopped. The bone-deep weariness they felt was now tempered by the joy of being pampered by a giant hairy mother figure. Before long, the threesome had settled into a happy life of daily work, regularly tempered by fun and parties on Friday and Saturday nights. Slugg had never been to a party, but he took to his first like a snail to lettuce. His body glowed with a happiness he hadn't known it contained. The life of a servant creature to The Masters had held few pleasures.

*

Whilst pottering around M'bali's garden in the dark, Wozzer's nose had detected a faint and familiar odour. He began tracking back and forth, snuffling vigorously. The smell intensified and stopped at a small hole in the mulch. It was under the spiky bush where he liked to rest on hot days. Wozzer was excited. That scent belonged to the funny man who liked playing chasey with him and jumping fences. Interesting! The old dog paused before beginning to flail at the earth with his great forepaws in case there were any more beings to play with where that one had come from. Minutes later, he unearthed the spacecraft. He gave it a couple of whacks to see if it did anything interesting. It didn't. He lunged to seize it in his jaws. They were underslung, designed by nature to allow him to breath if he latched onto a huge struggling beast. The thing was slippery, but he got an awkward grip on it and dragged it a short distance. But it was much less fun than the nice squishy ball he'd mislaid. He soon abandoned it in the driveway.

When the grinding, panting and slobbering finally stopped, the terrified remaining crew of the *Suzerator-6* heaved many sighs of relief and began to clean up the mess. The spa was full of random bathroom products.

Taurus

Sheep should avoid overseas journeys by boat
this week. Your cabin will be brutally cramped,
and the journey will not end well.

Fourteen

The long day passed in deceptive peace. A few cirrus clouds flirted across the blue of the sky, but it continued impassively refusing to spare the land from the sun star's unyielding fires. Heat haze shimmered over the roads, creating apparitions like waterholes in an unrelenting dry. In the stoic trees and bushes, animal life sheltered, flicking and twitching at an aggravation of flies. By mid-afternoon, a merciful breeze would waft from the nearby ocean, easing the patient wait of all the creatures below. Meanwhile, Wozzer slept, stirring in fitful dreams, on the cool living-room tiles.

This was one of the two days per week that M'bali worked at her physiotherapy practice. Her mobile had been switched off all day, but now she was free. She picked it up and woke it to see who wanted her attention. She had two voice messages. One from a new client seeking an appointment. The other was from Hayes. Her heart rate rose; she paced the floor. Why had she been such a cow the other night? Why was he calling? She fiddled about with the coffee machine, making herself a brew. Sipping it slowly, she sank into her favourite cane chair on the shady veranda. Sweat pooled between her breasts and channelled its way down her belly. Even that made her think of him and the slow tender way he had moved down her body with his tongue and lips until he had reached his target. As she tried to dismiss the memory, her hand was already grasping for the phone.

His deep voice disturbed her equilibrium even further. What was he saying? He was looking forward to seeing her again? When could they meet? God, she was reacting like a sixteen-year-old. Mind you, sex at that age had been all elbows, awkwardness and embarrassment—not flowing and natural as it had been with him. Maybe she should invite him over to see the farm when Roxy was here. That would be safe. No, Roxy would roll around laughing as she conveyed the scene to Jarrid.

Are you thinking what I am thinking esteemed reader? For god's sake woman just get on with it.

She finally did. He answered sounding excited. 'M'bali. Great. Sorry I ended your call so abruptly the other night. I'd like to take you out to dinner if that's okay.'

'I'm sorry too that I was in attack-bitch mode. My last few days have been unusually stressful.'

'No probs. Do you have any food preferences, allergies, or moral objections to consuming any particular species?'

'Thanks for asking. I'm broad-minded on the nutrition front.' No point in acting like a fussy eater on a first date.

'Great, how about I book us a table for tonight at the new little vegie place out in the forest?'

Vegetarian. How did he know? 'Lovely, I'll meet you there. Seven thirty?'

Esteemed reader, thank the stars and planets that's over.

Several hours later, M'bali cooked Zera a meal and took it to her room on a tray. The girl's facial skin still glowed despite her ordeal. She accepted the tray with brief thanks and closed her door. M'bali was relieved. The less she had to do with whatever they were up to the better.

Soon she was showered perfumed and scrabbling through her wardrobe to see if she owned any sufficiently rock-chick garments that she'd forgotten about. She didn't. It was a stupid idea anyway. She finally selected a simple shift dress. It caressed the lines of her figure without being too tight and was quite short without screaming 'take me now, you gorgeous beast.'

Before she left, she stooped to pat Wozzer who eyed her sleepily from his haven on the sofa and faintly wagged his tail. In her unaccustomed high heels, she strode across the veranda boards and crunched onto the gravel driveway. Seconds later she let out a yelp of pain. She had trodden on something and lightly twisted her ankle.

'What the frigging hell was that?' Now she could see it glowing faintly in the moonlight. With difficulty, she raised it up. It was a spaceship. A miniature spaceship exactly like the one she'd seen land several nights before—and so extraordinarily heavy for its size that it couldn't possibly be a child's toy. For several minutes, she stood, unable to think or move. But her habit of punctuality pushed her to keep going. She stowed the saucer in her leather tote. The *nids* inside clung to the bathroom fittings and cursed at having to clean up the rarking mess yet again. They had taken the opportunity to be up to all kinds of hominid naughtiness while The Masters were away—this housework lark wasn't as enjoyable as they'd once thought.

Half an hour later M'bali, conscious that she was a few years younger, was trying not to limp as the waitress led her to the table where a smiling Hayes rose to greet her. He kissed her cheek. 'You're limping. How did that happen?'

She sat and stowed her tote safely under the table. I just stood on an alien space craft was not a phrase she would allow to escape her lips. 'It's very minor. I stood on a bone my old dog left in the driveway. I'll ice and tape it as soon as I get home.'

The two chatted on happily for several hours about dogs, organic farming, where they'd grown up, how they both came to be living outside a remote hamlet in the woods. Perhaps you've been there, dear reader. You're half-listening to the words, and half-trying to suss out the intent behind them.

Hayes was warm, funny, and attentive. He filled her glass, but not too often, and he asked questions as though he were genuinely interested. Somehow or other, she ended up at his place which was a bit too conveniently, she thought on later reflection, down the road. Security lights raked the night as she followed him down his driveway. It was a flashy setup in an area where no-one even locked their doors. The house looked huge, but it wasn't the white modernist box she had anticipated he would own. Its façade was of local stone, and the whole thing hunkered down into a tree-clad hillside. She clambered out of the car. He came over and took her arm.

'Can't have you falling over things in *my* driveway, doll.'

M'bali resisted slightly but he was steering her towards a massive antique door which looked as though it had once belonged in a castle. Once inside, he directed her to a leather sofa fringed with huge squashy pillows. Her ankle was really throbbing now.

'Now young woman, I am going to attend to that sprain,' he told her. 'And don't start protesting. It's puffy and you know darn well what it needs.'

He left her. She sank back and looked around. It was a huge open-plan living area with a wall of windows facing the night. Comfortable, welcoming. His fridge was covered in photos of wildlife held on by an assortment of magnets. Not the usual harsh space-age kitchen featured in high-end magazines. Not space-age. Wrong word to think of tonight.

Hayes returned bearing a roll of bandage and headed straight for the fridge where he pulled out an ice pack.

'I love those photos. Did you take them?'

'Yes, one of the things I find a bit of time to dabble in down here.'

He came and stood next to her. She could smell his cologne. It was intoxicating. He casually reached down and her swung her legs onto the couch before sitting and quickly applying the ice pack. 'How long for? You're the expert.'

'Twenty will do.' She felt tense. Not her usual sociable, relaxed self.

'You really are going to have to learn to trust me, M'bali. I knew I was going to marry you the moment you told me about the way you honour your dead brother.'

'What?'

'I think you heard me perfectly well.'

'No, no, sorry. Never again. You've got the wrong woman.'

Reader, they'll either sort things out or spend the rest of their lives mooning over their choices. I'll leave them to it for a while.

Gemini

In a few weeks' time, the weather will
become far too chilly for little black flies.
Pester, pester, pester while ye may.

Fifteen

Just as he had promised, Gaz arrived at *The Briar Patch* at 4.30. This time he was not on foot. Two surfboards were anchored to the roof of his dusty ute. Clad in yet another pair of flamboyantly joyful boardies, topped with an equally riotous shirt, he strode in through the front door. He called out. 'Zera? Did M'bali tell you I offered to teach you to surf today?'

He waited a couple of minutes. 'Hello, Zera?'

She emerged wrapped in a green sarong tied at the armpits, her hair tousled with sleep.

'Hello, Gavin. Yes, she told me. This is so thoughtful of you to think of taking my mind off my worries. Is it alright if I call you Gavin? I like it so much more than Gaz.'

'Sure. That's what my mum calls me. I'll add you to the list.'

'I just need to slip into a swimsuit. I won't be long. On the kitchen bench are some delicious supplies that your friend has packed for us. You could take them to your vehicle.'

The habit of organising hominids runs deep in the space elite, patient reader.

'Supplies, you're getting the special treatment. That'll be the day when M'bali decides to provision *me* when I go off for a surf.'

'I'm just a humble paying guest,' said she, who seemed destined to be a queen in the celestial scheme of things. 'But you can carry them anyway,' she grinned.

Gaz did as bid, with an amused chuckle. How could he know that this kindly invitation was the worst decision of his life? She disappeared briefly while he stowed the picnic in his ute. Soon they were seated side by side, ploughing down M'bali's sandy track on the brief journey to the bitumen. He shouted over the engine's roar. 'I'm taking you to the bay break. It's easier for a beginner than the waves here.'

After a while, the vehicle was rocking through steep, sandy rises held together by woody, hard-leaved shrubs. Despite the harshness of the conditions, life bustled everywhere. Zera saw a flock of flying creatures in dazzling rainbow colours explode out of the bushes as they passed. 'What are those called, Gavin, those radiant beings?'

'Dunno, sorry. I failed ornithology at building school.'

Two pretty animals with gentle faces were feeding on the trackside bushes. Startled, they leapt to the left, thought better of it, then exploded back in great bounds, barely escaping the tonne of moving metal.

'And those?'

'Even I know them, they're kangaroos,' Gaz told her. They have the road sense of a drunken sailor.'

'Oh, but they're so magnificent. The way they bound so freely.'

'You really are a city chick aren't you,' he remarked, puzzled as to why she could not identify such a commonplace animal.

Zera didn't reply. She realised that she must not go on revealing her ignorance of the fauna in a country she was claiming to be her own.

With the Beach Bums' wavering falsettos about surfie chicks and fast cars setting the scene, the ute soon broke out onto a white crescent beach, fringed by a glittering sea which bowled gentle breakers at the sands.

'As I mentioned before, I've brought you here because it's a good place for teaching novices. The waves are small and well-formed, and there's no-one to laugh at you.'

'I think you'll find that I'm going to be rather good at this.'

'Pride goeth before a fall, butt over tit, into the breakers, young woman, as you will soon see.'

Gaz clambered out to begin the process of untying the boards. She joined him, managing to suppress a smile at the way the wind played with the loose fabric of his silly board shorts. He hoisted the two boards onto one shoulder and marched off, carrying them closer to the water's edge. Zera followed, struggling to put thoughts of Jeffrique's plight out of her head.

With the boards now placed side-by-side a small distance apart, Gaz asked, 'You've never tried this before, right?'

'No, never.'

'Then watch me closely and do what I do.' He knelt on his board and began to make paddling motions with his arms. Quickly she knelt on hers, mimicking his actions. When he felt she had mastered them, he began to show her how to leap into a crouch to catch a wave. Suddenly he was moving with effortless fluency. His height and muscled bulk, which made him seem awkward most of the time, were now transformed into something as centred and as poised as a dancer in motion. She shadowed his moves for a few minutes.

'I think I'm ready to see if you're any good as a teacher,' she suddenly said.

'Do you think you can manage to carry your board with your own dainty little hands?'

Without another word, Zera thrust the board under one arm, then strode off into the shallows.

'Don't be too hasty, hang on a bit,' he called after her. 'It's a bit different in the water. Let me show you.'

Ignoring him, she threw herself down and began paddling strongly. Turning to catch a small wave, she misjudged her time of entry, missing its passage entirely. The board, losing its forward impetus, sent her wobbling wildly as she tried to stand. Out of balance, she toppled into the surf. She surfaced to find Gaz by her side. Her board had run aground on the shore.

'Did you hear that?' he asked.

'Hear what?' she demanded, clinging to her board, which he'd had to retrieve.

'Two critters in the bush just pissed themselves laughing. You're willing to have a go, which is great. But just let me show you a couple of things, so that doesn't keep on happening. Even world champions learned from someone once. Firstly, this here object is a leg rope. Do yours up like this. Unlike Wozzer, I do *not* enjoy playing fetch.'

Matching the flow of the surf with his own fluency, he mastered several waves and swerved away at the exact moment he chose every time. Paddling closer to her, he called out. 'Do you learn by watching, or do I need to throw in a few words of explanation? Of course, I'm assuming that you're not above watching me.'

'Yes, I learn best by watching, and I did watch you flapping about in that ridiculous garment,' she replied. 'I think I've got it, it's quite straight-forward really,' she added confidently.

Gaz grinned. 'This, I will enjoy. Arrogance versus the ocean. Round one, I will referee,' he said.

He had taught many friends to surf, especially during his time in the city, but he had never seen anyone adapt to the ocean's rhythms as fast as she did. After a very few false starts, she rode the little break, time and time again, with an entranced half-smile on her face. Despite his astonishment at her skill, his eyes occasionally dwelt on how the light gleamed around the edges of her incredible body. She was way out of his league. Tearing his wistful eyes away, he paddled out further to take his own pleasure from the willing sea. Lost in their own actions which stole away thought, they both played alone in the waves for an hour or so. By then, cold was seeping into his awareness.

Paddling to shore, he called to her as he passed by. 'Come on you sea creature, that's enough. We'll scoff some of M'bali's goodies, then I'm taking you home.'

At the shore, she staggered a little as she tried to stand. His hand shot out to save her, yet he quickly let go as she gained her feet. Soon, wrapped in towels, they dropped to the sand to share the food and drink.

'That was totally amazing. What are you, part dolphin? Now I can see why you were so confident, much as I hate to admit it,' he commented.

Zera looked at her feet for a few seconds, then into his eyes as she spoke. 'I have no words to describe what that was like. It took me somewhere I've never been. I suppose that sounds silly to you.'

'No, not at all, I don't really have words for it either. All I know is that it's a big part of the reasons why I live here. I chose work that enables me to find the time to escape to the ocean nearly every day. It's that big in my life…and now it's made me cold, and I have a date at the pub. So, let's snack and run.'

Both attacked the small hamper with the appetite only vigorous exercise brings. Back at the ute, he strapped the boards onto the roof in silence, jumped in, and soon the big engine began throbbing.

He didn't seem the chatty type. Zera broke the silence as they rolled back up the track. 'Jeffree and I met a farmer named Matt Vigano in the *Quimby Quality Beefery*. He told us he wanted to grow genetically modified aneera, but some locals don't want him to. What do you know about that?' she asked.

'M'bali's the best one to ask about that stuff. She's an organic farmer.'

'How is that connected to aneera?'

At this point, my reader may notice that Gaz becomes a lot more verbally fluent in the presence of this lovely woman than he was with his mates. He was a smart guy. Context is everything.

'It's the opposite really. She's trying to get certification to farm naturally in every way. She can't use poisons, artificial fertilisers, or man-bred plants.'

'Does anything actually grow like that? I mean, can she make a living from it?'

'Yes, but its early days. She's still getting her system working. The farm isn't organically certified yet.'

Zera was surprised and intrigued. Nothing like this happened across all the many worlds she had visited. 'What does that mean exactly?'

'It means if she can prove to the authorities that her land and processes are totally natural then she can use that as a marketing ploy. You know—clean green. More and more people are looking for that.'

Zera did not know but wasn't about to admit it. 'I see. And are animals being genetically modified too?'

'I'm not sure. Mind you, I've seen on TV that they're talking about using it to get rid of genes that cause horrible diseases in people. I'm all for that, of course. And I know M'bali is as well.'

Snipping out unwanted genes made perfect sense to Zera. The cosmic elite didn't have a bad gene left in their bodies—not one that caused disease anyway. She sat thinking silently as life leapt and flew all around them.

Gaz was on a roll now. 'What does worry me is that big businesses are wanting to own the patents on our genes too. Owning the genes that God, or whatever, gave us. They didn't *invent* them. And, if they let their inventions loose in nature, they won't be able to take them back. I reckon there are bound to be some unintended consequences. It seems a dangerous game to me.'

Zera started out of her reverie. Every being in her world had genetic modifications of some sort—beneficial ones for the elite, brutal distortions of nature for the lower orders.

'What's wrong with it?'

'Seriously? You must have more faith in people than I do. Money rules. Who will protect poor people from the abuse of that power for profit? They could be bred to be too compliant, like slaves, or made into some terrible distortion of their nature.'

'What are slaves?'

'Unwilling, unpaid labour. Surely you know that's illegal.'

Now Zera was really startled, the most accepted orthodoxy of her world was being challenged and by a mere hominid. She had always thought that she and her family treated the creatures they owned exceptionally well. Struggling to appear calm, she controlled her voice. 'My stars, Gavin, and I thought you were just a surf-bum who could hardly string a sentence together.'

He laughed harshly. 'Maybe I live way out here to escape the darker side of our nature, if that's possible.'

Both lapsed into their own private thoughts. Zera had been shaken far more than she admitted. Her man and his family, the family she had just married into, had lordly rights over creation. The animals in their care seemed perfectly content and tractable. And yet some hominids ran away or tried to. Perhaps all was not as it had seemed. She dismissed the thought.

By the time they reached M'bali's hideaway, the warm light of the approaching sunset was warming the flanks of the pale gums in the garden to pink and gold. A flock of white birds had been feeding on the ground. They rose, contrasting their beauty with harsh screeching cries of protest at the interruption. Glistening palely, they decorated the dark wispy trees, waiting for another chance at the prized seeds and tubers below. Zera climbed out of the cab. Reaching back in, she extended him a firm hand. He shook it solemnly. 'Thank you,' she said, with an intensity that surprised him. 'You are an honest friend and a good teacher.'

He spoke tersely to cover his reaction. 'Well, ta for that. See you again sometime, I hope.'

At the sound of the throbbing engine, Jeffrique emerged from the house to silently wrap Zera in his arms. Over her shoulder he glared at the retreating vehicle and its hominid driver. How dare rarking chimpy-boy take his woman out behind his back.

Cancer

A mellow week for domestic dogs.
Follow your gut instincts, lie in the sun,
molest your squeaky toy and snaffle "lost" food.

Sixteen

With a startled sob, Zera leaned into Jeffrique, breathing the reassuring masculine scents of his body. They stood silently swaying for several minutes. At last, she managed to question him. 'What's happening? Why didn't you call me? Didn't you imagine how alone and worried I'd be?'

'My darling Zee-star, you can't seriously have thought I couldn't easily outwit hominid plod and get free. I didn't call because I thought you'd have more faith in me than that. It's all over, of course. I have no murder charge to answer, or any other charge for that matter. Now I'm free to enjoy my honeyflit with you, my glorious if foolish woman.'

She punched him lightly on the back in response to his teasing yet continued to plaster herself to his welcome form. He went on speaking, 'Anyway, I hear that you haven't been sitting here pining for me. You've been busy continuing your research into primitive hominid pastimes, such as falling off boards in the ocean with chimpy-boy.' Her face was buried in his chest. She did not see the fury in his eyes.

Zera detached herself from him. 'Yes, it was nice. But let's go inside now. I'm salty and tired, and I need a shower,' she replied.

He took her arm before they walked slowly through the garden into the house, where they found M'bali happily at work in the kitchen. She had pried a few select items suitable for a special occasion dinner form the freezer. Both sniffed at the sumptuous odours of her wine reduction which filled the living area.

'Mmm that smells heavenly. Now that I've got my man back, I've got my appetite back as well.'

'I don't usually treat my guests so well. But I've never had a guest falsely accused of murder, then released before. It's quite gone to my simple country head. I feel a celebratory dinner is in order.'

'You are so kind,' Zera began.

'Off you go and freshen up; fresh seafood waits for no-one.'

Now's my chance to pump them for a bit more information, she thought.

Sitting down to share a meal with M'bali was a very unusual experience for Jeffrique. Although some of the brighter hominids in his world seemed quite pleasant animals to him, most were just useful machines. Some had been modified to be gigantic, calm and obedient for farm work and building; some had been gifted fins and gills for underwater work; others received the benefit of a glow-in-the-dark function and huge eyes for working in mining tunnels. Anything the purchaser desired could be built in. Most unwanted qualities had long since been eliminated from their DNA. Except for that rarking curiosity which was infuriatingly difficult to eradicate.

Most hominid families lived in barn stalls when off-duty, although a few trusties were allowed semi-independent huts of their own in the farm grounds. Before his working life began, Jeffrique had occasionally been privileged to accompany his father on visits of inspection to managed farms to see the hominid beasts and their lower animal charges. A lordly visit to inspect the quality and growth of useful, but inferior beings, much as you might visit a farm and appraise the quality of the cows, pigs or sheep. Perhaps you don't hate cows. You may expect them to be treated quite decently by current standards; but not to be treated like people. You travel in an air-conditioned comfort wearing a seat belt; they travel squashed into an open truck. So, it was not merely a personal form of arrogance that led Jeffrique to look down on hominids. He was a creature whose outlook was limited by the values and experiences of the world he had grown up in. He thought what he did, and said, was normal and right.

In her innocent curiosity, M'bali had no idea what manner of beast she was dealing with. That night, he would no more have dined willingly at table with the hominid M'bali than others would sit on the floor to share a bowl of Crunchy Tuna Bits with the cat.

His mood was unstable for another reason too. He had discovered a dark secret on the extra day he had allowed himself to lounge about in Slique. If revealed, his father's wrath and rejection would engulf his life like a pyroclastic flow. And now Zera's clandestine surfing lesson with chimpy-boy had further inflamed his mind. He was barely in control of himself.

Zera was so ecstatic to have her lover back that she barely registered his mood. And dining with a hominid was not such a novel or confronting experience for her. She'd had many interactions with them through her work. Her family had even had a small one for a pet at one stage until it learned to open the cold store and gorge itself during the night.

She did not see hominids as something to despise—just as earthlings might not despise a horse or a cheetah. But she certainly did not see them as her equal. Generations of telomere management, genetic improvement, plus nano-chip insertions and replacement body-parts, had made the cosmic elite into a product they perceived as a unique and superior species. But at least these Earth hominids had lots more spark and vitality than the product as manufactured by *Genes-R-Us*. She was prepared to enjoy a celebration.

M'bali had laboured mightily in the kitchen. She would seduce these beings into honesty with her succulent dishes and fine local wines. She had prepared a spiky shelled creature in a fragrant sauce and two herb-enhanced salads. Soon her offerings were sliding down their throats, helped it on their way by a pleasing local white wine. They ate voraciously, occasionally murmuring complements which she felt were genuine.

'So, whereabouts in the mighty metropolis of Slique do you folks come from?' M'bali asked. Why not play their game and see what they said?

'We currently live in Garden Trove,' Jeffrique told her, naming an elite waterside address which he had researched whilst in the city. 'But I was born overseas, and only came to this state as a teenager. My parents were both killed in a car crash shortly after we arrived, and I've had to fend for myself since then. I own and run a big IT business. I've done very well financially, but you know I still don't quite get some of the local customs and jokes, as you may have already noticed.' He smiled winningly.

So, the story is that he's just an innocent immigrant lad-made-good living in Slique. And he's so bloody convincing. Almost. Let's see where I can push him.

'I have a close friend in Slique who is just desperate to find a good IT consultant. I'm sure she'd love your company's email address.'

A shocked silence followed. That was enough for M'bali. She went boldly on.

'I have no siblings now, but I used to have a younger brother named Jon. We were very close. He was killed, aged sixteen, in a car I was driving. He had wanted to be an astrophysicist and his passions were the stars, and the possibility of extra-terrestrial life. I struggle onto my roof at 3 am on most fine moonless nights, searching for a new comet to get named after him. It's all I can do to honour him…' She trailed off as the struggle against tears tightened her throat.

After a pause, she began again, 'I believe that I watched your ship land. I just wish darling Jon could have seen that instead of me.' Once more she trailed off, close to tears.

Jeffrique dropped his head. Unseen by the two women, his dark eyes flashed. He gained some flimsy control of himself and looked up. M'bali blundered on. 'Please tell me about your world... I mean, where are you from?'

'Indeed, we are not from your world.' The alien's eyes narrowed briefly. 'I respect your privacy, please respect ours. Zera tells me that you have been very kind to her in my absence. I will pay you extra, a lot extra, and then we will leave.'

Zera felt the need to add some social lubricant. She could see that M'bali meant no harm. 'I'll tell you a little about me. I have a PhD in zoology. I'm passionately interested in animal life. Your planet is quite enchanting to me in that regard. It's a truly unique place.'

'Zoology, what animals do you specialise in?'

Zera appeared nonplussed by this question. It took her several seconds to get out a reply. 'The higher primates,' she finally said.

'Which species?'

'Oh, er...'

'The higher apes in general,' Jeffrique cut in. 'Hominids to be specific.'

M'bali had no idea that this category included her. 'I'm insatiably curious. Tell me about them.'

Creatures like M'bali did not question the cosmic elite. Jeffrique exploded, 'They're the most rarking nosy, impudent beasts in the rarking cosmos and if you don't shut up...'

Zera finally realised her partner was on the edge of uncontrolled fury. She rose hastily, speaking before Jeffrique launch into action. 'You've been so very kind. We really must leave you in peace.'

'Thanks, but I've made dessert. Perhaps you'd like to eat it by yourselves on the veranda?'

'Yes, please. You are such a great host. You are making us feel like part of the family.' Zera tried to smooth things over by rising to help stack the dishwasher.

'No, no, not tonight. Not after the two days you guys have had. You go and sit outside in the cool and relax,' M'bali insisted. 'Wozzer may decide to come out and keep you company. I'll bring you dessert and coffee and then I'm going off to visit friends.'

She walked off, irritated by their reticence and puzzled at Jeffrique's fiery reaction to what seemed a few harmless questions. She hoped that the friendly old dog would make a thorough nuisance of himself, behaviour she would not normally allow.

'My rarking stars,' hissed Jeffrique, as he and Zera settled into the pillows of the cane chairs on the veranda. 'Now the smelly, hairy four-legged beast with the drooling mouth has been sent out to supposedly keep us company. What next? I'll be having a nice cosy chat with a fungus before I leave this hellhole of creeping life forms.'

'Oh, star-dream, he's quite sweet really. Look, he's wagging his tail. I think that means he wants to interact, and he's brought us a round thingy. He seems to want me to pick it up for some reason.'

'How revolting, Zee. It's covered in creature spit. Don't you dare touch it.'

'Jeffy-star, what happened in Slique? Why are you so angry?' She reached out a consoling hand.

'I've had more than enough of these beasts interrogating me.'

'Of course, I should have realised. This place is ruining our honeyflit. Let's get out of here. The universes are our playground and I want my boy back.'

Jeffrique now realised he would have to backpedal. He could not leave 3159XZ until he had dealt with it once and for all. He turned on his charm, judiciously mixed with a bit of trembling lip. 'Your boy will be back very soon, but I need a rest first. While I was in Slique, I saw that some surprisingly impressive mansions are for rental in the forest down here. The city elite fly here in their quaint helicopters to recreate themselves, so to speak. How about we hire a mansion and lie about making cosmic love for a few days. Lots and lots of luscious love.'

Esteemed reader, Jeffrique prided himself on his repeat performances in the sack—they were stupendous, as Zera would attest. Reading his face, she decided it would be wise to agree. The past few days had exhausted her own emotional resources as well.

He leaned forward to kiss her lingeringly. 'Great. If I get cross-examined again, I swear I'll permanently re-arrange someone's molecules before I can stop myself.'

On rising, Jeffrique aimed an irritable kick at the old dog. It connected. Wozzer yelped, lunged defensively at his ankle, and latched onto it, careful not to deliver a bite. Jeffrique's attempt to walk off failed. He had acquired an animated forty-kilo ball and chain. 'Zera, get this slobbering beast off me!' he hissed. She quickly ran a reassuring hand down Wozzer's back. He eyed her warily but let go. Fortunately for relations alien to Earth, M'bali had not heard their interchange.

This cosmic prince is surprisingly irritable for a boy on his honeyflit. Could it be that he is already feeling rattled by the dark secret he is desperate to hide from his lovely bride?

Leo

With cricket season now upon us,
an excellent week for seagulls.
Eat big but keep your eyes on the ball.

Seventeen

The town bench outside the *Quimbie General Store* was being warmed by even more elderly rear ends than usual. It buzzed with gossip. The young, and the technologically with-it, had already sent their gossip through the skies. By the time Jeffrique arrived back, some of the town had him convicted, not only of murder, but of embezzling the money for the fancy van as well. But local opinion was diverse.

In a small corner of the district, an area favoured by big men with aggressive tattoos, the reaction was as follows, 'Fuckin' coppers, arrestin' innocent people to get their fuckin' grab count up. Just as well the poor prick picked a good lawyer.'

Many more conventional residents of the town also took Jeffrique's side. They included the fair minded—he was innocent until proven guilty and all that. They also included the ones easily seduced by beauty; the ones who would never believe that their favourite movie star had sexually assaulted an under-age girl (the lying hussy), despite evidence showing clearly that he had.

Citizens who Dewar had caught for speeding applauded Jeffree's escape as though it were their own.

*

Once he was released from custody in Slique, the alien prince had decided to linger for another day. He booked himself into a fancy hotel (fancy by hominid standards anyway). He needed time for an investigation. He had to inform his daddy, the Creator-of-All-Things, that some bungler in his surveillance department had failed to notice life burgeoning on planet 3159XZ, fed by its fading red star. But before he did so he must be able to send a thorough and impressive report to the old man. How and when had unauthorised life started here? How thoroughly was the planet infested? Was this the only hot spot? With his data, the company would be able to act more efficiently when the *Planetary-life Enhancement Division* arrived and tidied the whole lot away. Maybe they could save a few of the brighter and athletic species for experimentation.

Reader, I can overlook his many boyish misadventures, but I'm somewhat alarmed by this train of thought.

Jeffrique applied his nano-chip-assisted brain and a pocket-sized quantum computer of sensational power to the problem for several hours. A hominid minion brought him a room service lunch and he consumed it absently as he worked. As he was tracking back further and further into the planet's history through eons of time, suddenly, the answer appeared.

'Oh, yessss! Got it!' he yelled after a brief pause. 'Pretty typical. A black smoker on the ocean floor has been nurturing primitive life. That must have been it. But I'd better concentrate and pick up a bit more detail.'

After a few space seconds, his cosmic aura glowed a frightened mauve. 'Rarking hell! The molecular remains of my DNA, old socks, apple cores and hamburger crumbs! It was me!' he shrieked. 'I started life on 3159XZ when I chucked my organic rubbish out of that evacuation portal.'

Jeffrique dropped his head to the table-top and began to cry despairingly. His father's rage would know no bounds. Waldorf's only deep sentimental attachments were to *Genes-R-Us* profits and a couple of his more memorable wives. A son like Jeffrique, a mere spawn of his loins amongst the many, could be dispatched to a shit-kicking job in some primitive backwater for eternity—despite his mother's protests. What to do? Should he tell Alpha Dawn and ask for guidance? That too would be demeaning—and risky. She was too fond of careless chatter.

He knew that the *Planet Demolitions Department* of *Genes-R-Us* could destroy 3159XZ easily enough. And he knew a few of the guys there, but no-one whom he could trust enough to keep his secret. The alien prince knew he would be blackmailed forever if one of those rark-heads got involved. And the products needed to do that were all locked up so securely that even he couldn't get hold of any. *I'll have to work out a way to kill everything myself. And I'll have to make it look natural*, he concluded.

Zera must never know. She thought he was perfect. She trusted him absolutely. He groaned and began crying angrily again.

Virgo

This week, whales will enjoy boatloads of tourists
oohing and aahing over your size and power.
Try to remember that not everyone is your friend.

Eighteen

Two days after Zera and Jeffrique departed her property, M'bali had a phone call from Hayes as she bustled about cleaning rooms. Before answering, she paused for several seconds, surprised that he was persisting after her defensive reaction to his marital intentions.

'Hi, doll. I've been wondering if you've been missing a sheet.'

He had souvenired one of her sheets? That was kinky. 'I'm not sure. I've been too busy to count them. I wash more sheets than you can imagine. Why do you ask?'

'I ask because I saw it partying in my audience at the Moobie Pub.'

'Please explain.'

'A very large hairy gent was cavorting in it. He seemed to be part of the ferals' table.'

'Firstly, there are no ferals, they are alternative citizens of this community. Secondly, how did you know it was one of mine?'

'Silk, very elegant blue stripes—quality rarely seen around here I would imagine. And it matched your very classy lace undies. I have a wonderful eye for colour.'

M'bali was silent for several seconds. Too many weird surprises had invaded her life.

Hayes filled the conversational gap. 'He seemed to leave with that couple I saw you chatting with at the gig where I first met you.'

'Jess and Rivers? They haven't told me—not that they'd know the sheets were mine. Anyway, I guess we've all been busy.'

He then persuaded her to let him come over just to go riding with her. They would canter down to the beach and along the sandy forest tracks adjacent to *The Briar Patch*. M'bali missed having a saddle companion but agreed with mixed emotions.

I don't know about you, esteemed reader, but I still have hopes for this pair. I just want them to sort it out when I'm busy doing something else.

She finished her chores then inspected the state of her hire rooms for minute faults. Having detected none, she hurried to have a shower and change before her next expected guests arrived. As she anointed her body with fragrant oils, her mind wandered over both his revelation about the stranger wearing her sheet and how to deal with Hayes's stated intentions. Dried and dressed in slim pants and a flowing blue top, she crashed onto the sofa clutching a wine. It was not her habit to drink alone but her life was getting odder by the minute. Her mobile rang. She jumped up and leapt across the room to grab it. It was an unfamiliar number.

'Hello, M'bali here.'

A breathless little voice which seemed vaguely familiar began speaking.

'Have you seen Gaz today?' Now she realised that the girlish voice belonged to Kasen, her friend's new squeeze of a couple of months. He seemed very keen on her but M'bali had only met her once, and briefly at that.

'No, I haven't. He does drop by here for coffee and a chat after a surf before work sometimes—but he doesn't always surf my break here. It depends on where he's working. You know Gaz, the board is always strapped to the ute.' Silence. She could hear the girl's ragged breathing.

'What's wrong Kasen?'

'He didn't show up at the job site this morning. His housemate said he left at 6.30 as usual. Packo saw him pass through town a few minutes later. He waved…'

M'bali's mind began racing over the possibilities. She knew Gaz well. He could be a creature of whim sometimes—but never about work. He'd never let mates at a job down without notice.

'What about his phone?' She was aware that he sometimes worked beyond mobile range.

'Lots of us have been ringing him all day. As soon as the guys didn't know where he was, they rang around.'

Gaz was a popular figure in town. His parents had farmed in the district for years, and he had grown up genial and easy-going, becoming first a sporting star and more recently a hero. As the key forward of the Quimbie Bulls football team he had scored six goals in their winning Grand Final against the Coffitup Cowboys the year before. This had included the goal of the century, a spearing boot through the middle after the siren, sealing the match. In little Quimbleton, this was practically qualification for sainthood. Naturally, he was a key figure in the local volunteer fire brigade, as well as a kindly all-round good guy who treated everyone alike.

M'bali quickly gulped all the wine in her glass. She was afraid to speak; afraid to think. She had not wanted Gaz to take Zera surfing. She had warned him off but had not been prepared to tell him why. She imagined that he'd have let out one of his great guffaws and teased her mercilessly for months.

Yes, astute reader, we both know who objected fiercely to "chimpy boy" taking his women to the beach in his absence. And we both know that the hapless Gaz isn't coming back. He has, to quote Jeffrique, had his molecules re-arranged. In other words, he was reduced to the stardust from whence he came. It happened on the highway just south of town. Gaz, singing country songs out of key and mentally planning his day, was overtaken by the white *Mercedes Sidebottom* van driven by the alien. Jeffrique was signalling him urgently to stop. Being a helpful lad, he did. Both men exited their vehicles. Jeffrique smiled before he spoke. 'Do you know what happens to insolent beasts who date my woman behind my back?'

'Mate, no offence. It was just a surfing lesson to take her mind off worrying about you.'

'Such altruism. I'll save you the trouble of saving maidens in distress again.' His eyes flashed and, before the hapless Gaz could move, he was turned to a cloud of particles which drifted slowly away on the morning breeze. His vehicle followed shortly after.

Unaware of all this M'bali tried to reassure Kasen. 'I've known Gaz for years. He was a cheeky little kid when I was a teenager growing up here. I know lots of his mates. I'll arrange a ring around too. You stay strong, darling. Do you have people looking after you?'

'Yes, my mum and dad.'

So, she was a local. M'bali couldn't remember her at all. After the conversation had ended, she stood up and poured herself another glass just as a vehicle crunched into her driveway. Judging by Wozzer's reaction, it wasn't a car he knew. She would somehow have to compose herself to welcome new guests.

*

Down at the town oval, the current coach of the mighty Quimbie Bulls, Steve Packer, known to all as Packo, had assembled his squad for an unscheduled meeting. Captain Gaz, his star player, had become like a son to him. The boys must be organised to spread out and find him. They would make a citizen's arrest of any turkeys who had him. And they'd manage to put the boot in a few times before Dewar turned up. He would understand.

Packo was a fine specimen of local manhood, a hairy beast anchored to the ground by calves like bags full of burgers. A famous footy player, and fiery orator, he had a great deal of influence over the youth and men of the town. He wasn't a bully; he didn't need to be. He had been club champion five times, and as such his opinion was valued.

But Quimbleton was no longer a village dominated by males, so not everyone in town was cowed by his manly achievements. Several indignant Quimbie mothers had objected to his use of the real "f" word during the last season.

'I'm not having my son speaking like a foul-mouthed bogan,' a new mother had yelled at him. She didn't really know what a bogan was, but she knew it wasn't good.

'Get real, Marcie. Your son learnt the "f" word in his first week at school. I'm not teachin' him nothing,' Packo had argued.

'You,' she said poking him for emphasis, 'are a role model to these boys. They idolise you. Kindly have the decency to show them how to behave like gentlemen.'

Packo, who did indeed behave like a gentleman when out socially in the presence of ladies, had responded. 'Jeez, Marcie this is a footy club, not an academy for little gentlemen. They know I don't talk that way in public. Why don't you girls go home now so your sensitive ears aren't offended?'

'Don't you tell me to go home, Steve Packer! I'm not one of your boys to boss around. I've known you since pre-primary, and what a freckly little twerp you were too.'

Several of the junior players looked shocked at their idol being thus addressed. A couple of the senior guys struggled to suppress a guffaw.

Yes, as Quimbleton struggled to solve the mystery of their boy Gaz's disappearance, the women of the town would have a role in the outcome. They might have a relatively minor role in the public life, serving afternoon teas and washing footy jumpers, but behind closed doors it was often a different story.

'Hell hath no fury like a woman scorned,' as some hominid wit once remarked. And they were all fond of kindly Gaz.

Suppressing a sob, Packo now stood up to his full height to address the sorrowful faces of his squad. 'Our mate is missing. He could be lyin' hurt somewhere. A tree fallin' across some bush track when he was goin' for a surf; an accident—some fuckin' visitor doin' a hit and run where no-one can see. We don't know. Wherever he is, we will find him. Who knows the tracks he drives down to surf?' A dozen hands went up.

'Good. Tell me where you're searchin' and I'll log it and put it on an onscreen map.' (He was not head of the Quimbleton Voluntary Fire Brigade for nothing. Drones would be scanning the district within minutes, scanning places his boys could not reach.)

In the C.W.A hall on main street, a similar meeting would be chaired an hour later by their president, M'bali. She was organising the members to phone every possible contact of Gaz who they could dredge up from their encyclopaedic collective memory. Then they would cater generously for the men as they returned to the town oval from the search. No normal work would be done in the little town that day.

M'bali was barely holding herself together. She felt sure that Jeffrique had taken Gaz and that he had most likely been stolen from their lives forever. Before the meeting, she had contacted Doug Dewar, warning him that her male visitor seemed the jealous type. 'He was furious that Gaz took Zera surfing. I saw his face out the kitchen window when he talked about it to her. They said they going to rent some mansion in the district, so I presume they're still here. I don't know whose place it might be.'

'I'll bloody soon find out,' Doug had told her. He liked Gaz a lot. He had often given free surfing lessons to troubled youth who Dewar was trying to steer to a safer path than breaking windows and joy riding in "borrowed" cars.

As we know, esteemed reader, they were not going to find Gaz. Dewar located the glamorous pile that Zera and Jeffrique were renting and drove out with his offsider to interview them. He could only ask if they'd seen the young man, and where they were on the day he disappeared. There was not a shred of evidence to implicate Jeffree Smith, or anyone else for that matter. The young woman had seemed genuinely upset at the disappearance of the man she called Gavin. And the bloke had been perfectly pleasant, even though he was being questioned by police so soon after his wrongful arrest. (Dewar was as yet unaware that his speeding charges had been dropped.) The old cop wondered what had set M'bali off to be so suspicious of Smith.

Reader, call it woman's intuition, call it what you will, she alone had the alien's dark number.

Libra

An excellent week for cane toad
travel and romance.
Avoid hominids with buckets on the 1st and 4th.

Nineteen

The search for Gaz consumed the townsfolk intensively for three days. After that, most had to report to their work. But many continued seeking clues to his whereabouts in their spare time for weeks. Their grief was heightened by the uncertainty as to what had befallen him and the lack of a funeral service to give them some limited closure.

On the evening of the second day, Hayes had arrived on M'bali's doorstep clutching a simple bouquet of wildflowers, a bag of takeaway food and a bottle. As soon as she opened her door, dishevelled and exhausted, he silently wrapped his arms around her. They stood together silently rocking for several minutes. He fed Wozzer, to the old dog's surprise, but stayed only long enough to give M'bali comfort and a meal. She felt far too strung out to be cynical and lay quietly against his chest until he disengaged himself and left for home.

Several days later, she was able to summon enough energy to suggest a visit to Jess and Rivers. On the phone organising a time, she questioned Rivers about the sheet thief. Not that the sheet itself particularly mattered. Where was he from? How had they met him? On the roadside? So, he couldn't speak their language. They hadn't told Doug Dewar. Didn't they think him highly suspicious?

Rivers had become defensive. 'You're surely not suggesting he had anything to do with Gaz's disappearance,' he snapped. 'Slugg is a lovely guy, and he has never left this property without us.'

'I believe you. But he appeared from nowhere like Zera and Jeffree.'

Rivers snorted. 'Not more little green men, M'bali. I thought you'd be over that notion by now.' He'd changed his tune. He and Jess were no longer singing from the same hymn sheet where she and aliens were concerned. She didn't blame him.

The following afternoon, she and Hayes made the forested trek out to the young couple's hideaway, ostensibly to deliver some new clothes to the rescued foreigner and also for Hayes to meet some more organic growers. On their arrival, they saw the pair in the distance carting mulch to tiny fruit trees. Suddenly, a woolly giant of a man lumbered past, effortlessly balancing a massive pole the size of a tree trunk on one hand. He smiled at them but quickly disappeared behind the house.

'He looked very fetching in your sheet. I'm not sure the lumberjack outfit does him any favours,' Hayes commented with a grin. M'bali had told him she was suspicious of this sudden new arrival, but not why.

They ploughed across the uneven paddock towards where Jess and Rivers were shovelling. Jess saw them first. She stood and waved, placing a hand on her aching back as she straightened. After the hugs and introductions, the four moved over to the shed-house. As they entered M'bali gasped in amazement, the place was orderly and clean, even the saucepans, once blackened, shone like silver. A delightful aroma of cooking filled the air.

'Wow, I don't know how you do it all. The place looks great.'

'All of this is Slugg's handiwork. He's a domestic goddess,' Jess told her.

'And as powerful as a tractor around the farm,' Rivers cut in.

As he spoke Slugg trudged through the door and glanced at them timidly.

'M'bali and Hayes, this is our saviour and friend, Slugg. He doesn't speak our language,' Jess told them.

The giant smiled and mumbled something but came no closer. M'bali extended the package of shirts and pants she had bought for him. Jess had warned her that he was exceptionally tall and bulky. 'For you,' she said. Turning to the girl, she added, 'He's even larger than I thought. I think he should try them on. If they don't fit, I can always exchange them.'

Rivers rose, and placing an arm around Slugg's shoulder, took him off to try on the new gear. The others sat at an old chrome and Formica table, scavenged from a roadside collection, to share the bottle the visitors had provided. Hayes plied Jess with questions about their plans for the farm which she answered with enthusiasm. M'bali noted how engaged in their enterprise she had become now that she was no longer exhausted.

When the man-mountain shambled out, he was grinning from ear to ear. He had managed to squeeze the shirt on, but it was too small to button up. M'bali rose and walked over to him. 'Let me see now—how much bigger does the new one need to be?' She gently spun him around, running her practised fingers over his shoulders and muscles. He blushed. Another pretty lady had touched him.

She turned him to face her again. 'Yes, much too small. Don't worry. I'll send you a larger size,' she said, smiling.

He smiled back. 'Xingblot ong da kuple.' Judging by his demeanour he seemed pleased.

As they ate his delicious food, M'bali noticed the devotion he showed to Jess and Rivers, and they to him. It was obvious why Rivers had gotten so prickly with her. She also eyed the strange talisman like a dog-tag which hung around the giant's neck. It was covered in a foreign script. Surely this was a clue to his origins. She would mention it to Jess when her partner was not around.

After a tour of the new house, she and Hayes were soon back in her vehicle, carrying M'bali's lost sheet, freshly laundered and folded. She drove in a trance. Slugg's muscles had felt human in shape and texture. But his overall height and bulk were outlandish. He must be eight foot in his socks. And he lifted tree trunks in one hand. Superhuman? She guessed he was Zera and Jeffrique's escaped underling. What would they do if they found out he was working for her friends instead of them?

'You're very quiet,' Hayes ventured after a few kilometres.

'Did you notice that dog-tag kind of thing around Slugg's neck? The writing on it wasn't any human script that I recognise, and I've seen most in my travels.'

'Can't say I did. I was too busy enjoying the food, and your friends. Your *alternative* friends.'

Scorpio

Cows will find this a great week for romance.
There is a lot of bull around these days.

Twenty

Day dawned once more on little Quimbleton, still sheltering in the arms of its forested valley, still seemingly so far from the troubles of the turbulent world. Weak early sunlight played along the furry edges of grass nibblers. M'bali had sat up late doing paperwork, worrying and, unusually for her, drinking. She turned in her bed to watch them blearily through the eyes of a rare hangover, until sleep reclaimed her. For once, the cacophony of wild birds could celebrate the start of morning without her help. A fresh burst of little black flies had hatched. They lurked hidden in the ferny forest, waiting for the warmth to rouse them. The early risers amongst good citizens of Quimbleton were already preparing the various beverages that began their days. 'Best time of the day,' they told each other smugly, as if their hour of rising were in some way connected to morality.

*

When the Merc finally pulled into the driveway of the mansion which Jeffrique had rented for their stay, Zera was greatly astonished. This was a far cry from the humble dwellings she'd seen in the Quimbleton township. As Jeffrique had noted, the general area with its forests and ocean was indeed a favourite holiday retreat for wealthy city dwellers. The owners of this home had not stinted themselves. As the heavily timbered front door swung open, they entered a marble atrium two stories high. Great floor-to-ceiling windows framed a one-hundred-and-eighty-degree view of a silky blue private lake embraced by the soaring pale-trunked trees of the forest. An elevator swept them upwards to the master suite with its vast ensuite bathing room.

'Look, a jacuzzi—with gold taps!' Zera exclaimed.

'Mmm, Zee-star our honeyflit is going to rise to new heights in this pleasure dome.'

They waded across the plush carpeting to an opulent bed, dwarfed by its setting. A crystal chandelier worthy of a palace sparkled above. The hominids of Slique were into *very* conspicuous consumption.

Zera took an appreciative breath, savouring the clean, fragrant air that only riches could buy; the quality of air to which she was accustomed. She was astonished that the humble hominid owner of this mansion enjoyed at least some of the comforts which only stellar beings enjoyed in her world. Who could have imagined what dreams and aspirations these creatures had for a better life? She would never be able to perceive a hominid family huddled together in their straw-filled pen in quite the same way again.

Jeffrique quickly located the spacious study, which was furnished with a glossy dark timber desk, and an array of sophisticated electronics (by hominid standards). 'Aha, command central,' he gloated. 'I have a quiet place to think at last.' As we know, he had no need for mere hominid computers, but he did need a hideout.

Emotionally he was no wiser than many hominids. From the depths of his brain stem, reptilian anger was just as capable of overwhelming Jeffrique as it was any simpler creature. Like many virtually fatherless boys, he was often filled with a formless anger, and a dark despair that he might never prove himself to that absent giant, the Creator-Of-All-Things. His father had been far more interested in sowing his seed than in taking the time to nurture and guide it.

Soon, in a sculptured leather chair, his clever child hunched over, lost in thought. Was his plan to eliminate all life on 3159XZ the only way he might redeem his innocent mistake? Much as his sneering attitude to mere beasts like hominids had been coloured by his life experiences, a part of him cringed at the thought of mass murder on a planetary scale. He was only temperamentally suited to being a small-time swindler and rake-about-town. Planetary genocide was more his father's idea of fun. Perhaps he could find another way. His mind swirled as he smiled and placated his lovely Zera. Whatever happened, he must not lose her.

Zera was yet to understand how much his brooding obsessions would take over the post-marital journey, which should have been so joyous. With the tender indulgence of new love, she would be happy enough to venture out into this new world alone once she had made a few friends.

'Just a little project I didn't have time to complete before we left home base,' he told her, while nibbling her neck persuasively.

Sagittarius

Black bears will wake from hibernation.
But if they go down to the woods on the 1st or 7th,
they'll be in for a big surprise, and not a pleasant one.

Twenty-One

Many galaxies distant, but still not too exponentially far away, an auditor was working in the surveillance division of *Genes-R-Us*. Of course, it wasn't actually called the surveillance division. It's much harder to spy on people if they know that you're trying to peek at them. So, auditor Quintis Quork's department boasted stationary letterheads which read—*Planetary-Life Enhancement Division.* If you were found to be a naughty little life-form, you got bumped off, which meant that the remaining breeding stock would be genetically inclined to behave better. They would also be scared shitless, which helped a great deal with behaviour management. A conforming lifeform was a good lifeform. Therefore, it was an enhanced lifeform.

Quintis was one of the more conscientious members of the brotherhood of auditors. When he received copies of observation data which was to be audited to see whether it had been responded to appropriately, he read all of it—and checked the maths. And he even thought about it, too. This made him rather more stressed than the average auditor, and not all that popular with his peers.

His wife, who massaged his knotted neck muscles daily, loved him despite his intensity and burning integrity, so he was happy. Not surprisingly, it was Quintis who noticed that signals, which could only have been generated by some cat-curious hominid life-form saying, 'Yoohoo, here we are,' were coming from planet 3159XZ, in the Alpha Megatauri sector. Not only that, the data also showed that these signals had been coming for eons of time, and no-one had investigated them. With his usual painstaking care, he focused the specialised life-form detection monitor onto 3159XZ. After his brief scan of what was now planet Earth, the machine almost exploded with lights, alarm buzzers and fresh data reports. He couldn't see any detail on the tiny blue planet, but his equipment could take in a great deal of data mathematically. Hastily he switched it off, to give himself time to take in this startling new information.

What he read was alarming in the extreme. Planet 3159XZ was so bristling full of life that it was a wonder anything there had room to move. 'Rarking whoopsie,' he muttered, 'how long has this been going on?'

All too soon, the answer was revealed, and it wasn't forty-two. It seemed that life had existed on that tiny, remote blue globe for over four billion years. He checked his figures again. Four billion years of unauthorised, unplanned living organisms had gone unnoticed on his watch. Cautiously, and with hope in his heart, he switched the machine on again. Lights flashed; buzzers blared. Quintis hit the kill switch.

'Bit of excitement there, Quork. What's going on?' asked a nearby colleague.

'Rarking monitor seems to be malfunctioning.'

What to do now? The answer was not straight forward. There were official protocols about whom he should tell, in triplicate, naturally. But it wasn't that simple. Any department which exhibited such gross incompetence for so long would simply be wiped out. The nameless and unknowable Creator-Of-All-Things did not go in for rewarding sacked incompetents with a generous termination bonus. He went in for disintegrating the whole team into the traditional "stardust from whence they came". Each family received a tasteful urn, featuring the company logo in classy gold-embossed lettering, in memory of their deceased member. This, of course, should have kept everyone in surveillance on their toes but where was a death sentence ever a deterrent to the foolish, lazy, or careless?

To report the long-unauthorised life, or not, Quintis agonised. Everyone knew that such lifeforms being freely available could grossly affect corporate profits. Choosing to tell meant an honourable death. To go on living would mean he must live with having failed to do his duty conscientiously. He pictured Kwinza, his lovely wife, waiting for his embrace and instead receiving a corporate death-urn. But how could he spend the rest of his days looking into her trusting pink eyes knowing that he hadn't owned up, and that he was not the man of complete integrity she imagined him to be? Had he asked Kwinza, she would have replied, 'Oh don't be so rarking stiff-necked. Of course you mustn't tell, you silly man. You're not leaving lovely me with three offspring, a mortgage, and a crock of dust.'

Poor old Quintis agonised in silence. Finally, he concluded as follows. 'I am not the man I thought I was. I cannot tell what I have just found out. I will never tell.'

Thus, he joined the rest of us who are not the man we thought we were, or even the woman. But perhaps my dear reader is leaping about and shouting, 'Bravo Quintis Quork, you are not just a corporate stooge! You are a hero! And you are a champion of free life.' That is certainly an equally valid point of view.

*

About a space-time month after Quintis' discovery, Alpha Dawn and Waldorf, the nameless and unknowable Creator-Of-All-Things, were having one of their rare evenings at home. On a good day, being married to Wally, as she called him (although not to his face) could be as tedious as being married to a man who has eight-thousand match boxes stored and catalogued in the garage. But on a day when some less-than-perfect being had ruffled his complacency, his tantrums shook the heavens and sent her scurrying to hide the children. Today was a relatively good day. He was apparently conscious, but not really present. His eyes were mostly glued to a screen which glowed with reports of the latest manufactured animals his boffins had dreamed up. One of the latest was a small hominid with an even-longer prehensile tail than had been previously bred. The earlier models had tended to lose their grip on trees at inopportune moments. Farming would become more economic because of this new one's ability to retrieve high-hanging fruit without the need of either a scaffold, or expensive insurance to cover the creature bouncing and breaking branches as it plummeted down. He occasionally let out a harsh chuckle of approval as a particularly useful deformation of nature came to his notice. 'Priceless,' he muttered as a new being arrived on his screen. Some tech genius had wedded a hominid brain and hands to a long scuttling thing with lots of legs. It could run up walls and fix the electricals at great speed. He must tell his boffins to create one with a spare pair of hands. Less time would be spent scurrying to and fro. He made a note of this potential money saver.

Dearest reader, such distortions are not a fate I wish for you and your children. Your rather novel shape is quite appealing and seems to work exactly as it is.

His queenly partner had been becoming increasingly puzzled and annoyed that she had received no recent progress reports on her darling boy's honeyflit. Even Zera, who was much more likely to put fingers to keyboard than Jeffrique, had not deigned to contact her. She had tapped at her wine glass with an immaculately manicured hand several times—failing to irritate Waldorf into communication.

'Waldorf, dahling,' she ventured several times. 'Waldorf!' she exclaimed. He allowed a reluctant uh huh, escape his lips. 'May I have your undivided attention, if that is not too much to ask?' When this lady dropped her usual drawl and addressed him crisply, he knew that a lack of response was futile.

'Yes, Kylee, my treasure.'

Alpha Dawn was not to be distracted by his careless use of her former name. 'I haven't heard a word from Jeffrique and Zera in an unfathomable period of time. I hope he isn't doing anything foolish.'

Waldorf laid his screen down and rearranged his privates. This gave him time to recollect which one was Jeffrique. A picture of his son's ravishing bride began to form in his brain. Ah, yes, he was that wild impetuous lad who had finally had the sense to marry well. 'From what I saw of the girl, she'll keep him out of the kind of mischief you fear. That one knows what she's about.'

'Indeed she does, but she is not his keeper. How do I get a view of the Alpha Megatauri area?'

He told her how. The following morning, after a night of heaven-splitting lovemaking during which she had seized the attention of every molecule in his being, she summoned a minion. 'Bring me my mauve gossamer gown; the one embroidered with star signs and planetary symbols of my own devising.' (Naturally, the term "devising" did not mean that Alpha Dawn had embroidered the design with her own fair hands.)

When she sailed into the foyer of the *Planetary-life Enhancement Division*, the inmates buzzed, fussed, and worried, awed by her queenly demeanour, her height, her cat-walk model deportment and the dazzling coronet perched on those sinuous locks. Why had this transcendent being deigned to manifest herself in their humble offices? Before this vision of girl-power had been forced to ask direction from the humble *nid* at the reception desk, a senior officer hurried to her side. 'How may I direct you, Your Celestial Graciousness?' he inquired.

'You may not direct me at all. But you must tell me who is the being responsible for surveying the Alpha Megatauri sector?'

'That would be Quintis Quork, Your Gracious Celestial…'

'Yes, yes, never mind the grovelling. Take me to him.'

Oh, dearest reader, what will become of poor Quintis if all is revealed? Oops, we can both guess the answer to that question.

Alpha Dawn and the senior officer walked for hundreds of metres through stark white windowless halls. When the wife of the Creator-Of-All-Things swanned up to his station, Quintis nearly lost his lunch. He stammered, he shook, he was quite unable to greet her appropriately.

'Quork, ma'am here would like to find out a little more about the remote corner of the Alpha Megatauri sector where her son is honeyflitting.'

Somehow Quintis managed to shuffle together enough functioning brain cells to cut the switches to the lifeform alarms before he homed in on the red star which warmed tiny 3159XZ and its eight neighbouring planets. He focused in further so that she could see the whole solar system.

'Why that is jarst the dahlingest little planetary grouping I have ever seen,' she drawled. 'I absolutely marst add it to my *Hororscope* work.' (We do recall how the spelling of the "H" word has varied over the years, do we not, dear reader?) 'Quork, you simply must assist me in my endeavours.'

Quintis nearly fainted. However, he quickly came to realise that this queenly vision could not understand any of his lifeform-detecting algorithms at all. She just wanted to see what her boy was up to—which was fortunately impossible at that distance. Now, distracted by the charms of the little planetary grouping, she wanted to shunt attractive spherical objects about to make them fit her cosmology. Quintis breathed sigh of relief. The boys over at planetary transport could handle that for her. He was home free—for now.

And the knowledge that life had busted all over the blue blob that we know as Earth would remain a secret known only to himself and Jeffrique—not to mention you and me, attentive reader. At least for a short time.

Capricorn

Feral cats will face hominid hostility on the 3rd and 4th. Turn up on an old lady's door acting cute and helpless.

Twenty-Two

One of M'bali's salient character traits was obstinacy. Her father had often told her in vain, 'I am firm, he is obstinate, thou art pig-headed.' This always extracted a wry smile but no reduction in her single-mindedness in pursuit of a goal. It was obstinacy that had carried her through the months when her brain was often patrolled by visions of her teenage brother's lifeless body being cut from the wreck. It also carried her through the period when Quimbleton's friendliness had turned to cool looks and conversations hissed just below her hearing level. Even as guilt had excoriated her self-belief to a shred, obstinacy would not let her crumble. She did not die of shame, or by her own hand. Gradually she came to believe the truth—that there was nothing she could have done in the face of a drugged driver racing around a bend on the wrong side of the road. Even if there had been a split second when she might have swerved the car off the road into the mighty trees of the forest, that move would have killed them both.

All she could do now was go on building a life in his honour. Yes reader, the hominid M'bali, in the way of such creatures, had an astonishing devotion to family. And Gaz Cooper had felt almost like to family to her—a part-substitute for the brother she had lost. Now a piece of inter-galactic shit had caused his disappearance from her life, and from his own. She moved automatically through her chores, banging and crashing in a state of suppressed fury. The spaceship of that smarmy murderer was in her possession. Should she replace it into the garden and hope that he flew away? Wisdom dictated she should do just that. But anger added force to her obduracy. No, she would stash it in her wardrobe and lock the door. Let's see what the evil piece of pond slime had to say for himself if he wanted it back.

Dear, M'bali, I for one do not wish to think about that.

*

Out in their rental mansion, Zera and Jeffrique had been struggling with their total lack of service *nids*. Neither had done a piece of domestic work in their lives and they were not about to do anything so demeaning now. The place was becoming a shambles and they were tired of dining out on the local hominid's idea of cuisine. One evening, as he lay abed listening to his partner's complaints and his own digestive system whining about these matters, Jeffrique took out his personal computer and summoned the *Suzerator-6*.

At that time of night, M'bali was also in bed—with Hayes. He appeared willing to accept a friends-with-benefits style of relationship, for the present at least, and had stayed the night. At last, passion spent, they now slept. Wozzer snoozed on his bedside rug.

On Jeffrique's command, the spaceship hummed into life. It collided with the wardrobe door at warp speed, splintered the wood, tore open the lock, and crashed out through the closed bedroom window. The old dog began charging about the room barking hysterically and blundering into things. The lovers awoke to this cacophony of terror. M'bali groped for the switch of the bedside light.

'What the fuck?' Hayes yelled, blinking in confusion at the sudden illumination. They both sat up surveying the state of the room. M'bali was shocked speechless. She knew at once the saucer had bashed its way out.

'Could something in that cupboard have exploded?' Hayes asked.

'No. There was nothing in there that could explode.'

Hayes was on his feet now. 'But the glass in the window has shattered too—and all the fragments have gone outwards. It's been hit from the inside.'

M'bali was shaking uncontrollably. Somehow, she managed to climb out of bed and reach for her kimono. 'I know what it was. Let me brew us a coffee and pour a slug of alcohol into it. We're both going to need it.'

Aquarius

If placed in a pretty glass tank,
lobsters are advised to make a scramble for it.
Those looks you are getting are not admiration.

Twenty-Three

When the two had reclaimed the bed, each clutching a mug, and the bewildered Wozzer had been comforted and permitted to join them, M'bali seized her phone. She opened it to *Picture*s. 'Firstly, I want you to look at the top shelf on the left side of my wardrobe. The one next to where the door has taken a bashing. Okay, now look at this earlier photograph of the same place.'

'I don't get it. There was a kid's toy spaceship on that shelf and now it's gone. So what?'

'That apparent kid's toy spaceship, only a few centimetres long, was incredibly heavy. I do manual labour most days, and weights twice a week and I struggled to lift it. No child could possibly manage it. On the night we first dated, it was lying in my driveway in the dark. I tripped over it and sprained my ankle.'

'But you told me that you tripped over one of Wozzer's bones.'

'I wasn't about to tell you I tripped over an alien craft on such short acquaintance.'

Hayes sipped his coffee. She could see his mind was in turmoil. She let him stew.

'This isn't happening,' he said. He sipped again.

She braced herself to tell him the truth. Until now she had not realised how much she did not want to drive him away by seeming to be some hick loony who saw aliens in every unexplained event. 'I've had a more than interesting time these last few weeks. I might as well tell you how it started. Then you can decide whether to flee the crazy lady or not.'

And then, dear reader, she told him the tale that you and I know so well.

*

In the *Suzerator-6*, a medic *nid* was treating one colleague for mild concussion and another for a broken wrist. The rest were frantically trying to clean up the chaos inflicted by the ship's collision with M'bali's wardrobe door. Aware that they were being summoned by The Masters, they had to get the place shipshape—and worse yet, they were going to have to explain the absence of Slugg in a few moments. Bickering over the exact wording of the story they had agreed to tell broke out.

'He left in the night. We didn't see him go.'

'First, you have to say he'd been quiet for a few days. Broody-like.'

'I know, but it wasn't like him to be broody. Slugg loved his work.'

'Yeah, but with The Masters gone there wasn't so much to do. Maybe that's why he was broody.'

Too late to straighten up the story. They felt the *Soozerator-6* cruise to a halt. The ship, and its contents, began the rather painful process, for a *nid*, of resuming normal size.

All too soon, the main hatch was opened from the outside and The Master strode in. He didn't look too cheery for a person on his honeyflit. 'Right, where's Slugg? We need some decent food in a hurry.'

The *nids* had hastily assembled into the greeting line demanded each time The Masters returned home. No-one answered—and then they all did at once.

'Where the rarking blazes is my chef?'

Now you know why gentle giant could cook up a storm in Jess and River's humble kitchen. Dear reader, Chef Slugg could produce a gourmet meal on the notorious planet 927GH2 in a sandstorm amongst falling asteroids. And he had, on more than one occasion.

The assembled crew were now gibbering. Nothing that came out of their mouths sounded like the truth to Jeffrique. 'Zera!' he yelled. 'Come in here a minute, please.'

She quickly appeared.

'Slugg's missing. See if you can get some sense out of these idiots because I can't. And you two, start unpacking the galley. Someone is going to feed us. And soon.'

The sous chef, who was new on the staff and whose skills didn't extend much beyond chopping and tidying up, ran frantically about seeking Slugg's recipe books.

Oh dear, oh dear. "Never come betwixt and between an alien prince and his chef" is a well-known intergalactic expression. And as true a little homily as was ever spoken.

Pisces

This week, meerkats will be fed up with the university
boffins who keep weighing them. Relax guys,
no predator will bump you off with them around.

Twenty-Four

A hominid can't be dealing with alien invasion all day and every day, however perplexing and scary that might be. Friends among the organic farmers' group had begun contacting M'bali, all alarmed at more down-to-earth developments in the district. They informed her that the aneera lobby group was escalating attempts to control local farming. Apparently backed by generous funding from their multinational supplier, they had begun to sponsor major community events and clubs. The Quimbie Bulls' oval was to be re-named Aneera Stadium in exchange for a generous donation to club coffers. A couple of new board members had begun to raise objections when the mighty Packo rose to his feet. 'I don't want to hear any fantsy pantsy greenie objections, thanks very much. If an injection of funds to help the might Quimbie Bulls win a flag is too much for your sensibilities I suggest you resign.' They did and were soon replaced by people who knew how to behave.

So, esteemed reader, it was Aneera Stadium now. That is a grand title to describe an oval of grass surrounded by primitive vehicles stuffed with bellowing, screaming hominids. Even so, such largesse from the aneera lobby would win friends, not only in tiny Quimbleton, but across the globe. Natural life would be distorted, and if some distortion proved to be unexpectedly harmful when let loose into nature, no-one would be able to take it back. Its burgeoning seeds would spread, out of control.

Until now, the organic growers' group had been loosely affiliated, but all agreed that they had to get together soon to form a cohesive plan against the strategies of their far-more-wealthy opposition. They gathered at the C.W.A. Hall in the main street, a quaint wooden building with no insulation. Meeting there was a test of the firmness of intentions in any season. The County Women's Association, which owned the building and was desperately fund-raising to restore it before it collapsed, had been a valued institution throughout the state for many decades. It had begun as a club where women could meet, exchange hand-written recipes, knitting patterns and stories about the amazing feats of their little grandies. 'Fiona is already speaking in sentences and she's only three.' A nearby member raised an eyebrow. Her Kriss had been speaking two languages since he was two. And he could count to fifty. But as the role of women in society had changed that conservative body had rolled with it. They still baked a great scone but now they were often a lobby group on local issues of concern.

As president of the C.W.A., M'bali had also invited a few of its key members to join the organic group, just on this issue. If an event were on the horizon, they would at least offer to cater. But she hoped they would pitch in more than that. Members of both groups straggled in, each working on their own version of Quimbie time. In the case of the more "feral" of the "alternatives", this was at least half-an-hour later than Quimbie central time. No-one was at all bothered by this. A spirit of tolerance prevailed.

The range of clothing on those assembled was quite startling to the uninitiated. The newbies included Klaire, the new chef at the *Quimby Quality Beefery*. Hayes had brought her along, both for her culinary contribution and to help her make friends. He found working under her gentle instructions totally refreshing after a series of male prima donnas modelling themselves on a famous television bully. They had tried his patience, which was considerable, to the brink of resignation on many occasions. He helped her shy introductions to a few attendees he knew.

To M'bali's surprise the group did not descend into the dreaded hominid-meeting speak. This phenomenon often seized even the most articulate citizens by the throat—making them waffle on, totally unable to keep to the business at hand. Perhaps it was the urgency of their cause because, with little stewardship on her part this time, they reached an easy agreement to hold an organic foods' day. It would feature both the raw and cooked produce of the valley, and Chef Klaire would co-ordinate that aspect. There would be rides of various kinds and other entertainment for the children. Stall holders purveying other products appealing to the teens and adults would be invited as well. It would be an event to rival the Quimbie show—the most exciting event on the town's calendar. Apart from the football Grand Final, it would be the only other exciting event on the little town's calendar.

Before the meeting ended, M'bali assumed her habitual organising role, ensuring that each area of the event was allocated to a person who would do something about it—preferably on Quimbie central time.

Give them bread and circuses. Who was it that spouted that pearl of wisdom, dear reader? Some wise but long-lost earthling leader I expect.

After the event, most stayed to catch up with friends. After a few minutes, chef Klaire excused herself. She had two kids, and the babysitter was only paid until nine. As M'bali wandered around chatting and introducing Hayes to some bemused friends, a piercing scream cut through the hum of conversation. She raced for the door.

In the darkness, Matt Vigano had been waiting. Word of this gathering had trickled through to him. His plan was to intimidate the more vulnerable members as they sought their cars so the lone exit of the new chick from the pub was convenient. As she hurried down the footpath he had jumped out from behind a bush. 'Listen to me, you fucking black bitch. You'd better bail out of cooking for that feral mob, whatever they're up to, or you'll be sorry. I know where you live.'

Klaire began to shake uncontrollably. She'd been just tough enough to get her kids out of the house, where they had been terrorised by her partner's unpredictable drunken rages; just tough enough to begin a new life for them in seemingly peaceful Quimbleton. Pictures of her children, brown limbed and vulnerable, flashed through her mind. She froze.

A blinding flash of blue light exploded in front of the pair.

'Lovely photo and video, Matt. I've caught the sun-damage on your left hand in particularly exquisite detail,' M'bali told him.

Vigano shoved past the little chef to propel himself violently at her mobile phone. M'bali side-stepped adroitly, sending Vigano's middle-aged bulk staggering out of control against a pile of bins left out for collection. He lay there groaning.

'They don't call me the cat woman of Quimbie because of my dappled coat and shiny whiskers,' she told him. Behind her she could hear half-stifled masculine laughter. She knew it was Hayes and whirled around to glare at him. He was convulsed but was trying to hold it in for Klaire's sake.

'You really do have to marry me, M'bali. I'll never have to live in fear of burglars again.'

Pounding with adrenaline she was in no mood to be trifled with. 'You're an idiot,' she told him before she walked over to Klaire, threw a protective arm around her and steered her back inside the hall. Once they were all inside, she locked the door. Within seconds, she was on the phone to Dewar. Her task completed, she turned to the remaining members who had stayed to dispense tea and sympathy to the frightened girl.

'The town is going to love these visuals and the little story that goes with them, especially Steve Packer's wife, Maddy. She's not at all happy about the aneera sponsorship, so she tells me.'

The following morning, her texts and emails were digested with breakfast all over Quimbleton and the surrounding district. Couples began to either debate or shout at each other, depending on the state of their politics and the state of their marriage.

Esteemed reader, these hominids will talk about the aneera lobbyist's actions for days. And talk can be powerful. Some say that money talks too. I don't personally believe that money talks—but it does give off a pungent odour, rather like a pheromone, which is strangely attractive to many. Let us see which prevails in little Quimbleton.

Aries

Another risky week for sharks.
Even with their little bitty teeth,
hominids will eat thousands more of you than you will of them.

Twenty-Five

While their sous chef quivered on the edge of a nervous breakdown in the unfamiliar kitchen, Zera and Jeffrique lay abed, waiting to be fed. The luxury of having a *nid* feeding them so that they could lounge about their mansion all day, copulating as the whim took them, had restored Zera to her usual happy equilibrium. As delighted as he was with his glorious partner's sexual availability, Jeffrique burned with rage over his missing chef, Slugg. Zera had managed to wheedle the crew into admitting that he had been absent for some time.

'I want my chef. And some piece of rarking primitive primate life knows where he is,' he hissed aloud as he anointed himself with unguents in preparation for his bride. 'I will reduce them both to the molecules from whence…'

Patient reader, enough of that. Neither you nor I can run shrieking into Jess and Rivers' shed to warn them, so we will just have to take events as they come.

After a few days of romantic delight and reasonably passable food, the couple were ready to socialise with little Quimbleton. Or at least Zera was. Jeffrique would have to placate her for some days before he retired to the study to plot a path to extinction for every organic molecule on Earth. She did not have to go looking for a social life. Their presence in the rented mansion soon led friends of the owners to their door. The bell chimed. A *nid*, clad only in a loin cloth, answered. He quickly scuttled off to fetch one of The Masters, leaving the visitor a little perplexed by the informal attire of the butler. Zera quickly appeared, smiling and dressed suitably, shutting down her visitor's mental speculations. A plump female dressed in abominably cheerful holiday gear was smiling at her.

'Hello, I do hope I'm not disturbing you,' chirped the woman. 'Gerard and Muffy told us you're here, so I thought I'd pop over and offer you some hospitality.'

Zera was thrilled. Friendly neighbours and a chance to study free hominids at play. A fascinating vista opened to her. 'How lovely, please do come in.' She stood aside to let the hominid toddle past.

Once they had sunk into the plush leather seating, the female introduced herself 'My name is Caroleena but please call me Caro, everyone does.'

By now familiar with the local beverages, Zera had travelled into town and stocked up at the general store a range of drinks and snacks. She offered the visitor a wide choice. The quaintly attired butler soon appeared bearing a loaded tray. Caro briefly wondered if his near nakedness meant that some kind of kinky sex was going on with the staff. Wait until she told the girls, and Gordi! The food was rather oddly arranged. She correctly concluded that this wealthy young couple must be widely travelled and very sophisticated in their knowledge of food cultures. They were—but not about this particular one.

After a period of seemingly aimless chat, during which Zera learnt more about hominid habits and Caro was charmed by the gorgeous girl's attentive interest in her life, it seemed that a new friendship had been made. After Jeffrique arrived from his study and worked his charms on her, Caro decided to invite the couple for a day out on her husband's boat.

'Have you ever swum with dolphins?' she asked.

At that point, Zera had no idea what dolphins were. But, of course, she could not admit it. 'No, but we would love to, wouldn't we star-dream?' Jeffrique managed a nod and a smile that involved his mouth but did not manage to travel as far as his eyes.

'Gordi and I would love to take you both out on our old stink-boat. There are some simply huge dolphin pods in a bay not far down the coast. But I expect you know that.'

'Actually, I wasn't aware they were so close by,' Zera told her.

They set a date. The chatty hominid soon rose to go, and the "butler" saw her out.

Jeffrique quickly decided that it was in his interests to go along willingly with the arrangements. The more friends and pastimes his partner developed outside the house, the more willing she would be to remain on this festering ape shelter while he plotted its destruction.

Two days later they cruised down to meet Caro and her husband Gordi at the nominated dock. To their amazement, the hominid couple were waiting in front of a handsome forty-foot motor cruiser. Being unfamiliar with the locals' casual slangy speech styles, Zera had expected the "old stink boat" to be a creaking dinghy covered in smelly fish scales. Her face lit up. 'Wow! Is that magnificent vessel yours?'

'She sure is,' the grey-haired male answered. 'Hi, I'm Gordi. Welcome abord *The Dugong.*' The couples exchanged handshakes. Jeffrique adroitly avoided hominid kisses. Like pashing a megazoid on 827KG he had told Zera. She had exploded with laugher at the thought.

'This old scow is my base for my diving and documentary movie business and our home-away-from-home on vacation as well,' Gordi told them. He seemed a competent being, for a hominid.

By the time the vessel had moved out of its river estuary mooring, they were all settled into chairs on the deck, drinks in hand. *The Dugong* began a stately buck as it forged through the ocean swells. A crew member navigated and drove, allowing the hospitable Gordi to attend to his guests. After their first drinks had been swallowed, he rose. Reaching into a small hold, he dragged out a pile of strange, dark garments and other equipment onto the deck.

'I guess you guys snorkel?'

'Why? No, but I'm sure we'll pick it up easily,' Zera told him.

'From what Gaz told me about your surfing exploits, I wouldn't doubt that for a moment.'

Zera gasped. 'You knew Gavin?'

'Certainly, a most affable fellow. I surf a bit and he was kind enough to show me a couple of great spots known to few. I can't say the other locals have been so forthcoming.'

This time, Zera was aware of her husband's frown. Perhaps he thought the locals should have been friendlier.

'Are you aware he has gone missing?' she asked.

Both the hominids looked shocked. 'That is just terrible.' Caro's voice was blurred with tears. 'I lost a son at about his age. Both lovely boys. That is so sad.'

Gordi nodded gravely. 'Bad business,' he said, but began handing out wetsuits lest the tone of the day be ruined. Soon both he and his wife were soon spluttering with laughter as their guests struggled into the constricting garments.

'My god, you look as if you're wrestling two giant boa constrictors and the score is reptiles four and people nil,' Caro managed between giggles.

'You're a funny pair. I can't believe that people with your opportunities haven't done this before.' This came from Gordi. The visitors were both wise enough not to attempt an explanation.

Despite his age and blood-shot eyes, Gordi was first to point out a small pod of dolphins cruising towards them. 'Here they come to surf the bow-wave. After all my time at sea, I still get excited you know, call of the wild and all that.'

'The silver-back meets the sea,' said Caro, affectionately rubbing a sun-worn hand through his chest pelt.

Jeffrique was slightly appalled. *Rark, now I'm going frolicking with fish*, he thought. *My acquaintances are moving further and further down the food chain.*

'What are my chances of being bitten?' he asked.

'Although you look like a particularly attractive morsel in that wetsuit, the dolphins won't see you as a floating banquet, Jeffree. Our fellow mammals seem to find us as fascinating as we find them,' Caro told him.

Zera suppressed a gasp. So, these were not mere fish, but mammals in the ocean. Intelligent lifeforms. As a zoologist she was both thrilled and amazed.

Soon, all four were over the side.

'Let them approach you, and don't touch,' Gordi advised. For half an hour, the sleek, finned bodies of the wild pod swirled and dived around them. Zera was soon twisting like wild thing amongst them, surfacing only to exclaim and laugh with delight. Jeffrique, enjoying the swim but not the animals, idly wondered what they tasted like. All too soon, the curious beasts had swept away, and the four clambered onto the old boat.

'They surf, too, you know. They're almost as good as I'm told you are,' Gordi told Zera as they settled back into the cabin, after a shower and change of clothing.

'You mean that I could surf...with them?' she asked in wonder.

'One day, if you're lucky, yes.'

'That puts a new meaning on playing with your food,' Jeffrique remarked, expecting this to be taken a sparkling piece of wit.

'I can't imagine think why you'd think we'd find that funny,' Caro told him coldly. She adroitly changed the subject but threw him appraising glances now and then. He worked even harder at responding to their friendliness. He sensed that Gordi was buying it, but the woman was suspicious. He watched her eyes tracking from himself to Zera and back. Despite his efforts, he was aware that the contrast between his strained cheerfulness and the genuine easy manner of his wife was clear to her. The rarking nosy hominid woman was doing the odds on their marriage. The impertinent beast should be whipped.

After the dolphin trip, a few days passed pleasantly by. Zera befriended a local couple she met while shopping in Quimbleton. They farmed a special fruit which they told her was made into a very popular alcoholic beverage on their property. Naturally, they found the girl charming, and she and Jeffrique were invited over for lunch. He continued to encourage this forming of bonds with the hominids—confident that her curiosity and friendliness would carry her through when he began to spend more and more time plotting in his study.

Jeffrique's rare patience was rewarded. She began to go out without him. He was not enjoying the tedium of his mental calculations about annihilation. Ambitious and intelligent though he was, he saw detailed work as for minions. Dreary hours of dull persistence were for not for him. He was becoming impatient to act—even though he had no idea what would work. To his astonishment his research so far had revealed that these pieces of ape turd had somehow managed to split the atom. A few of them must have some intellect that would be useful to *Genes-R-Us,* if harnessed and forced along the right channels. Perhaps he could kidnap a few relatively bright ones. That might get his father's attention in a good way. No, he could never confess their origins, and inevitably one of them would blab.

Following the nuclear trail in his research, he found that these earthling beasts had gone on to make bombs, rockets, and atomic warheads. Lots of them. And they were secreted in bunkers all over the globe. If left to their own devices in the galaxies, hominids were inclined to gather into tribes and bicker. Here he could see that this tribal bickering had expanded to encompass the whole planet in a constant stand-off. But this sabre-rattling now apparently involved missiles which could obliterate whole cities. *That could be very useful to me,* he thought. He decided that he would like to get hold of one of these weapons to see how it worked. Perhaps, if he could harness all of them at once, he could blow this orb of organic space junk to oblivion.

In the starry darkness of night, as Zera slept, he made his first impetuous move. The cosmic elite's nano-chip and computer-enhanced intellects had long since acquired the ability to analyse the molecules of an object and recreate it instantly at a spot far away. With a burst of mental concentration, Jeffrique focused with electrifying intensity on a warhead stored in an underground hidey hole. The resultant electrical field fused its wiring sending its military minders, from a dark super-power, running about like enraged bull-ants whose nest has been disturbed. Jeffrique would later have brief cause to regret that. An undamaged replica now stood, gleaming in starlit menace, in the dense forest a few kilometres away. Once he had done a test-fire he could calculate how many of these chimpy firecrackers he would need to extinguish life on 3159XZ entirely.

Taurus

Gorilla family life will be peaceful and rewarding this week.
Do not let diminishing forests dampen your day.

Twenty-Six

After the meeting in the C.W.A. hall, as she circulated meeting friends, M'bali had invited Jess and Rivers to lunch at *The Briar Patch*. She had asked for River's expert help, as a trained environmental scientist, with some issues about natural management of pests in her crops. The pair rarely allowed themselves time to socialise during the day, but she knew he was generous in sharing his scientific knowledge of how healthy ecosystems worked. Asking him for advice was a sure-fire way of luring him to visit and in return she would cook them lunch. Hayes was coming, not only to get to know her friends better, but because he was her witness to the spaceship crashing out of her bedroom. She would need him on her side because Rivers was going to take some convincing on the topic of visiting aliens. Although Hayes seemed to be understandably confused and dubious about it, at least he hadn't run off and left her. M'bali desperately needed almost anyone else to see Jeffree and Zera through her eyes. She felt alone, scared and slightly off-kilter in a way she had never experienced before.

Hayes arrived on Quimbie central time, and the young couple's old rainbow-hued vehicle came plodding up the hill a couple of minutes later. After their warm greetings, all four were soon tramping amongst the lush herb and vegetable beds examining leaves for holes and other signs of unwanted infestations. Rivers had a few laughs at some of her girly methods of construction involving pantyhose, pegs, and the odd hair clip. He offered her cuttings of a plant which attracted natural predator species to eat pests. 'You're welcome to come over and get some, we have heaps ourselves. They work a treat.'

She thanked him profusely. But before they could retreat to the cool of the living room, a battered four-wheel drive pulled up her driveway. As they all turned to look, a man dressed head to toe in khaki and holding a strange stick and a large sack clambered out of it.

'Oh good, it's Warren Stanton. Roxy had a snake rear up at her in the top paddock this morning. I asked him to come and remove it. He's an old school friend and the local herpetologist.' She waved. As he drew closer, he called to her.

'Hi, M'bali. What species of beastie has upset your Roxy this time?'

'Sorry, no idea beyond huge and scary. I didn't see it myself. Warren, meet Hayes, Jess, and Rivers, some of my organic farming mates.' She turned to the others, 'Warren spent his last years at school skipping class and listening to things rustling in the undergrowth.'

His eyes crinkled as he laughed. 'Hello, all. Alarmingly true, although I did manage to graduate despite that.'

'The beastie was in the long grass next to the central tree in the top paddock. Sorry I can't come up for a chat. I've got lunch for these guys on the stove.'

'No worries. It'll be less disturbed if it only senses the patter of my tiny feet.'

'Thanks, mate. Send me an account and we must catch up for a drink—soon.'

Warren nodded and with an affable flap of his free hand he set off walking.

'Not a job I envy,' Jess remarked as they walked to the house. In the cool living room, Hayes served drinks while M'bali grabbed trays of nibbles. She would wait patiently for her moment; the right moment to start talking about spaceships and aliens.

Can you imagine such a moment, esteemed reader, the moment when your cherished friends start to think you have flipped your lid?

Rivers now instigated a lively conversation about life in the district as outsiders. 'Most of the locals are okay. They've just been living in an isolated valley for so many generations that they think even Moobalup is a pit of dissent and strange opinions.'

M'bali put on her intently listening face—even though her mind and heart were racing. When she considered Rivers to be nicely warmed up, she rose and called them to the dining table for lunch. As they were finishing a luscious dessert made from her own fruit, fresh herbs, and cream, she pounced. 'Last time we spoke I was raising some concerns about where Slugg might have come from…'

Rivers groaned. 'M'bali give up. I really don't want to hear any more…'

Hayes intervened. 'This isn't about your friend, Slugg. It's about a scary and frankly bloody bewildering incident that I witnessed here. It happened in the middle of the night a few days ago.'

'I imagine M'bali is pretty full-on in bed,' Rivers countered.

'I'm not laughing, mate. I think you need to see what I'm referring to—and then we'll talk,' Hayes told him. He rose and led the way to the bedroom. M'bali followed with her phone at the ready to show her friends her photograph of the saucer *in situ*. Wozzer, attracted by excited voices, soon joined them. He slumped in the doorway in the tripping position.

The four stepped over his slumbering body as they emerged from the room quite a few minutes later. They subsided onto the living room furniture in a silence finally broken by M'bali feeling the need to defend herself.

'Look, I know this is weird, but do I look like the kind of fruit loop who sees…'

Jess intervened. 'I would say you are famously level-headed M'bali, so let's put together what we know. You watch the spaceship hover and appear to land, then it disappears. Straight after that Zera and Jeffree appear in bathers—he's walked kilometres on a hot morning with no sign of sweat. He's happy to admit to you they are aliens because, he says, no-one will believe you. Next thing you trip over a miniature but incredibly heavy version of the exact same spaceship in your driveway. You stow it in your wardrobe—what were you thinking, by the way? Then it blasts off in the middle of the night wrecking your wardrobe door, the lock, and a pane of window glass.'

'No chance of a successful insurance claim on that evidence,' Rivers put in.

M'bali smiled faintly and had to quell her urge to blurt out, 'Slugg appears from nowhere in the middle of all that. He's of outlandish height and strength and sports some sort of dog-tag in a foreign script.' She knew that he was too valuable and well-liked by Jess and Rivers for them to be willing to see a connection.

'Have you told anyone besides us?' Rivers asked.

'No, the arrogant prick was right—no-one would believe me. I will not be queueing up to be a laughingstock on my own turf. I've been on the wrong side of this town before.'

'What about telling Dewar? Don't you know him quite well?' Hayes suggested.

Rivers interceded. 'If these people, if they are people, have enough tech to get here, they are from a far more advanced civilisation than any on earth. We have no idea how dangerous they can be…'

M'bali interrupted his flow. 'I totally agree. I am firmly of the belief that he disposed of Gaz in some way. He took Zera for a surfing lesson while Jeffree was under arrest in Slique. I was looking out an open window when Zera was welcoming Jeffree back. I saw a look of absolute fury on his face as he commented on the lesson. And he referred to Gaz as "chimpy boy". I'm sure she missed the look because they were hugging. Gaz disappeared within a couple of days.'

'Well, we all certainly concluded he met with foul play. Out of character, no bank accounts used, no phone calls and all that,' Rivers admitted, frowning.

'So, we do nothing and hope they piss off?' Hayes asked. 'Where are they by the way? Has anyone seen them?'

'Yes, they've been socialising with all and sundry, including some of the Slique people with holiday homes here. Roxy, my farm hand, saw her at the store being charming and impossibly gorgeous the day before yesterday. She said that every male in sight was struggling to keep it in his pants.'

'She has a turn of phrase, your Roxy,' Hayes said.

'She's young—and observant.'

M'bali had found the whole morning a strain, as if the normal day-to-day worries of a establishing a new business were not enough. She rose and thanked them for their advice and company. All were thoughtful as they walked out to the rainbow vehicle.

'Don't forget to come out and get some cuttings, anytime,' Jess called as they began chugging away.

When she and Hayes were back on the sofa, she thanked him for his support. 'I'm a pretty tough chick but this business is doing my head in.'

He put his arms around her. They sat quietly for a while. She felt small yet safe cocooned in his embrace. At last, she spoke. 'I've decided to tell Doug. I don't care who they are, I am not going to stand around watching when I think one of my best mates has been disposed of.' She felt him tense.

'Babe, I know I can't stop you—but be careful how far you push this. Just remember that old Hayes could not bear to lose you. Okay?'

They kissed.

Reader, enough of that. This new intelligence landing on Doug Dewar's plate would be all he needed to complete a dire year. He had been having some alien-related troubles of his own—as you will presently see.

Gemini

This week, numbats will find it increasingly difficult to find one another. There aren't many of you left. Keep searching—you won't regret it.

Twenty-Seven

The spaceship story M'bali had related left Jess Kossick feeling more conflicted than ever about Slugg's presence in her life. Her confusion was partly fired by guilt over her failure to search for his family or friends. Wonderful helper though he was, she felt that he shouldn't be expected to be their farmhand, cook and maid-of-all-work indefinitely. In her earnest and idealistic way, she believed that he was entitled to a choice of staying or leaving. On the other hand, what if he didn't want to be found? This idea settled her for a while, but then her restless thoughts swirled another way. Someone might be worrying and missing him. But her sense of survival told her that the giant's helpful presence on the farm was probably saving her marriage.

Dearest reader, there were far too many "other hands" for her sweet simple hominid brain. Opposing thoughts ricocheted inside her skull, keeping her awake for too much of too many nights. She became obsessed by Slugg's dog-tag with its strange foreign script.

'Where do you think he's from?' she asked Rivers as they lay exhausted on their bed one night.

He was not an insensitive man. Although he sensed her anxiety, he wanted to push it aside with all his being. Their dream house was growing before his eyes and Slugg's dogged labour was hastening their journey towards a productive farm. Even more importantly than that, it was saving his marriage. His vibrant Jess was back, and he no longer dreaded the day she would drag her exhausted frame back to the comfort of her parents. 'No idea,' he told her with fake disinterest. 'He's perfectly happy here. He's free to leave. Stop worrying, honey.'

'Rivers, it does matter. M'bali is on the trail of whoever took Gaz, and you know if she gets her teeth into something she'll hang on tighter than Wozzer with a ball. If we can find out that the writing on his tag is a known language on

Earth—that would blow her alien theory about Slugg out of the water. We should pursue it.'

Rivers rolled towards her. 'Much as I esteem M'bali as a friend, her ideas about Slugg are unprovable speculation and not worth responding to. Come on honey, give me a big cuddle. It's been a rough day.'

Jess did as he asked. But she was not appeased for long. One morning, after a particularly restless night, she awoke feeling strung out. This alarmed her. She was on her way to feeling as exhausted as she had before the giant's arrival. She felt she must act. As soon as Rivers had left to toil in their field, she signalled to Slugg, pointing to his dog-tag. Then she pointed to her phone. He knew it took pictures. She used a waving finger to link the two. Trustfully he nodded. She pressed to capture the tag in its memory. With intent to hide her intentions from him, she made a great to do of making a portrait study of the giant at work in the kitchen. She would print it, frame it, and present it to him. A guilty present. Thanking him, with excessive smiles and thumbs up signs, she retreated to the alcove which served as the main bedroom. After a moment's pause, she began typing a message to Dewar. 'Sergeant Dewar, this tag belongs to our farm hand Slugg. He doesn't speak our language and we don't understand whatever he does speak. He is a great worker, but as you can imagine, it would be easier if we could communicate in words. Rivers and I would like to find an interpreter so that we can communicate better with him. I'm wondering if you know a way to get the tag translated. Regards, Jess Kossick. P.S. My husband and I are close friends of M'bali Hoyle,' she added, thinking that connection might prod him into helping. She pressed send.

Dewar read the odd request an hour later. Contacting interpreter services for civilians was not his core business—in fact it wasn't any of his business. But he already knew that this girl was a good friend of his mate M'bali, so he would pursue the matter as requested. He dispatched the photo by text to a friend at headquarters, with a note asking if he knew how to contact an interpreter. 'None of them needed down here, mate,' he typed to his mate. 'We all speak much the same lingo.' A message came from Slique several days later. It informed him that the inscription was not in any human script or language known to interpreter services. In fact, the interpreters had sent it all over the country as well as to colleagues overseas. They were baffled, but adamant, that the writing on the tag was in no Earth language—past or present.

The message made the hairs on the back of Dewar's neck stand to attention. This discovery was too close to home. He barely had time to process it when M'bali rang requesting to meet him. What she told him, and the photographs of the saucer that she shared, sent him home to the comfort of a bottle and the raucous company of his talkative rescued bird, Elviz.

Dewar and his wife, Ros, had lost their only child to stillbirth several years before. She was now forty-eight. There would be no more. Grief had driven him to work harder and drink more. He was becoming a habitual, if functioning, drunk.

Her sorrow had taken her on another path. Their baby's grave was in the small cemetery which lay in a bush clearing on a hilltop near the town's outskirts. Now she visited it daily; sometimes twice. Her escalating absences made Dewar uneasy and increasingly lonely. She began to pretend that the errands which took her from the house were merely practical.

'Where are you off to now, love?'

'Just popping into town for bread and milk.'

'Again? That's bullshit, Ros. I know where you're really going. Would you like me to drive you?'

'No.'

He knew from bitter experience that trying to talk her into getting practical help for her unfinished mourning was futile. What he had not realised was that visiting the tiny grave was not the only reason for her growing absences. One day, as he came quietly inside after tending to his vegetable plot, he caught a whispered fragment of conversation between his wife and her friend Gretel. His gut had churned. He had thought the two women only clung together to comfort each other in their loss but he was only partially correct. They had joined a fundamentalist sect, which he later found was based in a hidden compound in the bush outside Moobalup. He made secret investigations. It was a sect whose members had been conned into believing that their messiah would arrive on earth by spaceship. The leader was a fraudster known to the force for his past inept attempts to rob the unwary. Dewar had tried to warn her, but her sorrow and need for hope outweighed his words.

Every evening when she had left him alone, as the shadows of the forest began to take Quimbleton into their dark embrace, Dewar opened his first bottle.

Cancer

The stars are at a crossroads for hominids.
Exercise foresight this week, and every week.
Decisions made by you today will stay with you
and your descendants down the ages.

Twenty-Eight

Zera began waking each day with a wave of anticipation. Riding the wild surf with Gaz had been an unexpected thrill. To be at one with the ocean's power was a sensation almost as good as sex—but she wasn't foolish enough to tell Jeffrique that. Now she had swum with the dolphins. Most designer-animals in her world were docile and boring, no matter how exotic they looked. But these shining creatures had played with her; they had played with the ocean, surfing the bow wave in joyous leaps. Her conception of what other creatures could achieve was expanding daily. Jeffrique was unusually quiet. He told her he was troubled by his workload, so she decided to give him time alone to catch up.

Curiosity made her heart race as she showered in the fragrant bathroom. Dressed in a strappy sundress, and styled with her usual finesse, she raced downstairs to where he was already sitting moodily in the study. 'Don't worry about me today, star-dream, I'm going to leave you in peace. Caro and I are going on a girly shopping trip to Slique.'

Jeffrique looked up and took in her coiffed and perfumed presence. He paused. He did not want her going out without him looking like that. But his awful task was before him. He could not shirk it. 'Then come here and give me a proper goodbye, lovely wife.'

'See you for dinner at about seven,' she said from within his lingering embrace.

Caro and Zera sped to Slique in the hominid's sports car, chatting easily as women do. Zera learned that the hominid couple had travelled widely all over their planet with their two offspring. Was this urge to explore why the hominids in her world occasionally got caught digging tunnels or building escape primitive vehicles? Did novelty and freedom excite them as much as it did her and Jeffrique?

At many points during that day, she wished her Ph.D. supervisor was riding with her. Only he could comprehend her amazement that these lowly creatures had the mental capacity to imagine and build the sparkling city. On the way into the centre, mile upon mile of mansions with manicured gardens flashed by. Caro drove like a woman who could afford speeding tickets. Gordi had papered the guest's loo with her "trophies". Skyscrapers many stories high threw dazzling reflections back at the heavens. Caro parked the car then they wandered shopping malls full of artful clothing, jewellery, electronic goods and a myriad of foodstuffs. Hominids strolled by relaxed, laughing and clearly spending up big. Why had she not known that these creatures she had studied for so long were capable of so much joy and achievement?

*

At last, Jeffrique was free to inspect the rocket he had secreted deep in the forest. He strode out to where the *Mercedes Sidebottom* van was garaged and jumped in. It was soon jolting down a dusty forest track. He sent a couple of squashy bouncy things flying off its bull-bar on the way, but he raced on undaunted. As he swung around a sharp bend, he was forced to brake sharply. A vast pig weighing several hundred kilos was napping in the middle of the track. He blew the van's horn loudly and repeatedly. She eyed him serenely and was clearly in no hurry to move. Attempting to navigate around her rolling flanks, he spun the steering wheel to ease the vehicle slowly forward. To his annoyance, she struggled to her feet then executed a nimble side-step, blocking his movement with her bulk. He hit the horn furiously and was about to delete her from existence when two scruffy hominids bearing rifles held loosely by their sides, stepped out of the roadside bushes. 'Sorry about the hold-up, mate,' the taller of the two told him. 'Gladys here is trained to guard access to our mining lease. I suggest you don't proceed any further.'

'I am brim-full of curiosity to see your most interesting enterprise,' Jeffrique told him before he began yet another flanking movement around the sow.

The younger one, who looked like he hadn't bathed in a month or so, threw his rifle onto his shoulder and sent a slug flying through the windscreen. It missed Jeffrique's head by centimetres.

Dearest reader, the alien was really cross now. Enraged is probably a more appropriate term. An electrifying fizz filled the air, followed by the aroma of perfectly roasted flesh. Gladys was now reclining on a platter in a pool of apple sauce and steaming gently.

The older thug's lower lip began to quiver. 'I really loved that old girl,' he managed. The younger one's eyes flashed. He raised his gun to his shoulder and took aim at Jeffrique's chest.

You know what is going to happen as well as I do—both reduced to the molecules from whence, etc, etc. A third scruffy hominid had remained hiding in the dense bushes, witnessing the events. The disappearance of Gladys and her owners would send an angry ripple through parts of the community that no-one with any sense wanted to annoy. The alleged "mining lease" was a mature drug crop just ripe for the picking. A few men in expensive suites in Slique were going to be very cross indeed when the expected product was not delivered to them, especially when they found their guard animal had been roasted. (She was delicious, by the way. Waste not, want not.)

Jeffrique drove on unimpeded. He was not buying the mining lease story. *That's what happens when you come between ape-brains and their drug of choice—they get nasty. Leave them alone with any organic matter for a few days and they'll ferment it and drink it or dry it and smoke it.* He laughed at their weakness.

Quite a few kilometres past their illegal stash, and down another even narrower winding track, he located the rocket which towered above the surrounding trees. He threw open the driver's door and began walking about inspecting and analysing its capabilities. What the alien did not know was that in these southern forests many areas which looked totally wild and uninhabited were regularly traversed by a surprising number of hominids. Maybe the locals were taking a shortcut to Moobalup, walking the dog, stealing timber, training for a marathon, or admiring the flowers—whatever, some rarking nosy ape-brain was likely to pass by. And one did. A local fisherman, on the way to a secret stream to fish, came barrelling down the track and screeched to a halt. He leaned out of the cab and called in an easy manner, 'That's a pretty impressive skyrocket you've got there, and it's not even cracker night.'

You know the drill—reduced to the molecules from whence, etc. The man's wife would become distressed when his dog returned home, lame, exhausted and without her partner.

Irritated by these repeated intrusions into his train of thought, Jeffrique turned his attention back to the rocket and its support structures. He decided he would do a test-fire it to assess its capabilities. With little delay, he sent it roaring into the sky. Flames and dust blasted through the trees. At the level of Earth orbit, it homed in on a satellite belonging to a foreign power and blasted it out of the sky. Not a wise move. In some ways, the *Genes-R-Us* Corporation had it right about hominids. Left to their own devices they made some awful messes. Every major power on the little blue orb had excessive numbers of missiles hunkered down in silos and waiting to strike at, whoever. But blasting each other's satellites into itty-bitty pieces was not considered fair play. Several hostile countries began to track large fragments of the device as they showered down on a remote desert far away.

The fire ignited by the missile flared and crackled on the dry forest floor. It gradually rose, igniting peeling bark on the nearby trees. Sensitive creatures began to flare their nostrils, scenting the air. Fanned by a desert wind from the north-east, the blaze soon flew to the treetops. Shrieking birds fled desperately before it or fell, singed, to the ground. Creatures capable of hiding in logs, under bark or underground hunkered down. The larger and more mobile animals fled desperately before the flames.

Before long, the smoke plume was sighted by a fire-watching drone. The fire was heading towards several properties on the west side of town—including that of Rivers and Jess. The *Quimby Volunteer Fire Brigade*, led by Packo at breakneck speed, was soon closing in on it. They just missed Jeffrique's exit from the isolated track. He laughed as he watched them tear past him down the highway. If Norbert had been there, he would have re-noted the Mercedes' model, number plate and distinguishing marks out of sheer habit.

Leo

Mainly another steady week for chameleons.
Your "I'm a stick" pose will keep working.
But do not twitch on the 18th or 20th.

Twenty-Nine

The inferno saw little Quimbleton at its best. Packo and his crew hurtled down forest tracks towards the blaze. Many of the able-bodied men in town were fire volunteers, including Hayes. They tried to contact local property owners. Some responded, some did not. Out on their remote block, where only one corner of the highest paddock consistently had phone reception, Jess, Rivers and Slugg had no idea what was heading towards them. Leaving chef Klaire short of staff, Hayes rushed to throw on his protective gear and drove out to join the battle. He threw his big machine into Jess and Rivers' driveway and slewed to a halt in a shower of dust and pebbles. They were nowhere to be seen. He jumped out and ran for the house, shouting for his crew to inspect their firebreaks in his absence. Inside the half-completed dwelling, three surprised faces peered at him through a mist of plaster dust.

'Hayes, if we knew you were coming, we'd have baked a cake,' Rivers told him before he took in the uniform and the worried demeanour of their sudden visitor.

'Fire coming towards your eastern boundary, on current wind direction anyway. How are your breaks? Are you prepared enough to stay and fight?'

Judging by their horrified faces they were not prepared.

'No, no, no, this can't happen to us,' Jess wailed.

'My boys and I are here to defend your property. We'll clear breaks, and backburn if we can. There's no immediate danger. You can help if you want—but if I tell you to leave, you'll have to go.'

All four ran outside. Jess was frantically miming to the giant, trying to make him understand. A soon as the men began working, Slugg understood what was required. He ran about felling trees with his own force before Jess used an old grader, normally used to clear paddocks, to shove them away from the forest wall. In astonishingly little time, they had cleared a substantial break. The wee-wah of sirens had preceded two other units from the Quimby brigade which roared past the boundary on their way to neighbouring properties.

As sometimes happens, a change in the wind swung the flames in another direction and the property was saved. Packo and several units of the brigade battled on in the forest, managing to extinguish the blaze in a few days with the help of a little rain. Wildlife volunteers combed the blackened ruins looking for singed creatures to save or euthanise.

Hayes was left with the memory of Slugg felling trees and lifting impossible loads again and again. *No-one can do that*, he thought. The idea would haunt him even at work. Yet in other moments it did not seem quite real.

M'bali was beginning to believe she had picked a good one this time. She was left with a mental image of this man, who she was longing to trust, racing out to face the flames and save her friends.

Reader, I'm left with wanting to get on with my story.

Virgo

An excellent week for the few surviving bald eagles,
and many more to come.
Gorge on those salmon right up to pussy's bow.

Thirty

When it became safe to enter the fire ground, several senior figures in the Quimby and Moobalup brigades began an investigation into how the blaze had started. They puzzled over a wide area where large trees lay flattened in a circular pattern. It looked more like a blast zone than an area sprinkled with accelerant by a pyromaniac local with a grudge against life. They sent photos and reports to Slique and soon Dewar was being asked questions about locals with an affinity for explosives. He was unable to name any—which meant there most probably weren't any.

After a few weeks of futile investigation, the incident was classified into the too hard box, pending a cold case review, perhaps a few months down the track. On someone else's watch with any luck.

Several notoriously flaky members of the community, who were known to live in a haze of substances, reported having seen a missile streak into the blue firmament. As they often saw insects crawling up their limbs and the odd dragon, their observations were dismissed as fanciful.

*

Over a passable meal under the crystal chandelier of the dining room, Jeffrique and Zera discussed their day. She was more radiantly excited than he had ever seen her—out of bed, anyway. 'Star-dream, it was so exciting to see what these clever Slique hominids have been able to build and create when left to their own devices.'

Esteemed reader, inter-galactic boffins used to argue about the extent to which hominids could think, much as you wonder about Fido or Kitty's mental capacity after they have done something particularly devious. When some hominid subject with electrodes hanging off his head remarked, 'Bloody oath we can think, lady,' this was not taken as scientific evidence of their ability. And their elaborate attempts at escape were only taken to mean that the naughty genes hadn't quite been engineered out yet.

Jeffrique appeared to be looking fascinated by Zera's discoveries about the ape-brains. He was only fascinated by her shining violet eyes and how the light played upon the bone structure of her face.

'Look at this, star-dream. I took so many photos and videos.' She thrust a camera in front of him. 'If only I could write an academic paper about what they can do. It would revolutionise our scientific understanding of their capacities.'

Jeffrique dropped his eating implements. 'Rark no! I mean I totally support your career, but this planet is meant to be lifeless. You can't tell anyone. Your precious hominids will be bumped off or cloned and modified the instant his gracious celestial rarking daddyness finds out about them.' He watched her mood sink at his words. He went on, 'So we won't tell, will we? We'll just relax here for a while then whizz off and enjoy our honeyflit amongst the stars.'

Zera sighed. Her eyes filled with tears. 'You are so right; we must not tell. But I am allowed to have regrets.'

But those tears were about more than mild regret. She was beginning to be consumed by an inner turmoil. Yes, hominid behaviour had once only been of academic interest to her. Now, the foundations of her deepest beliefs were being challenged. Gavin, Caro, and even the nosy M'bali, had been so kind and welcoming to her. After befriending these free, unmodified hominids, she did not want to imagine them being used only as beasts of burden or domestic slaves for the *Genes-R-Us* elite. Zera could not say a word about her feelings to her husband. Genetic manipulation and cloning were the basis of his family's business empire. And now she was allied to that by a marriage she had assumed would last for eternity. She had believed that married couples should hold no secrets. Now conflict about her forbidden opinions began to torment her.

Jeffrique too was anxious. He was going to need a welter of time in his study to interpret the results of the rocket firing. But he would have to keep accompanying her on forays into this rarking, festering life-pit or she might begin to question what he was up to.

She might indeed. She very well might.

Libra

Polar bears had better evolve back
into the grizzlies they came from, in a hurry.
And don't invest in ice futures.

Thirty-One

Sergeant Doug Dewar's life was about to get more complicated. After witnessing Slugg's impossible strength and endurance, Hayes had phoned him to add to his dossier about the giant. Apart from the perhaps dubious alien invasion aspects of the story, there was a possible illegal refugee hiding out on Jess and Rivers' remote property. He was obliged to investigate such matters on his patch.

Dewar's best home companion sat on his shoulder throughout breakfast accepting an occasional almond or titbits of toast. Elviz was a cockatoo with dark feathers and a crest which shot up and down according to his mood. Years before, the sergeant had noticed him, bald and squawking, under a roadside tree. He had given him over to the care of a local wildlife expert who later reported that one wing had been damaged in his fall from the nest—he could fly a little but would never be mobile enough to survive in the wild. By the time he was a fledged adult, the carer needed aviary space for incoming cases, so Dewar had elected to look after Elviz himself. The bird had become an excellent mimic and his cheerful chat often lightened the cop's life—but not always. This morning he struggled to hold onto a rational thought as the Elviz launched into a hymn in the wavery soprano voice of his wife, who was still slumbering in bed. He needed to get away from the hyper-religious atmosphere and the sorrow. Elviz was devoted to him and would try to flap outside in pursuit as he left the house. He slipped his hand under the bird's feet and stood up, intending to confine him, not in a cage, but to another room. As Dewar lumbered towards his prison door the cockatoo twigged what was about to happen. 'Spawn of Satan. Do not mock the sacred word!' he commanded. This alarmed the cop. He began to wonder how many members of the cult had visited his house in his absence. He knew that such organisations worked hard at alienating their possible recruits from family and friends. Miserable as she had become, he did not want to lose Ros. It wasn't easy being a cop in a country town—you had mates, but only up to a point.

With Elviz confined and still hurling abuse, Dewar set off for his four-wheel drive. Half-an-hour later his white vehicle, now embellished by the red dust of the unpaved road, pulled up outside Jess and Rivers' boundary fence. The bushes rustled and moved with the passage of startled animals. He could see the young couple stooped over a tree they were planting. Rivers looked up as the sound of an engine sent birds screeching for shelter. The cop had passed their place before but had never stopped. 'Bloody Dewar. What does he want?'

Jess knew she had to confess in a hurry. 'He might be here about Slugg…' she began, hopeful he would forgive her.

'Why the fuck should our farmhand concern him? Tell me you haven't blabbed to Dewar.'

'I think Slugg has the right to a choice. He seems so lost, and we don't know who's missing him.'

'You silly cow…'

As Dewar approached with his powerful waddle, Rivers tried to rearrange his face into a mask of innocence and welcome.

'G'day, you two. That house of yours is looking pretty impressive.'

'Yes, thanks to our farmhand and friend Slugg,' Jess told him.

'That's just who I was hoping to talk to you about. Where is he?'

Rivers was failing to get control of his expression and his mouth remained closed in a tight line. Jess was still angry at the way he had spoken to her. She was not going to back up his silence. 'He's in the kitchen of the old house cleaning up and preparing lunch.' She yelled the giant's name.

He soon ducked out of the doorway. 'Yez, Jezz?'

She signalled for him to approach. He began to do so, looking at the newcomer with his usual bland friendliness. Dewar extended a hand which disappeared into the giant's huge paw.

'This is just a routine visit,' Dewar lied. 'Headquarters have a bee in their bonnet about illegal refugees at present. I just need to see his papers to check where he's from.'

'We haven't seen any papers. Who asks their farmhands for formal identification?'

Dewar knew plenty of employers who checked the *bona fides* of potential employees, but he made no comment about that. He slid his phone from a pocket, opened it and held up the photo of the tag. 'Concerns have been raised because no-one has been able to identify this script.' Concerns had been raised for a few other reasons as we know only too well. The fact that immigration had never cleared anyone named Slugg, or even Slug, was just the icing on an increasingly mysterious cake.

'We don't know what the script is either. All we know is that he's a lovely friendly guy who works hard and minds his own business,' Rivers cut in, indirectly suggesting that the cop do the same.

'Zera and Jeffree,' Dewar said, watching Slugg's face for a reaction. The giant's eyes flew open. He backed away slightly but was too subservient to run.

'What the fuck are you frightening him for?'

Dewar pointed at the sky then at Slugg. 'You, Zera, Jeffree.' He waved his arm upwards to the heavens.

The giant began to wail. 'No, no, no. No go back!'

He'd got the response he wanted, now Dewar tried to de-escalate the situation. 'Look, I don't want to upset him. I can see he's worked hard for you. I'm going to talk to Jess a bit in the old house.'

Rivers could not suppress a glare as his wife and the cop trudged across the uneven field together. Jess was silent. Once inside at the old Formica table, she poured the cop a cup of tea. 'What's going on?' she asked, trying to look nonchalant, but failing miserably.

'Your Slugg arrived in the Quimbleton area at the same time as Zera and Jeffree Smith. Those two are under suspicion for reasons I can't reveal. When I mentioned their names, he became anxious. What can you tell me about him?'

'Not much. The little of our language he knows I taught him. We found him by the roadside between here and Moobalup. He was wearing only a sheet which we later found he had taken from M'bali's clothesline. She isn't fussed about that. The poor man must have been robbed of everything he owned—including his identity documents.'

Dewar sipped his tea and gave her space to go on or face an awkward silence.

Jess babbled on hopefully, 'He's kind and gentle. He loves to work, both in our fields and in the house. He's the most domestically skilled man I have ever met. He even cleans the toilet, for heaven's sake.'

Esteemed reader, any female anywhere across the galaxies will understand at once that Slugg is a man of great virtue and value.

'Even our friends love him. He dances, he sings,' Jess dribbled on knowing her words were to no avail.

'Your Slugg seems to be some kind of illegal immigrant in this country. I'm afraid he will have to go into detention pending further investigation. By the way, do you have another name for him?'

'No.'

Dewar had no idea that these people were aware of M'bali's alien story. He decided that he would not mention the "a" word in case it created unnecessary panic. But panic had already been created.

Jess jumped up and ran for the door. 'Rivers! Tell Slugg to run!' she shrieked. Her partner mimed running to Slugg and they were soon crashing off, forcing their way through the dense undergrowth.

Dewar sighed. 'Not your best decision, Jess. Now both you and Rivers will have to come with me to the station for questioning.'

Other eyes had seen Slugg singing and laughing in the pub on the night he was picked up by Jess and Rivers. They saw a long-haired, bearded man in a strange robe. Later, they had remarked upon this to their cult leader, Nigel Cuthbertson, the well-known fraudster, who had now designated himself as Yuewath-Sahib, prophet of the coming messiah. He lifted his scrawny body to its full height. 'You fools!' he boomed in the preaching tone which he rarely dropped. 'It is the chosen one! He has come to us!'

Dearest reader, poor innocent Slugg. Now he is wanted by the local fuzz, an annoyed alien and a bunch of deluded fanatics.

Scorpio

This week, domestic cats will have it made, as usual.
Put down that bird, or mummy will be cross.

Thirty-Two

M'bali had launched herself back into her busy life. It was proving an excellent distraction from her speculation about what might happen when Dewar intervened in the lives of alien beings with unknown powers. Inviting Hayes to ride with her in the forest and along the local beaches had proved, to her surprise, a great success. He rode well, was gentle in his handling of her precious young colt and did not exude a stream of endless chat frightening the wildlife away. That was a great improvement on the behaviour of some of her female friends.

They were now relaxing in the cane chairs on her wide veranda sipping coffees after such a ride. Wozzer was recovering from a sulk over not being allowed to accompany them. He could no longer keep up, but that did not temper his wounded feelings. M'bali absently stroked his head.

'That gallop along the beach was great. But, sorry to say, I won't be free to ride for a week or so,' Hayes announced, looking a little tense.

'I'll miss that. You're particularly nice to be with. What's up?'

'My daughter is coming to stay.'

'Daughter? You said you'd never been married.'

'It is possible to conceive a child out of wedlock, M'bali.'

'Sorry, I hate sounding like a small-town prude.'

'Accepted. I must say I hadn't noticed the prude bit at all.' He grinned wickedly.

'So, tell me about your daughter.'

'She's seven, and her name is Bree. Her mother and I were together a few years ago when I was on the road. Annika was a rock photographer then and she wrote pieces for a few trade magazines. We were both twenty-three when the kid was born. Best thing that ever happened, by the way.'

M'bali smiled.

He went on, 'Being on the road with her worked out for about three years. We were young, we made it happen. But the relationship was foundering, and we had to get Bree into pre-primary so she could make some stable friends. Annika and I broke up, but we've remained on okay terms. She's settled in Slique and has another guy now—fortunately I approve of him as an outlaw stepfather. I get to see Bree when I get up to Slique on weekends, and on school holidays as well.'

'Wow, you are full of surprises. A nice one in this case. I guess it's a bit too soon for me to meet her.'

'Yes, it is. But hang in there and it'll happen. You two will get on like the proverbial. She's action woman, into martial arts and she rides like a pro. That was how I started with the equestrian thing. It was a way to connect with her, but now I love it too.'

Hayes was not ready for his precious daughter to meet his new lover. Her stories about aliens seemed superficially plausible and yet he lay awake some nights doubting and wondering. Was there something mentally wrong with her? Had the wardrobe door and window been smashed by some trick piece of technology beyond his grasp?

M'bali flinched a bit at the "L" word. She wasn't quite ready to trust love yet. 'So, I guess Bree is why it was so important to you that I honour my brother?'

'Yes, I'm a very family-minded unreliable retired rock god.'

'Hah, hah.'

Enough of this flirtatious hominid drivel, dear reader. I have a cosmic story to tell. Let's cut to the chase.

'Anyway, what's the news on Dewar and Slugg?'

M'bali squirmed in her chair and sighed. 'It isn't getting any better. Doug told me that the guy has no identification papers of any kind. He told him he'd have to go into immigration detention.'

'So, he's locked up?'

'No. Jess and Rivers freaked out when they heard Doug wanted to take Slugg and they told him to run. He's hiding somewhere in the forest.'

'Pretty futile move, I would say.'

'I agree. Fortunately for them Doug isn't the kind of cop to instantly call for the dog squad. He likes to be trusted in the community because that way he gets told lots of info on the quiet, and that won't go on happening if he gets officious. He's giving them a bit of air and hoping sanity will prevail. Maybe Jess will talk some sense into Rivers, or maybe not. Losing Slugg would be an awful blow for them both. Trying to cope with the new farm before he arrived was tearing their relationship apart.'

*

Out in the wild woods, the only genetically modified hominid at large on Earth was curled in a foetal position inside a camouflaged tent. The previous day, Jess and Rivers had made their weekly trip into Quimbleton to buy supplies. Following Dewar's intervention, they could no longer take the giant along. After a pantomime of brief sentences and lots of gesturing, they convinced him to hide in the forest and lie low while they were away. At least, they thought they had. As the rattle and hum of their rainbow vehicle receded into the distance, he emerged and plodded towards his workplace. His inescapable dutiful streak was driving him to continue cleaning and cooking in the shed-cum-house.

Holding an armchair in one hand, he was humming to himself as he vacuumed when a group of blue-robed men and women barged into the room. Most of them threw themselves at his ankles with ecstatic cries. Mistaking them for a posse sent to capture him, he froze, whining pitifully and muttering in his own language.

'The messiah is speaking in tongues!' the fraudulent Yuewath-Sahib cried.

Reader I can't help all the exclamation marks. He always talked as though he was addressing the masses from a pulpit.

Like a giant creature afraid of mice, poor Slugg could only stand helplessly as they danced and sang around him. So great was his fright and confusion that he lost control of his bladder.

'He sheds the sacred water,' one of them cried, reaching out to dabble his hand in the massive puddle. They were mistaking the wild-eyed terror on his face for religious ecstasy and in their noisy ravings they missed the sound of the rainbow van returning. Jess and Rivers could hear the commotion from many metres away. They tore into the room having no idea who these people were but prepared to take them on anyway. Rivers registered the terror on the giant's face at once.

'Get the fuck off my property before I call the cops!'

'He is our messiah. He has come from a galaxy far away to save us,' the leader told him.

Well reader, Yuewath got part of that right, anyway.

'He's not your bloody messiah, he's our friend. You are trespassing. Get out.'

'Blasphemous hound! Do not swear at the chosen one!' the leader boomed.

Jess pulled out her phone. 'I'm calling Dewar right now,' she threatened. It was pretence, she was only stabbing in random numbers. But it worked. Yuewath instructed his followers to leave. He was too "known to police", as the force diplomatically put it, to stay. He could not afford to draw untoward publicity towards their secret compound deep in the woods. The disciples straggled out, but not before trying to take Slugg with them. He resisted with all his considerable strength. Several left clutching small pieces of fabric torn in the struggle from one of the shirts M'bali had bought him. These would soon be declared religious relics, framed, and displayed for worship at cult headquarters.

It took Jess and Rivers several hours to calm Slugg. He could not comprehend most of their words but sensed their protective concern.

It was with even more difficulty that Rivers persuaded him to return with him to the isolated tent at twilight. Soon darkness fell like an enveloping blanket and the rustle and thump of creatures feeding in the night began. That had been terrifying enough. Now these crazy people might try to drag him away while he was alone. He wept and called for his distant mother.

Sagittarius

It's never a good week for most farmed pigs.
But the slop will be exceptionally tasty on the 21st and 26th.

Thirty-Three

Despite the canker in their midst, life sailed on peacefully for little Quimbleton. Luscious leafy odours from the nurturing forest filled the early morning air. The early risers sniffed appreciatively before savouring a smug cuppa on their verandas. Loving couples with their minds on other things, lingered abed knowing they would not have to tear out of the house to make a frantic commuter dash to work.

Such rural quiet was not calculated to thrill a lively seven-year-old who has never been allowed to be bored or had to amuse herself. Fresh from the delights of Slique, Bree arrived to find that her father still had not bought the promised horses. His explanations about the time, money and labour involved in setting up a rural business naturally fell on deaf ears. After a period of sulking, she announced that she wanted to learn to surf. Having endured far too many glares and sighs, Hayes, although somewhat annoyed that she had been so indulged by her mother and stepfather, phoned M'bali to see if she knew any of the town's surfers.

'As it happens, I do. I wouldn't have thought it was your thing though.'

'It's Bree's thing. Suddenly, right now—if you see what I mean.'

'Okay. You know how I teach martial arts at the high school once a week. Gaz's close surfing mate Richo is the Phys. Ed. teacher there and my work falls under his control. For both those reasons, I know him pretty well.'

'You like?'

'Absolutely great guy. Laid back, great sense of humour and very patient with bright, lively kids. I presume you have produced one of those.'

'Indeed. Do you have his number?'

The following afternoon saw Richo, Hayes and Bree wading down a deep sandy track to a gentle bay break. The obliging teacher had brought a small board outgrown by one of his boys. Bree, a wiry child featuring Hayes' spiralling curls in a lighter colour, whined a bit because her first lesson only involved paddling motions and learning to stand on the board on the dry white sand of the little cove. Hayes lay back letting fine grains slip through his fingers as he had as a child. He watched with amusement someone else having to work their way around his spirited daughter.

Eventually, he saw them move to the water. After much laughing and spluttering, she managed to briefly stand several times. Hayes applauded. Richo left her to practice and dropped down on the beach beside him. 'Good to meet you, mate. We all took old Gaz's disappearance pretty hard, but M'bali did especially. You know she used to babysit sit him years ago?'

'No, I did not know that.'

'Yeah, he was kinda like a baby brother to her.'

Hayes nodded. He was somewhat relieved to know that was all Gaz had been to her. He had no ambition to be second best to an invisible corpse.

Richo kept up the casual chat, but he was waiting for his moment. With Bree still happily giggling and falling off the board, he took it. 'Has M'bali ever mentioned to you that a bright object fell out of the sky towards her place a few weeks ago? A mate and I saw it from the ocean. I wondered if she might have been out comet-watching and seen it too.' He hadn't mentioned it to the lady herself, figuring that she would see right through him and dig out the embarrassing truth in front of his workmates.

Hayes took a few calming breaths before he replied. 'Did you happen to see a large shiny flying saucer by any chance?'

For a moment, Richo thought he was being teased. 'Er, no mate. Just a big light comin' down.'

'M'bali saw a silver saucer hover over her garden and disappear. We have subsequently recovered it.'

'You're jokin'?'

'Never been more serious in my life.'

'Okay, well, Mick and I saw it too. We shut up about it because we thought everyone in town would tease the hell out of us—too much weed last night boys, that kinda thing.'

Hayes quickly recounted the story so far, including the mysterious Zera, Jeffree and Slugg. 'Dewar knows about all of this because we think one of them may be connected to Gaz's disappearance. He gave Zera a surfing lesson while Jeffree was locked up in Slique. M'bali says the guy was not well pleased, to say the least.'

Richo was silent for some time. He frowned and scratched his shaggy locks as he tried to take it all in. An alien had disappeared one of his best mates?

Hayes went on. 'The last thing we want to do is panic the town—or give away the fact that old Dougy is investigating them. They're socialising with a few locals, and you know the rumour mill. We need you to keep absolutely stum—for the present anyway.'

'No probs, mate. No-one would believe me anyway.'

Hayes left considerably relieved. Others had seen the spaceship land. He loved M'bali and he had wanted to believe the whole alien landing scenario but some cautious and secret part of him had doubted her a little. He had not been sure he could cope with a manipulative or even hallucinating partner after the difficulty of extracting himself from the crazy drug scene of the rock-music world.

If M'bali had known about his reservoir of doubts, her insecurities and tendency towards anxious flight would have overwhelmed her.

Now let us hope that Richo does not yield to the temptation to blab to Mick his fellow witness of the landing. If that boy indulges in his usual unguarded chat when he's smoked a few, the cat will be even further among the seed-eating birds, so to speak.

Capricorn

Another great week for anteaters.
Despite what hominids think, insects rule the world.
You will never go hungry.

Thirty-Four

Jeffrique had obtained a vast amount of data from the missile launch but, to his huge frustration, had not been able to sneak enough time to analyse it. For some time, he had been bombarded with increasingly irritated messages from Her Celestial Motherness, Alpha Dawn. Fortunately, both he and Zera had reason to fabricate their replies. His wife wanted to protect the rarking hominids and all the fluffy, shiny, feathery things that cluttered up the place. As we both know, best reader, Jeffrique created this mess, and his parents must not find that out.

Together the partners spent a few minutes working on a brief but plausible response from each of them. Jeffrique wrote, 'Greetings, celestial mumsy (a cheeky greeting seemed safe and amusing from this distance). So sorry about the lack of response from us. We've had some serious equipment failure in the communications area and the *nid* who's meant to fix it has been down with some local germ. You know me, I don't do hands on, so we've been off-air for a while. Anyway, we are cruising through Alpha Megatauri, as you know. We are in a safe little planetary system and we're having lots of swims in an ocean of high cosmic standard. Both well and blissfully happy. Much love, Jeffrique.'

Reader you and I can both see that he carefully refrained from mentioning planet 3159XZ.

Zera's note followed the same theme but included some nice girly comments about the exquisite shades of colours in the pretty planetary system which she knew Alpha Dawn would appreciate.

But in her galaxy, not exponentially far away, Alpha Dawn would be very annoyed by the paucity of both those replies. 'Token effort, dahlings, absolutely token effort. Ah will not be brarshed off in this manner. Where exactly are you and whart exactly is going on?' Experience told her that a silence from her most impulsive son should be investigated. No sooner had their meagre messages arrived than she was back on her machine letting them know how she felt and demanding further explanation. Neither replied. Jeffrique was too plagued by worries and Zera was not about to encourage a nosy mother-in-law.

Jeffrique had been dutifully socialising for days in order not to create suspicions in his partner's mind as to what he might be up to. They had been out most of the day and he was about to retreat to his study when the phone rang. Zera answered cheerfully, murmured a few words then spoke to Jeffrique, 'Stardream, Gordi's camera team have finally got the right weather for a night shoot in the forest. They've asked if we'd like to come, and I said of course we would. That's okay, isn't it?'

'Yes, sure. Tell Gordi thanks for the opportunity.'

When she put the phone down, Jeffrique had dropped his social charm. 'Since when do you make arrangements without discussing them with me?'

'Sorry, I thought you'd enjoy the adventure. You could have refused.'

He raised his voice. 'You mean I could have been the one to spoil your fun and slight your friends. I didn't do that, not that it's appreciated.'

Zera came over and hugged him, murmuring endearments. He gave in. At least, she now owed him some time in the study.

A few hours later, they were bouncing along a winding track as Gordi steered expertly towards his hide. Jeffrique's brain spun with figures which Zera and Caro's excited exclamations kept scattering into disarray. 'Rarking women and rarking furry little useless blobs of protoplasm,' he muttered to himself. Fortunately, the roaring engine obscured his comments.

Once in the hide with the night-vision camera team, silence was compulsory. For some time, equations streamed uninterrupted through Jeffrique's skull. In the soft infra-red light, a creature with a pretty face, dominated by enormous eyes, came crawling down a tree to the ground where it began snuffling about in the leaf litter. A smaller version of the same thing soon joined it. Jeffrique felt grateful that the enforced silence meant that the women couldn't start oohing and aahing over the baby. A great bird swooped through the night on silent wings. A distant shriek signalled that its prey would be no more. A little scurrying thing with a plumy tail came tearing into the clearing sending the other creatures fleeing back up the nearest tree. Many small animals emerged from the leaf litter and began creeping about, hunting and mating. They watched for hours. Well, some of them did.

The complexity of what he saw reminded Jeffrique how difficult it would be to wipe out absolutely all life on 3159XZ. The larger animals were not really the problem. It was the tiny unseen things he began worrying about. They had the ability to secrete themselves into safe places such as deep crevices and the ocean floor. What if he couldn't destroy absolutely everything? The unauthorised process which you call evolution, and which he called a rarking nuisance, would start the whole circus of life back up again.

Gordi delivered them back to their rented mansion at 4 am. Zera was far too elated by all those new creatures going about their business unimpeded to be able to sleep. But she stopped chattering as soon as she realised that her husband was exhausted. 'You go to bed, star-dream. I'm just going to write my diary,' she told him.

Diary? Jeffrique will have to find a way of "accidentally" destroying that before they return home, or the faeces could hit the twirly thing in the Creator-of-All-Things' office.

The following morning as the chef *nid* scurried out, having delivered them a breakfast tray to enjoy in bed, Zera the zoologist was still enthralled by what she had witnessed. 'Just imagine what there is to see on the rest of this gorgeous planet.' Her hand reached out for the on switch of a primitive hominid search engine. Before Jeffrique could devise a plausible protest, she had quickly found a site on which a drone camera swept over a plain of golden grasses where vast migrating herds of animals plodded their way to water. A tawny beast rippled like molten metal over the ground as it stalked them. Its young, heavy-footed bundles of fluff with savage teeth and playful charm, hid in a tangle of grass and fallen branches. Elsewhere, in a jungle clearing, a particularly large and hairy group of hominids lounged about, grooming each other another or stripping branches off trees on which to snack. Their babies rolled about playing adorably.

Adorably? This, esteemed reader, is a Zera-centric view of Earth to which I may or may not ascribe myself. I shall leave you to form your own opinions.

Zera went looking for more, not noticing that she was putting her husband right off his Korn Krispies. In a land of ice and snow, a predator beast with massive paws hunted. Sleek sea creatures with bulging eyes shot up through their breathing holes in the ice to snatch a breath of air before it pounced. In the oceans, reefs made patterns of colour in which a myriad of swimming creatures darted and cruised. The beauty of it. The wild, crazy diversity of it. Zera was stunned.

She decided to explore the almost microscopic. Branching fungi-like organisms lay hidden underground sending sustenance to the trees. Pale eyeless things hunted other eyeless things in the darkest of caves. Luminous beings as frail as cobwebs hunted in the ocean depths.

These were the very last straw for Jeffrique. How could he totally wipe out things that were so deeply protected? 'Enough, please, please enough. My head hurts. I can't cope with these late nights.'

Surprised she turned to face him. He had always been up for an all-nighter in the past. 'So sorry. Are you ill, star-dream? I must say you don't look it.'

'Well, I rarking well am sick. I'm sick and tired of you twittering on about illegal lifeforms that could hugely impact the profits of the business into which you have recently married—in case you hadn't noticed.'

Zera's eyebrows rose. 'It's a bit early in that marriage to start speaking to me in that tone.'

'And it's rarking early in the same rarking marriage for you to forget where your loyalties should now lie.'

'Don't you dare address me with a mouth full of abuse. I'm not some little space bimbo you picked up in Bar-bariq.'

'I could have sworn that was exactly where I picked you up.'

Zera was not easily riled but now she was furious. 'I manifested myself in your favourite tacky little haunt because I thought you were a worthwhile catch. Perhaps I was wrong.'

That cut him to the core. Jeffrique had all the insecurities of any boy with a cold, absent father. He could not cope with the idea of losing her. He dropped his head. 'Please don't let us fight like this.'

Zera had all the self-confidence of a beauty who has been loved and cossetted by both parents all her life. She did not want to fight either, but she would not have her enthusiasms crushed by him. 'I know *Genes-R-Us* has made some amazing beings. However, as a scientist, I cannot help but see that they are all one-trick ponies, designed for a limited purpose. And they don't have the joy and freedom of interacting freely with one another. Can't you at least respect how exciting that is for me as a zoologist?'

He tried to hide a dismissive frown as he launched into describing a parade of creatures which his own family company had created.

She jumped off the bed. 'I'm not attacking your family's achievements, or you. I'm just observing things that excite me. Why can't you respect our differences and leave it at that?'

Jeffrique jumped off the bed on the opposite side and began fumbling with clothing he had discarded on the floor. 'I'm behind with my work. I need a couple of days in my study—then I'm going to deal with this rarking heap of pestilence for once and all. And then we're getting out of here.' He tried storming off with dignity but tripped over his trouser leg and fell sobbing angrily to the floor.

Esteemed reader, sometimes even members of the galaxies' elite say things they do not mean in the heat of an argument. And sometimes they let slip things that should have stayed tucked up inside their elegant skulls.

Zera was wise enough withdraw from the battle and work at patching things up after this, their first serious quarrel. She comforted him, got the chef *nid* to make him a coffee then encouraged him to catch up with his work.

As soon as she could seize a moment when he was out of the house, she would hack into that computer of his. It was ruining her honeyflit. What was he doing on it anyway? What had he meant by dealing with Earth once and for all? Was it just nonsense spouted in the heap of a quarrel, or something worse?

Aquarius

As ever, a challenging week for desert cacti.
As the climate changes, more deserts are coming.
You'll be just the guys to fill them.

Thirty-Five

Saturday had dawned, warm but slightly misty, on little Quimbleton. Despite the risks of driving in such poor visibility, Dewar's wife Ros was already dressed in her best black church-going attire. From the bed, he gazed at her wearily through eyes narrowed by a throbbing hangover. 'You're looking very dolled up, dear. Something special on out at dingbat headquarters?'

Not a wise approach perhaps, but his own.

'Yes, something extraordinarily special is happening. The chosen one has arrived on earth at last. We are preparing our humble hall to greet him. I am doing the flowers today.'

'Say what? You mean someone has seen your messiah from outer space? Is he small and green by any chance?'

'No, indeed. I am told he is of magnificent size, build and presence, beyond anything a mere man could attain.'

Something clicked in the cop's brain. 'Big hairy gent is he? Wears a robe occasionally?'

'Don't mock me, Douglas. The messiah is real, and I believe that his appearance is exactly as you so flippantly suggest.'

Now he knew their "messiah" was probably Slugg. And what in heaven's name *was* Slugg? Was he connected to the disappearance of Gavin Cooper? 'Please don't go out there Ros,' he begged. 'You have described someone who I am investigating. He may be more dangerous than you can imagine.'

'Now you're being silly, Douglas,' she snapped. Despite his further pleading, she picked up her best handbag and left.

Dewar spent the rest of the day alone at the old wooden kitchen table, hunched over his laptop computer and sipping a high-octane brew straight from the bottle. He had distracted Elviz by strewing seeds and nuts over a large rug on the floor. With his beak full, the bird could only manage an occasional "hallelujah" as he found a particularly delicious morsel.

The cop already knew that Slugg had neither a birth certificate nor immigration papers. It was easy for him to discover that the so-called Zera and Jeffree Smith didn't have them either. Or tax records. He knew that Papadopo, who had interviewed them in Slique, was a well-reputed officer. The man had established that Smith had definitely not murdered Jo-Ellen Lambert but surely he should have also discovered that the pair were illegals of some kind as well. Why had he let Smith go?

Dewar had met the police chaplain a few of times socially. He decided to risk ringing him at home. Chappy had been about to settle in to watch a boxing match and was not well pleased to be disturbed.

'G'day, Chappy, I was the officer who originally arrested Jeffree Smith for the murder of Jo-Ellen Lambert. I've heard on the grapevine that your guys up there who interviewed him both went off on sick leave the next day. Is that correct?'

'Doug mate, you know I'm bound by rules of confidentiality not to blab.'

'Understood. But I am now investigating Smith in connection with the disappearance of a Quimbleton local. Can you give me any insights into his character or behaviour?'

'All I can say is he seemed perfectly civil and cooperative to the office staff. I have no idea what went on in that interview room because it seems that the electronics were down. Browning and Papadopo have been unusually reticent with me about what went on behind closed doors, but I can tell you that both remain considerably shaken and unable to work since that day. The powers that be are getting a tad pissed-off about that, mate. I've been pumped for info by officers higher up the food chain than your good self. What can I do if men won't talk?' Chappy excused himself with a lie about a family birthday and was soon sprawled on this sofa bellowing instructions at his favourite athlete.

Dewar spent an hour thinking about that conversation. Was this Jeffree fellow perhaps the head of a drug cartel? Had he intimidated them into silence for that reason? Surely someone in headquarters must have a memo on their desk telling them to investigate what lay behind the breakdowns of two reliable officers. He was all too aware that the police force, as usual, was understaffed and overwhelmed. No doubt the memo would be responded to eventually.

He knew where the alleged Smith was staying. Should he go out and arrest him and his wife as illegals? If they really were aliens, and had disposed of Gavin Cooper in some way, what powers might they have to hurt him? Or Ros? Dewar had seen enough television documentaries to know that any being capable of arriving on Earth in a spaceship from far away was from a far more advanced civilisation than his own. The more he thought about that the more frightened and wary he felt. Perhaps it would be best to rely on the locals for info about their activities. He decided to word up a few reliable sources to keep a discreet eye on them, without telling his contacts why.

He could keep this Slugg under a bit of surveillance himself. The giant seemed an amiable enough fellow. If he borrowed a mate's car, he could hide it around the corner then follow his wife the next time she took off for cult headquarters. Maybe that was where the Slugg fellow was hiding out now or would be soon.

Pisces

Jaguars will find conditions favourable
for kills on the 1st and 4th of this week.
You're running out of rainforest fast. Eat up.

Thirty-Six

Out in flat blackness of the forest night the entire fabric of the camouflaged tent was quivering as Slugg's massive body, which it could barely contain, trembled against it. Every evening his situation only seemed bearable for as long as Jess and Rivers lingered for a chat and a drink with him before retreating to the farm. The horrors began as twilight stole his sanity away. Unseen and unimaginable creatures began to rustle, slither, crash, and occasionally screech all around his fragile shelter. Coming as he did from a controlled world where nothing disorderly moved about in the darkness, he had no means of making sense of any of it. The lost world of his past, once seemingly so dull and confining, now seemed safe and welcoming.

He lay awake crying for hours. Sleep claimed him briefly, but he woke to feel something with way too many legs racing up his left thigh. He screamed and jumped to his feet, ripping the tent pegs out of the ground. The entire tent and its cover of leafy boughs came with him as he took off, stumbling in what he thought was the direction of the farmhouse. Within seconds, he had run head on into the bole of a tree and knocked himself out cold.

Led by their borrowed hound, which was following the scent trail to his hideout, eight members of the cult found him there. Yuewath-Sahib was carrying a stash of some ether-like substance hidden under the robe disguising his puny body. He had intended to administer it, as discretely as possible, to make the giant more amenable to reason. If he said he was going to deliver a messiah to his followers, there bloody well was going to be one. And soon.

It took all eight of them a couple of hours to manhandle the sleeping giant to their wagon. They dropped him several times, but he didn't stir. Once he was in the cult hearse (the only vehicle of a size and shape able to accommodate him) the leader instructed the others to seat themselves and buckle up. As soon as they did so, he snuck back and threw a rag soaked in anaesthetic over Slugg's face.

As they set off, the rumble and crunch of their departure caused Jess to stir in her sleep. 'Rivers,' she hissed. 'Rivers!' She poked him sharply.

He groaned.

'I just heard something big drive off. I think Dewar's got Slugg.' In some ways, that would have been a relief to her. She had been half-heartedly trying to persuade Rivers to hand him over for days. But whoever it was, they were too late. The sounds slowly faded to silence. After agreeing to contact the cop first thing in the morning if the giant was indeed missing, the couple soon sank back into the deep sleep of the weary.

By the time the fake Yuewath-Sahib had negotiated the winding tracks to cult headquarters, dawn was breaking. Dewar was waiting. He had followed Ros there a couple of days before. From her increasingly excited demeanour, he had gathered that something big was imminent. Her hymn singing had escalated overnight, sending Elviz into endless sympathetic trilling. 'Oh lord, won't you buy me a *Mercedes Sidebottom*,' he warbled, slightly failing to grasp the situation.

Glad to get out of the house, Dewar had risen early again to stake out the place from a twiggy clearing in the undergrowth. He watched as the hearse rumbled close by, carrying what looked like a huge corpse in the area usually filled by a coffin. One alien down, two to go? Perhaps a relief, but it wasn't that simple. For one thing, he had a job to do. If entered the compound and intervened in the cult's activities, Ros might never forgive him. But they were already stealing both her physical presence and her devotion, so he had little left to lose. He decided to throw the dice. If he could get these bastards for kidnapping or murder Ros might cease being under their spell. The massive electronic gates of the compound had closed before he could reach his hidden vehicle. Too late to get inside now, but he had dredged up a phone number for old Yobwank-Shithead, or whatever Nigel Cuthbertson was choosing to call himself these days. Later in the day he would call on him to open the gate, then burst in with reinforcements.

The sergeant was not the only one who knew that Slugg had been carted off in the night. Although he was the only hominid who knew it. When Jeffrique finally seized a few moments to himself, he saw that his hand-held device had been triggered by passing close to Slugg's microchip as they returned from the night shoot. Now he had the co-ordinates of where his chef *nid's* journey had ended. His defection had been a festering sore of annoyance to him since the

Soozerator-6 arrived at the house without him. Telling Zera he needed a drive to clear his head after work, later that day he set off in pursuit of his property.

Yes reader, just as you or I would set off in pursuit of Deisel or Fluffy if we saw them being nicked by a passer-by from the back garden, Jeffrique took off to demand his domestic animal back.

Dewar, his female offsider, and the Moobalup detective arrived at the high-walled compound in late afternoon. Despite a phone call from the sergeant demanding that they be allowed access, the gate remained closed. The fake Yuewath-Sahib had captured his prize, and he was being feted for delivering that prize—he was not about to open the massive gate to anyone. Festivities and chanting had gone on for hours around the sleeping giant. And Nigel Cuthbertson was now officially the one true prophet of the messiah. He had even called to tell his mum. His father had seized the phone from her and told him to cut the crap and come home. That was but a small blight on his triumph.

Slugg had woken about midday. He rose muddle-headed then shambled off to find a toilet. Once relieved he drifted into the shambolic galley and gazed at it through a calm haze of fading anaesthesia. Not up to his standards by a long way. Despite the pleading and chanting of his acquired followers, he resolutely cleaned up the place, inspected the supplies cupboard, and cooked lunch. Only then did he accept their offer of a shower and a nice pink robe.

Now delighted by The Chosen One's culinary skills, the members were tucking in when the cops battered in the gate with a ram and ran inside yelling. Dewar's female offsider ran for the back door accompanied by the detective, who fancied her. A powerful and commanding presence, she put her shoulder to the door and raced in, followed by the 'tec admiring her heaving buns as he ran.

Dewar arrived ahead of them just in time to see Slugg trying to serve dessert but being manhandled and shouted at by Jeffree Smith. The alien saw him and raised a threatening arm. The cop dragged out his gun. 'Halt or I'll fire!' he commanded. Instantly, both were gone. His colleagues came panting in to find Dewar holding his service pistol, a hole in the ceiling, and a mob of screaming deluded dingbats running around the room. There was no kidnapped giant to be seen. 'He was here. I witnessed a struggle. He's been forcibly abducted.' Dewar insisted. 'Search the place.'

The cult members said not a word to back him up. Neither the alleged victim nor the alleged perpetrator was found on the property. A righteously angry

Yuewath raved, 'Police brutality! Invasion of privacy! You haven't heard the last of this!'

When that got no response, he threw himself to the floor. 'My heart, my heart!' he shrieked clutching his chest. One of his female acolytes willingly performed mouth to mouth and chest compressions.

Dewar's colleague, Detective Atkins, spread the story by phone, with many humorous asides. He texted freely to mates in Slique. 'There was the fat prick, red in the face and gibbering about an invisible abductor. He's into something stronger than beer now.'

Sadly, this moment would come to define the attitude of headquarters to Doug Dewar for the rest of his career. Once a fine reliable officer—now too often drunk and unbalanced by the threatened loss of his deranged wife.

Esteemed reader, little Quimbleton, and indeed the whole of planet Earth, had just lost the aid of the only officer capable and willing to seek help from on high. By "on high", I mean police headquarters, and even higher than that, the might of the country's armed forces.

Aries

Another wonderful week for peacocks on country estates.
Don't shriek too much on the 6th—
his lordship will have a hangover.

Thirty-Seven

Before M'bali could leave the house to work in her field with Roxy, her phone rang. It was Jess, crying uncontrollably. When she finally managed to speak, she said, 'Someone took Slugg last night…even his little tent has been torn from its moorings.'

M'bali knew the story of Doug Dewar's visit to the young couple and the giant's flight into the woods. She had tried to counsel Rivers to surrender him. 'For one thing, he can't live out there in winter. And even Doug will have to bring in the dog squad eventually.'

She set out to visit them immediately, this time leaving a text message for Roxy to warn of her absence. When she arrived, both were huddled in the shed-cum-house looking miserable. Now that the angel whose work had saved their marriage was gone from them the kitchen was already beginning to descend into chaos. Rivers seemed full of remorse that his futile attempt to shelter the giant had led to his being seized in the night. 'There were so many broken sticks along the way, and the ground had been trampled by lots of feet. I feel so bad. He must have been terrified.'

'Do you think Doug finally got help to get him out?'

'We don't know. I've left a message but it's too early to expect a reply.'

It was much later in the day when a weary Dewar, who had been up and on duty since 4 am, followed by filling in a sickening amount of paperwork ever since, texted back.

'I did not remove your friend from the forest. His disappearance is an operational matter. I am unable to divulge any further information.'

He had descended into cop-speak which, as we all know, is a jargon unto itself designed to baffle and deter nuisance inquiries. Did this mean that Slugg had been seized by someone else? By Jeffree so-called Smith? Jess and Rivers sat together in silence, scared and baffled.

*

While Jeffrique had been away on a supposed drive to clear his poor weary head, Zera had taken the opportunity to hack into his computer. As she had suspected, his password was easy for her to crack. Pet nicknames, birthdates—quite ridiculously careless. 'I guess he trusted me not to peek,' she told herself as she trolled through his search history and stored documents. 'Silly boy, I'm not that virtuous.'

What she found froze her fingers above the keyboard. 'Gathering All the Nuclear Weapons on 3159XZ to Destroy All Life—A Feasibility Study,' he had typed. There followed a plethora of algorithms and calculations that she lacked the mathematical skills to fully decipher. But his typed conclusion was clear enough. Yes, if he detonated all the hominid's bunkered weapons, he could create a nuclear winter blanketing the life-giving rays of the red star for many years. Most creatures would die quickly by blast, or slowly by starvation. But, so far, he lacked data to be sure that all life in the deepest oceans or caves could be totally wiped out. Possibly further experimental rocket firings would answer this concern—or perhaps there was an easier way. Even his quantum-powered calculator could not provide an answer on present information.

As Jeffrique strode up the front path, followed reluctantly by Slugg, he was anticipating a hero's welcome. He had restored their chef *nid* to his proper place in the universe. Before he could insert his key in the front door, it flew open.

'You vile two-faced rarking piece of space shit!' Zera yelled. Her lovely face was contorted with fury as she waved his computer wildly above her head.

He knew at once what she had done. 'You've hacked into my private computer and *I'm* two-faced. How dare you! You ape-fancying little bitch.'

Slugg, who had been cowering behind as their voices raised in temper, bolted past Zera as fast as his over-sized legs could carry him and headed for the kitchen for a little culinary therapy.

He needn't have worried. Neither of his owners had any interest in him at all in this moment.

'What crazy psychopathic thoughts have driven you to destroy life on this beautiful place that you know I love so dearly? Do you hate me that much?'

'I love you more than there are words to say. I couldn't tell you because I couldn't bear to lose you…' Jeffrique's rage was fading now, replaced by an overwhelming fear and sadness that she had discovered his darkest secret. For minutes, he was unable to find words. Zera waited, still furious, for some explanation of his treachery.

'I have to, I have to…you don't understand. Your father isn't a terrifying, cruel bully with the power to destroy everything you love. My old man's tantrums shake the very stars. How do you think that feels to a child? Don't moralise at me from your safe, spoilt little life.'

'Slugg! Two coffees, pronto,' Zera yelled, hoping to defuse things a bit.

By the time the assistant chef scuttled in and deposited her request on the low table, Jeffrique was trying to explain his youthful error of hurling his boy junk out of a portal, the alchemy of it sprouting into life, and all the implications of that for their future. She interrupted him. 'How long have you known that you accidentally began all life here?'

'A few weeks. I found out when I was in Slique researching how and where life had begun. I thought my father might notice me and praise my diligence if I investigated it—then I could direct the company's intervention.'

'Did you intend to report life on Earth to *Genes-R-Us* right from the start?'

'Here we go again. The spoilt little girl whose daddy thinks the stars shine out of her bum. I've got to tell, or he'll disown me. The self-titled creator of all rarking things, including me, is my boss. It's company policy. How do you think the old bastard built up the empire he has today? Not by being half-arsed about gene control, that's for sure.'

Now Zera was furious again. 'Even before you knew that you were implicated in life beginning here, you chose not to tell me that you were going to turn this glorious place over to the gene police? To total control and slavery? I'm your wife and you didn't think you should tell me?'

'I assumed you knew. You're a smart lady, and you chose to marry into the business model. And as for this slavery word, that has no meaning in our world.'

'Don't you mansplain to me. I know rarking well that slavery isn't perceived to exist by your precious company.'

Well, dearest reader, Zera's world view has changed beyond her partner's comprehension. It had been a hasty marriage, powered more by lust and ambition than rationality and knowledge of who they were hitching themselves to for eternity. Now the rudder seems to have fallen off the love boat.

'If you love me as you say you do, we're going to get out of here and say nothing about it back home,' Zera demanded.

'Impossible.'

'It is not impossible. Life has burgeoned here for billions of years and no-one in the company has noticed. They are that incompetent.'

'Easy for you to say, but you have no idea how it is for me. *The Planetary-Life Enhancement Division* of the company works day and night. They will find that there's unauthorised life on this place eventually—incompetent as they apparently are at times. I couldn't handle living with that axe hanging over my head.'

'Life enhancement, is that company-speak for genetic manipulation and control?'

'Describe it any way you like, wife, his bloodhounds will find this dump one day. And when they do, my father will explode like stars colliding, sending me, and maybe you if you stick around, to the farthest reaches of the most hideous galaxy he can think of. We will lose our friends and live our lives in disgrace and poverty. Or I will, anyway.'

'I would stick by you, Jeffrique. I can work. I can support us.'

'Live off my wife, in disgrace, estranged from everyone I know for eternity—I'd rather die. I've heard enough. This festering pool of ape life has to go.'

Zera stood up, seized his quantum computer, and hurled it at the nearest wall. A crash followed by tiny tinkling sounds signalled its demise.

Reader, hopefully he won't be able to work out how to destroy sweet little Earth now. But, as my story isn't over yet, perhaps he will.

Taurus

Grasshoppers will find the whole week excellent for hatching.
Hominid crops are ripe and ready.
Beware of planes spraying nasty substances on the 8th.

Thirty-Eight

Meanwhile, life in little Quimbleton was humming along peacefully enough. Summer was cooling into autumn and more early mists swirled through the valley playing hide and seek among the trees. Fungi sprouted from the forest floor in a bewildering array of shapes. Little Reece Schultz had an experimental nibble on the wrong one and had to be hurried off to the Quimbie Hospital by his worried but irritated mother. ('How many times have I told you, blah, blah, blah,' he heard.) Most of the trees were not becoming clad in the glowing colours of fall because trees around Quimbleton didn't go in for such frivolities. The little black flies were not thrilled by this chillier turn of season and wandered sluggishly about. But every farmer in the valley moved with fresh energy and smiled as showers replenished their precious water supplies.

The team working on the organic foods' day had met a couple of times. M'bali was delighted that chef Klaire had chosen to stay with them despite Vigano's threats. Her professional skills of organising staff were proving invaluable. She could smooth ruffled feathers, cajole, and sometimes lead firmly from the front. Along with the most skilled cooks among the C.W.A. women, she had put together a delectable menu based on the local produce of the season. Everyone knew what their roles would be on the day—who would do salads, savouries, cakes, smoothies, and desserts. Along with some of the like-minded teachers, M'bali had sourced entertainers suitable for children of all ages. Hayes and his band would sing but he had also called in a favour from a younger rock group in Slique. (At thirty, he was a little past it for some of the younger teens, and the ones who fancied skinny seventeen-year-old boys.)

Working on a shared project had allowed M'bali to see him in broader contexts. If he was only pretending to be warm, thoughtful, and funny, it was a very good act. Her friends liked him and kept passing on irritating advice. 'That one's a keeper. Don't worry about his age, you still scrub up well,' one of them advised her.

'Thanks a bunch. You've made me feel particularly ravishing—for my age,' she replied.

Her pal looked embarrassed and apologised. The ill-concealed jealousy of a few members of the golf club gave her a warm inner glow. She could never forget how vicious a few of them had been over her role in Jon's death all those years ago.

*

In their marble-lined mansion, Zera and Jeffrique battled on. Conflict had made their sex life even hotter—as conflict often does. They had not actually swung from the chandelier, but that wasn't for want of trying.

When they were not making love, Zera was consumed by worry. How could she trust him now? She had never seen a roller-coaster, but her emotions were lurching down and hurtling back up again exactly like a racing carriage in an amusement park.

Jeffrique had resumed their outings and social life with a better grace. They had swum together in a quiet cove and made out passionately on the white sands. He hadn't even complained when the little black flies assembled and circled languidly around his head—or when fine grains of sand invaded body parts not designed to receive them. This unusually temperate reaction made her doubly suspicious.

To discover on her honeyflit that she had married a totally different husband to the one she had thought he was had been an overwhelming shock. Zera understood his dismay that she was not the blindly loyal wifey he had assumed she would be either.

And Earth had changed her view of the cosmos and her place in it. It was a change so radical as to be almost traumatic. She wanted to run from it, but she could not. How could she fit back into the world of casual cruelty which his parents, and indeed her parents, the elite of *Genes-R-Us,* saw as their right to control?

One afternoon, he disappeared for several hours. When he returned, he appeared more relaxed than before he had left. He threw himself onto the sofa and demanded alcohol from a house *nid*. She walked over and sat next to him. She looked sadly into his dark eyes. 'What are you planning, Jeffrique?'

'You know what I am obliged to plan. The details of how I achieve it need not concern you.'

'Please, star-dream, surely you cannot murder our friends here. They have been so kind and welcoming to us.'

'Look, if you're so concerned, we'll take them with us. I'm sure they could find a useful role somewhere. The possibilities for travel are endless. They'll blow their minds.'

She would not respond to such an unworkable suggestion. They would soon be found out and killed. That tack hadn't worked on him, so she tried another. 'Gordi says there are billions of hominids on Earth. They call it genocide to kill so many of them and it is the vilest crime imaginable. Surely the sweet man I married could not bear the weight of living with that on their conscience forever.'

Zera could see that had struck a chord. He took a quick gulp of his wine. 'It's awful. I feel sick about it. But it's you and me or them. I have to choose us, or our rarking life won't be worth living.'

'Don't you dare implicate me in your decision. I want no part of it.'

He glared at her. She dropped her head to try to hide her tears.

Now he could not hide his anger. 'Don't try girly tears on me. I suppose you've conveniently forgotten what Gordi told us your lovely hominids are doing to this planet. They have filled the oceans with plastic trash that is causing countless other animals to die slow, horrible deaths. They are wiping out other species and destroying wild habitats at a rate my old man would be proud of. They are filling the air with blanketing gases that are holding heat in and slowly incinerating everything alive. And they're too rarking selfish and ignorant to sacrifice anything much to stop it. That's your precious rarking hominids left to their own devices—slowly destroying what they should treasure.'

'I can't argue with that. I know Gordi has travelled the globe job as a wildlife photographer. I know he has seen all those horrors. But what you're planning is even worse...'

He interrupted. 'So, you want this slow, terrible demise of the planet's natural world—as opposed to a quick, merciful ending delivered by me.'

'That is not the only choice. We're far more technologically advanced—we could stay and help improve things much faster.'

'You live in a fool's paradise. We can't intervene. Feral hominids are tribal. Some of the tribes are as big as countries now—but they're still tribal animals. If we choose one side, the other side will hate us. They have no unity.'

'You can't just deny responsibility. This creation is yours, Jeffrique. You made life on this lovely wild planet.'

'Don't you rarking dare blame me for a mistake I made as an innocent child! This chimp exhibit is not rarking mine. It's out of control. Your *lovely* hominids have weapons stored all over the place to blow each other to pieces many times over. And they've killed millions of their own kind before. Wake up, Zera. These feral primates on 3159KZ are not sweet, lovable domestic pets.'

'What about all the other innocent creatures—the dolphins, the kangaroos, the elephants, and all the wonderful creatures I showed you online? And the plants, they are extraordinary too…'

Jeffrique leapt to his feet. 'You have chosen your side. You can stay here and die or leave when I do. Now rarking leave me alone.'

Zera stood, taking a few steps towards him. She stretched out her arms, attempting to wrap them around him. He hurled her back onto the sofa.

'Do not mess with me!' she yelled. 'I'm not some sweet lovable domestic rarking pet either!'

He strode across the room. She saw the study door slam shut.

Reader, our male alien acquaintance got in a few salient points there. However, I don't think it's gaining him any ground at all on the marital happiness front.

Gemini

This week, the portents are dark for
battery hens. Be thankful life is short.
Hope is not yet at hand for most of you.

Thirty-Nine

Zera lay face down on the sofa for several minutes, her heart racing. Weeks ago, he had shoved her aside in anger so he could take over the driving in Quimbleton. This second time he had been more forceful. Luckily, she had landed back on the couch rather than smashing her head on the marble floor. She would not stick around to be subjected to a third assault. Angry, scared and bewildered she longed for the shelter of her distant parents' arms. What would the gentle folk who had raised her so well advise her to do? She must not ask. She must spare them this.

After her tears finally ceased, she lay there for several minutes more. When she rose, stiff and awkward from her torment, she saw Slugg seated on the floor with his body weight barring the study door. He was shaking with fear yet had plodded out to defend her. Her eyes welled with tears. Being a messiah for a few hours seemed to have given him a whole new view of his powers and a large dose of courage.

Zera signalled frantically for him to move away. He did not. She raced off to the bedroom returning several minutes later with a roughly packed suitcase. Standing at the open front door, she beckoned for Slugg to come with her. He hesitated. She flexed a bicep and pointed to herself—symbolising that she too had power. To her relief he began lumbering barefoot across the marble towards her. The study door remained shut.

Once outside, they clambered into the Merc van. She told him in *nid* language to leave his door slightly open. He complied. Zera eased off the brake, put it into reverse and let the heavy vehicle slide backwards down the sloping driveway to the road, hoping it wouldn't begin screaming indignantly about its doors being open before they were out of earshot of the house. They slid onto the road. She swung the wheel and gunned the heavy vehicle in the direction of *The Briar Patch.*

When M'bali opened her door, her eyebrows rose in astonishment. She saw the lovely Zera, always so immaculate, in a state of dishevelment with tears coursing down her face. The giant, Slugg, stood behind her, whimpering and muttering.

'What's wrong?' she demanded suspiciously. Was this a trap?

'I have left Jeffrique... I mean Jeffree. He threw me around.'

M'bali knew that Wozzer, her protector, was standing amiably behind her. One scream from her and her would turn into a raging demon. A weakening aging demon.

'Is that all? Surely you can go somewhere else. You have money, a vehicle. I have a partner and he has a child. I cannot put their lives at risk by allowing you in.'

Well reader, things have certainly advanced on the romance front in our absence.

'He's going to wipe out all of you—everything, everyone on Earth. I can't stop him. I stand it,' Zera cried. Her legs buckled and she began to fall. Slugg caught her in his arms.

What to do? M'bali signalled to the giant to enter. He shambled inside and laid the unconscious girl on the green sofa.

When she had revived enough to talk, M'bali spoke to her firmly, 'Tell me what is happening. I must know. But you cannot remain here. I will give you food and other supplies and then you'll have to go.'

Zera nodded grimly. 'As you know, we are alien here. My husband is the son of the founder of the *Genes-R-Us* company which owns and controls all life on all planets in all the galaxies—except here on Earth.' With many pauses and breaks for crying and drinking coffee, she related the whole dark story.

When she was done, M'bali was silent for several minutes. She was far too shocked to cry. 'And he killed Gaz, didn't he?' she finally managed. She could see that Zera was genuinely shocked.

'Why do you say that?'

'I say it because, when you and Gaz returned from your surfing lesson, I was looking out that window and I saw your husband's reaction to it. You were in his arms, and only I could see his face. He was angry, very, very angry.'

'I have married a monster,' the girl whispered.

Sympathetic as she was to Zera's plight, M'bali would not risk her loved ones, Wozzer included, by allowing her to remain on the property. That decision seemed a little ridiculous, even to her, in view of the fate that allegedly awaited her world—but she was yet to fully believe that the alien had the power to carry out threats made during a marital spat. She loaded Slugg up with a quantity of fresh produce to take to the van. Then she supplied Zera with directions to a location so deep in the wilderness that even most locals had no idea it existed. Because the old forestry track was heavily overgrown, she found it a great place to walk the dog without being annihilated by speeding vehicles. 'Don't use your phone,' she warned her. 'I'm going to tell the police, and hopefully they will call in special forces to arrest your husband.'

'You don't understand. They can't hurt him. He has powers to eliminate them far beyond anything you can imagine.'

'We'll see about that. Now go. I have work to do.'

Reader, I do admire the M'bali hominid's guts and determination, but she seems to be a little optimistic on this one.

Cancer

Squirrels should keep an eye or two out
for low-flying raptors on the 9th
and low-running dogs on the 12th and 13th.

Forty

As soon as the pair had driven off, M'bali ran for her phone. Much to his irritation, she'd had Dewar's home mobile on fast dial for some time now. An increasingly estranged wife and an alien who could be there one second and gone the next were doing his head in quite enough. And that bastard of an outer-space cowboy had made him seem unhinged in front of colleagues. On top of all that he did not need an agitated woman urging him to make dangerous arrests based on little credible evidence. Although, he had to admit it was seeming more likely to him that this "Smith" character did have something to do with the disappearance of M'bali's mate Gaz. He'd seen the creature in action before his own eyes—even if his colleagues didn't believe him. But she could push at him all she liked, that didn't mean Dewar was queueing up to be next on the missing person's list. He wasn't a coward, but he wasn't a reckless fool either.

When his home mobile sang its greeting, Elviz joined in. Dewar swore, 'What the fuckin' blue blazes now?' He had been attempting to complete his washing, a task formerly done by Ros, and a gutful of high-octane booze was not helping his ineptitude. One of his white shirts was now pink and several other garments were now the size of a much smaller man.

'Yes, Dewar here,' he slurred.

M'bali Hoyle began raving at him. The female "alien" really was an alien. She had left the bloke alien because of domestic violence. The girl alien said that bloke alien was planning to destroy all life on Earth. Dewar sat down to collect his thoughts. M'bali was still yacking and telling him what to do. Automatic pilot kicked in. 'I will have to take a formal statement from you on these matters. Can you be home at 1600 hours this afternoon?'

'Of course, I can be frigging home. You sound pissed, Doug. Maybe you should send someone else.'

'I will be at your property as arranged.' It was now midday. He had four hours to sober up.

Long before the police vehicle rolled up her driveway, M'bali had assembled Hayes, Jess and Rivers to listen to her recording of Zera's hideous tale. They were speechless for some time. She refilled their glasses.

Rivers spoke first. 'This is something way beyond even the police. It's an invasion by some kind by very foreign power. We need the army, special forces or something.'

'We sure do. How drunk was Doug?' Hayes asked.

'Slurred voice, I-can't-quite-follow-what-you're-talking-about drunk. But that was nearly four hours ago.'

Soon he was waddling up to the front door. M'bali thrust it open before he could knock. She pointedly took in his appearance.

He was standing at attention and staring her down. 'I'm fucking tickety-boo, thanks for asking. Are you going to keep me standing here?'

'Sorry, Doug, come in. To say I'm on edge would be the understatement of the millennium.'

In the living room, he was confronted by three anxious faces also giving him appraising looks. He saw the drinks. 'I came here for a formal interview with M'bali, not a bloody party.'

'I recorded what Zera told me on this device. They've already heard it because we've all had encounters with these beings, whatever they are. We all have evidence to add.'

Dewar slumped into a deep chair and didn't bother to argue. She placed a strong coffee before him and tapped her phone. Zera's faltering voice told her tale again.

When it was over, he remained thoughtful for some time. M'bali opened her mouth to speak but he held up a warning hand. 'Only one of us here is an experienced investigating officer accustomed to dealing with the police hierarchy in Slique. Let me digest what I just heard,' he said.

M'bali fidgeted and frowned. Hayes clasped her nearest hand and held one finger of his other hand to his lips. They waited.

'Coffee and brandy, anyone?' she asked when she was unable to bear the tension any longer. Three cups were held out to her.

'I will have to take this phone as evidence…' Dewar began before she could move.

'Not my phone, I can't do business without my phone.'

He raised his eyebrows at her in a gesture that was clearly unsympathetic. 'Those who achieve rank in the police hierarchy are very-down-to-earth practical people. They are not paid to believe fairy tales or write musicals.'

She suppressed an urge to interrupt. He went on, 'When they hear this girl's story, the obvious conclusion they will come to is that she is a paranoid schizophrenic, a sadly deluded young lady who thinks evil beings are coming to get her, and the planet. Aliens are not an uncommon theme with such folk.'

M'bali couldn't help herself, she exploded. 'Bloody hell, Doug, I saw the spaceship land. So did Mick and Richo. And it wrecked my wardrobe door and my bedroom window.'

'I believe you. Understand, I am putting myself in the shoes of city cops hearing this tale. You know as well as I do that country towns are hotspots for crop circles which they claim were made by visitors from afar, and for sinister lights in the sky from planet Zog.'

'But not Quimbleton, Doug.'

'Not the core of Quimbleton, no. But a couple of ferals—you know the type I mean, not you two, Jess and Rivers. A couple of ferals, probably sky high on some kind of jungle juice, saw a huge rocket take off out of the forest near Moobalup not so long ago. I had to record that in my log. No-one on the force got at all excited about that, I can assure you.'

'You mean to say you aren't going to tell anyone? We need the army. We need special forces, and pronto,' Hayes put in.

'We do, I totally agree, I'm just trying to explain why we are unlikely to get them.' Dewar did not intend to add that his colleagues had recently seen him with a gun drawn on an invisible assailant abducting an invisible giant in a pink robe. Or that they had undoubtedly smelt his breath on a few mornings lately.

The others broke out in a frustrated babble. He ignored them. He held out his hand.

'Hand over the phone, M'bali. I'll get it back to you as soon as I can.'

She passed it to him then saw him to the door. 'You will try to persuade them, won't you?'

'Trust me, I'll be selling it like a fuckin' vacuum cleaner salesman.'

After he left, the terrified babble continued.

*

Dewar drove back to Moobalup slowly, taking in the quiet beauty of the forest and lush farmlands along the valley. He loved the place. He'd hoped to retire happily there one day with Ros. At the front door, he called hopefully for his wife. The house was empty except for Elviz who greeted him with delighted shrieks. When he released him from his day room, the bird flapped onto his shoulder, raised his crest, and nibbled his ear affectionately. Dewar stroked him absently as he sank down into his old armchair to type.

A couple of hours later, the Police Commissioner was meeting with his senior colleagues who had the recording and Dewar's report.

'Douglas Ross Dewar, long-serving, reliable officer as I recall,' his deputy suggested. He called up the sergeant's photo and record. 'Yes, that's him. Usually pretty sound.'

'I suggest you read the most recent entries, sir.'

He did. 'I see. The wife sounds very disturbed according to the detective down there. She seems to have left him—belongs to a cult waiting for some messiah coming from space. There are reports of the sergeant being on duty the worse for alcohol in recent weeks. And he seems to have drawn a gun in unreasonable circumstances lately. In fact, he put a bullet into the ceiling of the cult headquarters.'

'Another cult down there in the woods. What do we know about it?' the commissioner asked.

'Cult leader, so-called, is one Nigel Cuthbertson, well known to us for various kinds of inept frauds. He's done time before, but we probably can't get him for this one because he's calling it a religion. Dewar has valid reason to keep an eye on his activities. We don't want naïve kids persuaded away from their parents. That could get all over the press pretty quickly—kid's stolen, cops doing nothing about it. But he needs to keep his domestic circumstances out of it, and his weapon holstered.'

'What about this tape, the girl's story,' the commissioner asked.

'Paranoid schizophrenic, most likely.' There were murmurs of assent.

'And the corroborating evidence from the other witnesses?'

'Organic farmers, every one of them.'

'A bunch of hippies saw a flying saucer land. It was big, then it was small, but they can't produce it now because it flew out of a wardrobe. Let's face it, the area is famous for whacky weed plantations hidden in the forest.'

They all laughed.

'Dewar urges us to contact the P.M. with a view to bringing in the army. Anyone here willing to put their reputation and career on the line to make that phone call on the basis of the information we have?'

They laughed again. 'Perhaps after we get a clear snapshot of the little green men posing in front of their spaceship?'

They laughed again.

'What's the detective's name down there?'

'Atkins, sir.'

'Suggest he keeps a quiet eye on Dewar.'

Leo

Salmon will have an excellent week in patches.
Beware of bears on the 24th and 25th,
and big noisy things with nets on the 19th.

Forty-One

The following morning, Sergeant Dewar received a message from police headquarters telling him there was not enough evidence to proceed with his request. Atkins enjoyed a discreet phone call telling him to keep an eye on Dewar.

Dear reader, how small and puny the good citizens of Quimbleton seem to be in the face of far greater power in the hands of a bitter alien with daddy problems. Of course, the safety of Earth had always been relative—a rogue asteroid could wipe out most of its cargo of life easily enough, as could the eruption of a super caldera creating a years-long winter snuffing out life. But nobody much thought about things like that, or even knew about them.

The residents of Quimbleton had now discovered that help to save their lives, and the planet, would not be coming from their government. M'bali rang her local member of parliament who made sympathetic noises as he took sparse notes. If the police thought there was no serious issue, he had more urgent constituency problems on his plate than the nonsense she was going on about. The rubbish bins on Quimbleton's main street were inadequate for the influx of warm-weather tourists, and too many visitors were parking illegally on the verge opposite the supermarket.

M'bali, Hayes, Rivers and Jess had a sombre meeting after work that evening. They all felt helpless, and no-one had much to say. Wozzer, sensing the atmosphere, mooched about trying to dispense comfort but was gently pushed away. He finally settled onto his big cushion in the corner with a pointed sigh aimed at M'bali.

'I for one am not going down without a fight,' Hayes announced. 'I have a child to protect and protect her I bloody will.'

That raised a spark in both Rivers and Jess. They had talked and wept overnight about the loss of their dreamed of children, the ones who would thrive on the farm and make all their sacrifices worthwhile. 'I say if we're going down, we're going down big,' Rivers declared.

A little energy returned to the room. M'bali sat up frowning with concentration. 'But what can we do? Zera says he has powers beyond anything we can imagine, and he's quite capable of working out another way to destroy our beautiful planet.'

'But can she be trusted? She's a pretty smart alien too…'

'I saw her when she arrived at my door. She was devastated at how he had treated her. And Slugg was protecting her. I don't think he was acting.'

That convinced Rivers. 'We need a plan. Who do we have on our side?' he asked.

'No-one yet. Jeffrique is a smarmy bastard, and he's horribly handsome. All teeth and trousers as they say. Some of the town like him, and they'll take his side no matter what we say.'

'True, but lots will see him as a privileged city wanker—it's his word against us hard-working locals who…'

M'bali interrupted. 'Yes, but Zera seems very well-liked. She's been in town shopping quite often and always has a friendly chat. I think we should hold a town meeting and play her tape to everyone (when Doug gives my phone back). We could get hold of Richo and Mick to support our story and we can show everyone the picture of the saucer and what it did to my wardrobe. And I'll throw in that I'm convinced he got rid of Gaz. That'll really get them going.'

Everyone nodded. 'Nothing to lose. Not a bloody thing,' Hayes concluded.

*

Little Quimbleton was abuzz, a rare occurrence in this staid rural community. There had not been so much shared emotion in town since Marilyn Rogers discovered a clandestine swingers' group in her living room. Returning unexpectedly from a shopping excursion to Slique, she tripped over a pile of bodies more connected than a clutch of saw fly larvae writhing in a tree. After the tangle of limbs separated, four of them proved to belong to her own darling husband. Sobbing hysterically, she had managed to get in some amazingly accurate blows with her tennis racket before being disarmed by a burly farmer who was clutching his genitals for protection with the other hand.

'I always knew that Maz had a great forehand, but her backhand was inspired that night,' one of the participants was later to confide to a friend. For weeks after that it was difficult for anyone to watch her playing tennis without having a quiet smirk.

Reader, this time little Quimbleton was venomously abuzz. Most of its citizens had believed Zera's story. The bastard had wiped out their Gaz, hero of fire and footy! This was personal. They were exceptionally infuriated to hear that the government was not going to do a thing to protect them. Yet another case of the bloody city ignoring rural needs. As usual, they would have to fix things themselves.

The town quickly mobilised all its resources. Had they not combined to save Quimbleton from bushfires many times? Had they not banded together to attract more citizens and save the school when the government threatened to close it? Had they not all pitched in to fund and build their massive aquatic and sports centre to keep bored kids out of mischief? Yes, they bloody had, they told one another. Like an enraged swarm of bees protecting a hive, Quimbleton would descend upon Jeffrique with everything it had.

Bravo Quimbleton. A very commendable attitude, but I fear I may not enjoy the result.

Down at the footy club, Packo would marshal his troops. The volunteer fire chief (also Packo) would do the same. The C.W.A. ladies would soon meet in their fragile little hall. Many of them were farmer's wives and crack shots when dealing with an unwanted piece of vermin. When the rumour circulated out into the forest, hairy men with lots of aggressive tatts remembered what that prick had done to their friends and to their beloved guard sow, Gladys.

The cult, all too aware that the alien had kidnapped their messiah, had been whipped up into a frenzy of prayer by Cuthbertson, alias Yuewath-Sahib. This had been his most profitable scam ever—in fact, it had turned out to not even be a scam. His messiah, Slugg, must be a real alien with superpowers because he could disappear at will before their eyes. Or at least at someone else's will.

Doug Dewar oiled his service pistol and sighed over the futility of it all. He contemplated putting it to his temple, looked at Elviz, and changed his mind.

Virgo

This week, turtles should be wary of many things—
rogue fishing lines, plastic bags, speedboats and
hominids bearing down on them with assorted weapons.

Forty-Two

Out in his rented mansion Jeffrique had been unable to summon a rational thought for days. In his own limited way, he did love Zera. He had never felt so lonely in his life. If he managed to destroy all life on rarking 3159XZ, it seemed he may have to return from his honeyflit alone. Concocting a story about her accidental death to explain her absence to his parents kept him awake at night. His ears tuned into the slightest sound of a distant vehicle—perhaps she would repent and return to his arms.

He waited in vain. Out in the hidden van, Zera was still fuming at his deception. His arrogant assumption that she must do as he wished or be shoved around fuelled her fury. Sometimes she had doubts. Was her determination not to return to Jeffrique reckless? Why choose to die for the sake of a little blue speck in the cosmos she had not been aware existed until a few months ago? What if she returned to him, escaped the destruction of Earth, but left him again as soon as they returned home? Slugg cooked her delectable morsels to tempt her appetite. She refused them all.

Meanwhile, Jeffrique finally summoned enough concentration to deal with his main anxiety—how to avoid his father's wrath. His mother sent him several more annoying messages demanding a response. He ignored them.

For a few hours, slumped in the big leather in his office, he tried to think without the aid of his quantum computer which Zera had successfully destroyed beyond repair. His nanochip-assisted brain was not adequate to the task. He would have to restore the now-hidden *Soozerator-6* to its normal size; it contained many times the computing power of the contents of his head. Too bad if any visiting hominid saw it.

Several stories high, it was towering in the garden when Caro and Gordi dropped by for a visit. Both Jeffrique and Zera had failed to return their messages. The rumours that their new friends were dangerous aliens were preposterous so perhaps they needed help. At least, that was what they had thought until they drove up and saw the saucer gleaming among the trees. 'Fang it, Gordi!' Caro yelled, borrowing her teenage son's vocabulary. He fanged it.

Inside the vessel, Jeffrique was unaware of their passing. He finally had a brilliant idea. His mother's messages had somehow reminded him of those far-off days when he had made a tiny planet and wafted it around his room with just the power of his mind—until she blundered in and swatted it away. Why hadn't he thought of that before? With all the *Soozerator-6's* computing power assisting his mind, he could tow 3159XZ far closer to its red star. The oceans and rivers would evaporate turning its surface into a hellish cauldron of fire. Soon even the rocks would melt, then gasify. No living being, no matter how tenacious and well-hidden, would survive.

Dear reader this is a very unfortunate turn of events for sweet little Earth. You may have seen, as I have, documentaries where hominid experts taught their disabled clients to switch on electric lights and appliances using only the power of their minds. Sending messages by mind power has been done. But this is on a far larger scale than you or I could have anticipated.

Jeffrique was not entirely delighted with his idea. It seemed it would cost him his wife. What kind of father would intimidate his son into making such an awful decision? His kind of father, he concluded bitterly.

Libra

Bison will continue having a peaceful graze this week.
Buffalo Bill has long gone to his maker,
along with every other slaughtering cowboy.

Forty-Three

Tiny Quimbleton remained furiously energised and obsessed. Not much everyday work was being done. The seeds of autumn crops waited in sheds to be planted. Tourists wondered in vain why the pub and most of the shops were closed and the friendly locals either refused to answer their queries or came up with something preposterous as an excuse. 'Anniversary of the birth of Gertie, the town's patron saint,' someone lied.

Matt Vigano and members of the aneera lobby had been at the town meeting. This homicidal alien nonsense, if true, was an abominable nuisance now that they had obtained massive sponsorship from the multi-national which manufactured the magic bean. Much as it peeved them to be on the same side as the bloody hippy greenie aneera-doubters, they were not about to let all their good lobbying go to waste. Armed with a ferocious quantity of toxic farming chemicals, they were going to give this alien fellow the shower of his life.

As his boys came in and spoke to him, Packo's computer screen rippled with increasing quantities of data. His lists included who had a rifle, who had bulldozers to flatten the alien's headquarters, and who had masses of inflammable material to use when they to set fire to the rubble. As fire chief he did not wholly approve of this strategy but needs must. At least, he and the boys would be there to stop the blaze careering into the woods too much.

Out in their forest dens, the men decorated with lots of aggressive tattoos were not in on these plans. But they had come up with an idea of their own. Wearing gas masks, they would sneak up to the mansion and throw a few smouldering torches laced with good forest-raised dope through the windows. That would send the alien prick into a happy land so peaceful he would barely feel it when they battered down the door and skewered him for the barbeque. Noble guard sow Gladys would not be allowed to die in vain.

Jeffrique would have laughed if he heard of these plans. He would reduce the lot of these rarking ape-brained peasants to you-know-what the instant he saw them. His nanochip-assisted reflexes were faster than anything they could imagine.

*

M'bali had been on her old green sofa clinging to Hayes and Wozzer for some time. She had believed Zera when she told her that Jeffrique could destroy any puny hominid attackers in an instant. The battle would be as unequal as those in hominid history when poor souls with stone-age spears had tried to defend themselves against invaders armed with muskets.

'Marry me,' he said, after a long period of silence.

'Frigging hell. Is that all you ever think of?'

'That, and Bree, and how to keep fungi out of my crops.'

'I will. If we survive. We aren't going to survive—which is a problem.'

He kissed her. 'I will die a happy man.'

'As I have told you before, you're an idiot.' But she could feel the tension in his body. He was only being flippant to protect her. She nestled even closer.

'Ah yes, but I'm your idiot now.'

Hayes stayed for a couple more hours, both far too worried to make love. After he left, she adjusted her position until she was curled up around Wozzer's smelly body. 'God, you need a bath, baby,' she told him just before sleep claimed her.

She awoke an hour or so later with the seeds of an idea. Warren Stanton. Yes, her old school friend and eccentric snake catcher Warren. He could supply exactly what she needed. But first she would have to sneak out to Zera's hiding place in the very early hours of the morning. Her help would be crucial to the plan. But could she be persuaded to go along with it?

Scorpio

Horses will find this an excellent week for racing.
None of you will break a leg
or get flogged too hard over the finishing line.

Forty-Four

It was finally 3 am, the hour when all the good citizens of Quimbleton (and most of the bad ones) were finally asleep. There would be no night on the tiles searching for comets for M'bali. She had advised Zera not to use her phone, so she would have to arrive without warning. The poor girl would probably be terrified at the sound of her vehicle, but it had to be done. As she drove it occurred to her that the Merc van might be armed in some way. With nothing to lose, she drove off.

The entrance to the track was so overgrown that she had to scout back and forth to relocate it. Ploughing down it in the dark became a nightmare. The parallel lines of earth compacted by tyres remained bare of growth, but the regrowth sprouting down the middle was so dense she frequently had to get out to examine it more closely before she was willing to force her vehicle over the top. Confused animals, caught in the headlights' dazzle, slowed her down again and again. She became increasingly alarmed in case she was being followed. As she realized she must be approaching the hiding spot, she slowed, wound down her window and began yelling over and over, 'Zera, it's me, M'bali!'

At first, the only answer was silence. Her mind raced over the worst possibilities. Finally, she heard an answering call. The girl was still there. And alive.

They met in a relieved hug. M'bali could feel how alarmingly thin she had become in such a short time. Slugg stood behind Zera, a wall of flesh in the starlight. After they clambered inside, he began bustling about making coffee.

'I risked coming out here because I have a plan. But I need your help to carry it out.'

Swiftly she explained Warren Stanton's occupation to a woman whose rulers had eliminated every inconveniently lethal animal from their world. 'He's an old friend. He trusts me and he's promised to bring us his fastest and crankiest reptile.'

Zera was unsure. 'You mean he has a creature which can instantly poison Jeffrique with a bite? I find it hard to conceive of such a thing.'

M'bali pulled out her phone and showed the girl some startling photos and articles. Zera laughed for the first time in days. 'They certainly look the part. What else can we do? I'll try it.'

Sagittarius

This will be a very irritating week for reptiles.
Shedding your skin is such a drag.
But soon you will be all shiny and new.

Forty-Five

The following morning dawned cool and misty. Zera lounged in the doorway of the Merc, sipping a coffee and sniffing the delicious leafy odours of the forest. Finally, she had a slender thread of hope. By the time she had made herself look glamorous, the mist should have cleared. She spent a little time scrabbling among the few clothes she had fled with to find a garment loose enough to hide her thinness. Slugg gently removed it from her hands and began fussing over it. He would get the creases out as best he could while she showered.

Wearing a little more makeup than usual to disguise the shadows under her lovely eyes, she surveyed herself in the small bedroom mirror. *Hopefully, good enough to intrigue and distract a sex-starved mate*, she thought.

In the soft autumnal light, she set off. At M'bali's place, she deposited the reluctant giant. Wozzer was thrilled to see him and rushed off to find his ball. M'bali hugged them both before they went inside to flesh out their strategy. She quickly noticed the giant trying unsuccessfully to hide his fear. 'Please tell Slugg that Wozzer loves him. He just wants to play.' Zera spoke in his own language, but Slugg didn't appear convinced. The big slobbery thing had tried to mate with him before, he was sure of it. M'bali called the reluctant dog to heel. He obeyed but spat out his ball in disgust.

Half-an-hour later, Zera emerged from the house carrying a basket. It was the kind of goodies basket that the hominid heroine Little Red Riding Hood was carrying when she was bailed up by the wolf. Hominid cultures the galaxies over have a Little Red Riding Hood story—under an incredible variety of names. Warren Stanton, the herpetologist, emerged after Zera. As usual, he was dressed head to toe in khaki, wore unfashionable glasses, and didn't much bother about his hair. In fact, he looked exactly like the amiable rural boffin that he was, and an unlikely rescuer.

'Thanks again for the lend,' she told him with tears in her eyes, 'I'll promise I'll look after her.'

He climbed into the back of the vehicle and wedged his small body as best he could under a bed.

'Good luck,' M'bali whispered as she and Zera hugged farewell.

'Trust me, I can do it,' the girl assured her.

*

Zera's hands were shaking but her mind was clear as he drove towards their mansion. On the way, she stopped to message Jeffrique that she was coming and was willing to talk more reasonably. She did not want to allow him time to think. He replied tersely that he would see her soon.

To her relief he allowed the electronic gates to open, and she parked the vehicle inside. Her heart was thumping. Would he insist on searching the van before he allowed her in? Preoccupied with acting as though he was not thrilled at her re-appearance, he failed to be suspicious. Her first obstacle was down. They embraced briefly and walked inside. Zera flashed him a warm look to distract him. She was horribly aware of the weight of the basket on her arm.

Warren loved every one of his creatures. It had taken a couple of hours and a few beers to persuade him to risk one of them in the interests of saving the planet. But he had always found M'bali to be bright and level-headed. Although this was a weird situation, he had decided to trust her judgement. Inside Zera's goodies basket one very cross snake lay curled on her heat pad. Rosy the reptile had been in the process of shedding her skin for a couple of weeks. It had not been easy. Firstly, there had been the writhing and pushing to break the skin on her head—then the long, slow process of pulsing and squeezing her way out of the whole worn-out hide enclosing her six-foot-long body. She had not felt like eating for days. Now she had been shaken and joggled about in the confining basket. Rosy belonged to the most venomous species on earth—and when the lid was lifted, the first thing she saw was going to cop a feel of her fangs. It was Zera's job to see that her victim was Jeffrique.

Zera took a couple of steps towards him, jiggling the container as she did so.

'Star-dream, so wonderful to see you. This basket contains your very favourite—Mahpia Mooncake, baked with love. Let me show you.'

At striking range, she lifted the lid. Rosy shot out like liquid fury. Taken by complete surprise, Jeffrique had no time to react. She latched onto his arm and sank her fangs in hard. He screamed. There were no predator animals left alive in his over-managed world.

'You rarking treacherous bitch! Get this thing off me.' He could not vaporise Rosy. She was imbedded in him.

'Not yet. It's okay, her venom will take several minutes to catastrophically clot your blood.'

He was hysterical, shaking his arm and trying to hit at Rosy with his other hand. Terror and agony were throwing his aim out.

'You rarking murdering little bitch.'

'I have no wish to watch you die, Jeffrique. Outside in our van is a hominid with the antidote to her bite. As soon as you swear that you will not destroy Earth he will come in and administer it.'

Already he could feel himself starting to lose control of his muscles. His eyelids were drooping; he feared he might soon fall. 'Okay, I won't destroy festering ape-shelter. Now tell the rarking hominid to come in and do what he has to do.'

'I have to be sure you mean it, Jeffrique.'

'Of course, I rarking mean it. I'm planning a long, happy life. Without you.'

'Promise?'

'Yes, I rarking promise. On my mother's life, I promise.'

Zera strode to the door and called for Warren who came running in carrying the anti-venom already in a syringe. He quickly injected the alien and helped him to a chair. Only then did he carefully remove Rosy and expertly thread her back into her shelter. 'Don't worry. It'll take effect pretty quickly.'

'Don't rarking worry. I'll give you don't rarking worry.' Before he could reduce the brave herpetologist and his reptilian ally to the molecules from whence they came, a familiar female voice cut through the air.

'On your mother's life, indeed. I heard that.'

Capricorn

Naughty sons of Her Gracious Celestial Motherness,
Alpha Dawn, should have learned by now not to ignore her.
This is an insult up with which she will not put.

Forty-Six

Well reader, I have never been more gratified at the sudden appearance of a venomous female reptile. And now Alpha Dawn has turned up as well.

Her Gracious Celestial Motherness had brooded on her son's repeated failure to respond to her messages for some time. The only thing that had stopped her from arriving sooner was the thought that society considered it appalling bad manners for a mother to land in the middle of her son's honeyflit.

But her annoyance was equalled by her concern that her impetuous youngest boy had done something foolish that he wished to hide from her—yet again. She had always considered Jeffrique her problem child, the one most damaged by his father's harshness and indifference.

In order to arrive at a galaxy not exponentially far away, it was necessary to have one's molecules replicated—a very taxing experience at her age. And not ideal for the complexion. 'My dahlings,' she cooed to her house plants as she gave them a final sprinkle, 'Mumsy will have to just moisturise herself and bear it.' She moved on to the darting creatures in the fish tank which covered one long wall of her apartment. 'My poor harmble creatures. All that banging abaht breeding and squabbling—and your little lahves are so short. I do hope my Hororscopes bring you sahm comfort.' A passing fish eyed her glassily and swam on.

She swanned into her dressing room and surveyed the length of its dazzling array. 'Agoutha, fetch something grand for mah arrival on 3159XZ.' (Jeffrique's comment about swimming in the ocean had told her exactly which planet in the little galaxy the miscreants were visiting.) 'A selection of something sweeping in gold will do, so kind to the complexion.' Her personal maid-of-the-dress scampered off. She arrived back several minutes later, puffing as she pushed a rack of assorted flimsy creations dripping with jewels along the heavy carpet. She curtsied. The girl was engineered to be plain but had an excellent eye for style and cut.

'You may leave, Agoutha. Check my travel accoutrements and pack a few little things for yourself.'

Alpha Dawn reached out an elegant claw and began rifling through the selection. 'Mmm, spun moonlight on the waters,' she murmured, selecting the palest shimmering creation.

She slid into it. 'Naht bad, Kylee, naht bad,' she told her reflection.

On arrival at her departure point, she saw that Quintis Quork was already waiting (terrified but trying not to show it). 'Quintis sweetie, you have been sahch a big help to me in finding the raht planet. It's only raht that you have a little visit too.' He nodded. His tearful farewell to his wife and children had taken all his emotional resources.

*

'I repeat, what exactly have you sworn on your mother's life, young man?'

Jeffrique could not form an answer. The treatment was slowly coursing through his veins dispelling the toxin—but his mother's arrival was one shock to many.

'I can see quite clearly that you two are not getting on. Zera, perhaps you can enlighten me. How has your honeyflit turned into this?'

'Most Gracious Celestial Mother-in-law, you have had a tedious journey. Please accept a seat and some refreshments and I will be happy to enlighten you,' Zera suggested.

The toxin was still making it difficult for Jeffrique to control his mouth and tongue. 'You keep your rarking mouth shut, you treatherous bithch. I haven't finished with you yet,' he lisped.

Alpha Dawn swept him a look. 'I will not countenance that attitude to your wife. That you managed to secure this treasure has been one of the best surprises of my life.'

She sank into one of the sumptuous chairs and gazed around as the house *nids* raced to serve her. An astonishingly spacious and aesthetically pleasing little hominid home, she noted.

While Jeffrique sat glowering, Zera poured out the whole story of their honeyflit. It took a couple of hours. As normal function returned a little to Jeffrique's muscles, several times he began to interrupt. He could still barely control his tongue. 'As you thee, my wife wants to save thith feral pit of uncontrolled rarking life. When you tell father, our lives won't be worth living. She hath decided to throw away her glamorous life, her pothition in society, and be catht off by all her friends.'

His mother managed to quell him with a look, several looks, until the whole tale was told. She seemed surprisingly amused. 'For some reason, you assume I tell your father everything, Jeffrique?'

'Well, don't you?'

'You seriously imagine that a woman of my sparkling intellect is a simpleton who tells your father everything? Wally-the-wonder-god knows what I deem it safe for him to know. Now go on, what exactly are you planning to do to little…Earth, is it?'

'I will push it closer to its old red star with the power of my mind—and a few select computers. Its very fabric will fry. It will turn to gas.'

'That won't be happening, my son. Quintis dahling, come here. Explain to my boy in mathematical terms whaht our little project has been. With the help of those simply gorgeous planetary movement people, of course.' Stammering, poor Quintis slowly managed the task.

Alpha Dawn turned to Zera, 'In layperson's language, my dear, I have already had this dahling little solar system positioned exactly as I want. It will allow them to get maximum benefits from my *Hororscopes*. Earth will stay revolving exactly in the orbit I chose. My celestial designs will NOT be tampered with.'

Jeffrique staggered to his feet. 'He'll find out. The *nids* will blab. Do you want to get us all turned out of society? You rarking idiot women…'

'Now, dear, I had hoped you would outgrow those little tanties. I feel we have promoted you beyond your capacity to cope…'

'He will divorce you!' Jeffrique shouted.

'Jeffrique, please calm down. Are you familiar with the expression "Happy wife, happy life" perhaps?'

'What are you drivelling on about?'

'I am Wally-the-wonder god's favourite and principal wife. This is because I am stupendously, dare I say cosmically amazing, in bed. The result of my talents is this. I don't interfere in your father's business, and he doesn't interfere in mine. NO MATTER WHAT.' Alpha Dawn had not raised her voice in pronouncing those last words, it just felt to everyone assembled that she had.

No boy wants to hear about his mother's talents in the sack. That part of her message made Jeffrique's addled brain spin like a cake mixer on whip setting. As a result, the more salient part of her message failed to reach long-term storage. In other words, her main point was lost to him.

Zera had instructed Warren to phone key people in Quimbleton to inform them that their attack was now unnecessary. Full of adrenaline and various helpful substances, many of them were extremely disappointed. Unfortunately for Jeffrique, the men with very aggressive tatts were not on her call list. A succession of bangs signalled their arrival with the drug canisters. Several windows shattered and a dreamy smoke began to fill the air. Jeffrique, already weakened by Rosy's venom, felt his powers beginning to fade. He struggled to his feet reeling towards the *Suzerator-6* (the one with the gold taps and the jacuzzi.) Everyone else in the room also jumped up and fled outside.

It was minutes before Zera noticed he was not with them. Too late. The spacecraft rose above the trees, hovered, then shot off to Earth orbit. In his deranged state, Jeffrique was beyond reason. When his mind had cleared, and his strength had returned, he would carry out his plan of destruction.

Zera ran sobbing holding her beseeching hands to the sky. All too soon he was just a tiny shining dot winging his way across the heavens. (Or he would have been if it hadn't been broad daylight.)

Esteemed reader, I expect you are rather put out at this turn of events. I am most disappointed myself. Will the boy never grow up or listen to his old mum?

Aquarius

This is the dawning of the age of Aquarius,
both for little Quimbleton and
Earth's precious cargo of life.

Forty-Seven

Jeffrique's test-firing of the stolen rocket from the forest had caused widespread agitation throughout the parts of the Earth where earthling technicians in one military/industrial complex were paid to feel paranoid about what other earthling technicians in other military/industrial complexes were up to. There was a lot of money to be made from war. And a lot of money to be squandered on mistrust and paranoia as well.

His experimental rocket had brought down a satellite, and the tribes considered taking pot-shots at satellites to be frightfully poor form (although machine-gunning the children of other tribes, or spraying them with toxic chemicals, were both allowed by all too many of them). In silos all over the planet, sleek missiles were prepared in case the intransigent, whoever it was, tried anything else unsporting.

As soon as the *Soozerator-6* began to orbit the Earth, it was instantly detected. In many languages, messages were relayed instructing the unidentified craft to land and surrender. It was instructed to land in so many places that its computers went into a bit of a tizzy. Jeffrique laughed bitterly. He ignored every message and every alarm. His ship was equipped with the most sophisticated missile defence systems in all the galaxies.

Unfortunately for the youngest son of the founder of *Genes-R-Us,* there are just so many missiles that any defence system can disable or deflect at once. Four hundred and sixty-five sleek destroyers shot out of hidden bunkers and homed in on his refuge. Hundreds of them struck the *Soozerator-6* in unison. Jeffrique was reduced to the star dust from whence he came.

Star Dust, one of my favourite earthling songs. I need so much to hear its story of a nightingale who sings happy tales in an earthly paradise.

Pisces

Honeybees will find life is improving this week.
Hominids have finally worked out that bumping you off
as collateral damage from crop spraying isn't very smart.

Forty-Eight

Unaware that Jeffrique had been dispatched by far-too-many missiles, little Quimbleton had several hours during which everyone blamed themselves, and everyone else, for letting him escape to annihilate them. They fumed and accused. If this, if that—not to mention those old favourites you should have, then I could have. Naturally, the key players in this debacle came in for the most flak. As most of them were women, one half of the community was even more accusatory than the other. Anger was slowly joined by terror as reality dawned.

Those closest to the alien were bombarding themselves with the most harrowing blame and regret. M'bali was distraught that her plan to save Earth had failed, putting Zera in a position where she blamed herself. The girl cried bitter tears over her chosen love who had betrayed her. He had proved a frail vessel to carry the burden of his wife's expectations. She shed as many bitter tears over the lovely blue planet and its innocent cargo of life, but what could she do now but flee with her mother-in-law?

Alpha Dawn held her tenderly. She had lost her precious boy to an unknown fate. His path through life had been like a spinning firecracker bouncing from one impetuous error to the next. 'I offered to pay for the best counselling many times. Just as many times he refused, my dahlings.' She did not believe for one moment that he still intended to destroy the planet from his orbiting haven. How could he, Her Gracious Celestial Motherness was on it?

The first news bulletins of the following day revealed that an alien craft in Earth orbit had been obliterated by countless missiles. Little Quimbleton had to change feet in the blink of an eye. Zera was a hero. M'bali was a hero. Alpha Dawn was a hero. Rosy was a superhero and would soon receive many gift-wrapped rodents in the mail. Unfortunately, she preferred them alive, and Warren had to hold his nose and rush to the bin every day for several weeks.

Now Zera shed more tears over her role in the events leading to Jeffrique's death and her joy that Earth had been saved. Alpha Dawn, in her own grief, still took a moment to puzzle how she might explain his son's death to the so-called Creator-Of-All-Things. At least, it would take Waldorf quite a while to notice that he was short of a son. By then, she would have her tale concocted. Quintis, and other minions, would be very handsomely paid for their silence. The odd threat would help too, she concluded.

In the cult's forest hideaway, Yuewath-Sahib was having his finest moment. He had urged his followers to pray for the destruction of the alien who had stolen their messiah—and yay, forsooth and all that, he was dead. He was showered with garlands, kisses, and cries of adoration. But his total triumph would be short-lived.

As soon as he could cadge a lift, Slugg journeyed out to be re-united with Jess and Rivers. Dewar had guaranteed that he could stay with no further investigation, and Zera had released him from servitude. The giant was free for the first time in his life. He had spent several nights pondering life and the meaning of it all—which proved to be a problem far beyond his brain to contemplate. He came to realise that although he loved Jess and Rivers he had greatly enjoyed being worshipped as a messiah as well. What's more, the cult members were huge fans of his cooking. Over a cup of tea in the new kitchen, with Zera translating, he told them his new plan. Would they mind if he spent every Sunday out at cult headquarters?

Jess rose and tried to envelope as much of him as she could encompass in a hug. 'You silly old alien, we just want you to be happy. And when the farm gets going properly, we will pay you—back-pay and all.' Their partying went on for so many days that the neighbours were forced to stop complaining and join in.

A one-day-a-week messiah proved to be an economic problem for Nigel, alias Yuewath. The resident cult members all figured they might as well just go home and only visit headquarters on Sundays when the food was superb. And Nigel had been charging them rent. Now he would have to make a new business plan—perhaps he could run a religious B&B for seekers from Slique. Those city types were fussier, the place could use a coat of paint and a few giant photos of The Chosen One. He started getting quotes.

Ros slid quietly through the front door to find Dewar despairing over his lonely fate. She tiptoed behind him and planted a kiss on his right ear. 'So sorry, dear. I won't ever leave you again.'

Elviz, who had not missed her at all, flew onto the cop's other shoulder where he burst into her least-favourite song, 'Hyperspace bypass to hell,' he shrieked. Dewar raised a finger to caress the feathers under his crest and smiled.

When life finally settled to close to normal and her emotions had stopped rocketing around uncontrollably, M'bali insisted that Hayes propose to her again—properly, and with all due ceremony. He happily complied—romantic location, on one knee, sparkly beverage, his grandmother's ruby ring decorated with old brilliant-cut diamonds. All that hominid nonsense. For a year or so, Bree would not be too impressed at the entry of another female into her father's life—but she would mellow. She and M'bali were apparently fated to be soul sisters. I have no idea what that means.

Forty-Nine

There will be no Hororscope today.
The author is taking a short break.

Our brave, if obstinate, heroine's immediate problem after Jeffrique's demise was finalising the arrangements for the organic produce day which was imminent. It was to turn into little Quimbleton's celebration of being alive. Vigano initially refused to have Aneera Stadium set up for the event—but had to give way under the force of the town's disapproval. A sea of stalls and carnival rides soon engulfed it. Packo walked around fussing about the state of the turf but, after a few insults and glares were thrown his way, he decided it would be best to put up and shut up about dents in The Bulls' precious sod. Klaire and the C.W.A. ladies laid out an organic feast the town would reminisce over for decades.

The big day dawned for triumphant little Quimbleton. Honeybees buzzed and dived into the forest flowers, showering themselves with pollen. In the autumn chill, the little black flies decided to stay napping until later—possibly next summer. Leaves sparkled in the morning dew as the town rose to drag out festive garments which had not seen the light of day for months.

Quimbleton knew how to work, and it knew even better how to party. Hayes sang until his throat felt like burning cinders, and every able-bodied citizen danced until the Quimby Bull's precious turf was worn to a sea of mud. They paused to eat the sumptuous food and quench their thirsts, and then they danced some more. Little kids rode on their fathers' shoulders and even Norbert and Francis rocked their walking frames from time to time. Zera, M'bali and Alpha Dawn, still shaken from the death of Jeffrique, watched quietly from the sidelines. The two alien women cried to see hominids have such fun. The celebrations raged until another dawn broke over a town sated and happy under the retreating stars.

Dearest reader, is your lovely mind bothered about the comet our heroine so longed to find and register in her brother's name? Have no fear. When Alpha Dawn heard about M'bali's search on behalf of Jon, she waved a jewelled hand at the firmament. 'You want a new comet, dahling. I'll have one pop up right above your little house just as soon as I get back.' She didn't forget. For decades, astronomers would puzzle mightily over how Comet Jon Hoyle had come to be gift-wrapped.

Zera remained on Earth to help save the planet from the environmental messes created by those silly hominids. In public life, she manifested herself as a famous television naturalist—David somebody, as I recall.

Dear and esteemed earthling reader,

I, your narrator, am Commander Zud Vulpeloc of the Kiva Subversives. We are few, but our technical surveillance skills are greatly superior to those of my deranged younger brother Waldorf and his abominable Genes-R-Us. We deploy those skills to track every movement of that fiend, his offspring, and all they seek to harm. Unfortunately, we have limited powers to help.

As you are already aware, your planet is monitored by that lethal tool of Genes-R-Us the Planetary-Life Enhancement Division. Fear not, Alpha Dawn has fixed that problem by means of a few well-placed bribes and threats.

But, with all due respect, you earthling hominids are making a right royal fuckup of your glorious blue planet without Waldorf's help. Many alarm bells are ringing if you are willing to listen. From afar, we can see that Earth's lungs, the Amazon forests, are being burnt, sending out more CO_2 than they save. The overheated oceans are driving increasingly unpredictable and wild climate change, destroying food and safety for people and animals. There are about 8,000,000,000 of you and only 50,000 wild elephants (down from 5,000,000 a hundred years ago) and that devastating trend towards extinction is echoed across the planet. Do you really want the only animals left alive to be in zoos? Habitat loss and human burning of fossil fuels are undoubtedly the causes.

If that doesn't make you want to give tardy politicians a kick in the pants and find out how to lower your own carbon footprint, then, sadly for the planet and your children, you're dreaming. What is the worst mistake you can make at this time? Ignoring an unpalatable reality.

Alpha Dawn and I are increasingly sad witnesses to an unnecessary and escalating catastrophe.

With warmest wishes and hopes for your future,

Commander Vulpeloc
K.S. Headquarters

Ingram Content Group UK Ltd.
Milton Keynes UK
UKHW020608140723
425125UK00006B/263